Ery trit ure Vel'dulan elau sery prue

Plavi un er weh ery sik o ure

Tro bak o skice en leth o wea

Cm fer en shew ure vise un er

THE LOST KINGDOM OF MOORA

By Robert Ryan Cruce

THE LOST KINGDOM OF MOORA

Cover by Robert Ryan Cruce
Map by Solis Rachels and Robert Ryan Cruce

Visit the author's blog at
www.journeyaboardthesalvation.wordpress.com

First Edition

ISBN # 9781520796710

In memory of my grandfather, Stephen Cruce, and my great aunt, Pauline Smith. Dedicated to my grandmother, Evelyn Cruce. Thank you all for supporting me through the years.

Special thanks to my father and mother, Mike and Debbie, my sister Faith, my brother-in-law Shawn, and to Solis, Justin, Lyndsay, and Lara for taking the time to read this while I was writing it and giving me feedback.

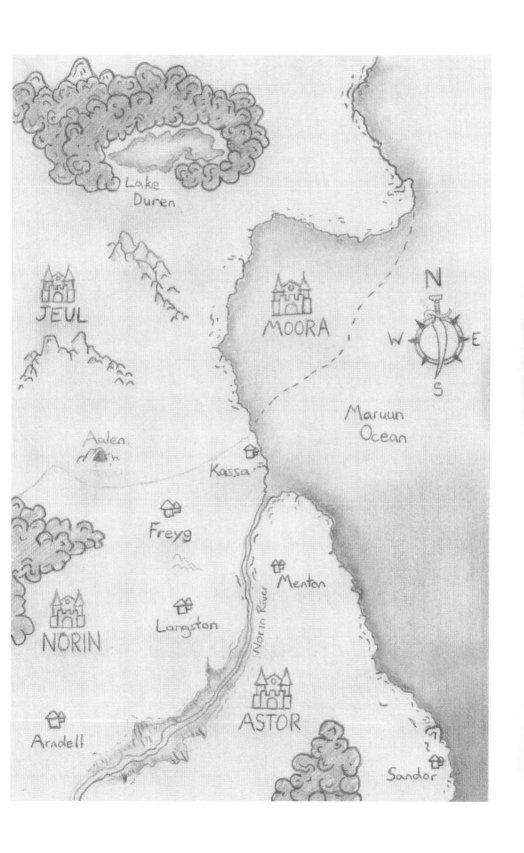

PROLOGUE

A DEMON'S PRICE

The knife slipped quickly into the guard's back and was easily pulled out again. Tecuul Boaruun removed his left hand from the guard's mouth. No sound had escaped his lips, and no one would discover Tecuul's escape until he was gone from this prison. While gently lowering the corpse to the floor against the bars of the cell, he removed the keys from the guard's belt. After opening the cell door, he pulled the dead guard inside and went about the task of swapping his clothes with his former jailor.

Tecuul stripped the guard first and then himself, placing the lifeless body in the drab gray shirt and pants he had been given during his stay. He put on the green shirt and pants of the prison guards, buckled on the sword belt with the sheathed short sword, then pulled on the black boots and gloves. He finished by putting on the few pieces of black leather armor given to guards for their chest and shins, as well as the helmet, which fit snugly over his head with ample room for his pointed elven ears. Long dark brown hair had been tucked into his shirt to mimic the shorter hair of the guard, and the back of the helmet covered the back of his neck so it wouldn't be noticed.

The freedom this disguise offered would afford him a little bit of time to gather a few supplies before making his full escape from the city. During the past three years, he had plenty of time to think about what he would do when he had gotten free and now he could set his plan in motion.

After shutting the cell door behind him, Tecuul took a moment to look around at the other empty cells. He had seen others come and go in the prison, but none of them had committed the hard crimes Tecuul was guilty of. None of them ever had the threat of death for their deeds. Once sure that there were no witnesses to his escape, he began his ascent up the gray stone stairs and away from the dark and dreary elven prison that had confined him. Thoughts of his betrayal to his kingdom and the failure of his plans fueled Tecuul's rage. They should have executed him when they had the chance, but now they would all pay.

Tecuul stopped a moment to let the twisted smile fade from his face and to focus. He hadn't known which guard he would replace until a few moments ago when he decided now was the time to make his escape. However, he had studied all of the guards' voices and mannerisms to prepare for this moment, so it was of little matter which one he had to kill. With his freedom from the magical barriers of his prison cell, he could now use his magic to disguise his voice perfectly.

The pleasure of being able to feel that power again brought a genuine smile to Tecuul's face. All of the elves were naturally attuned to magic, and he had felt empty without it. If not for his strong will and resolve, being denied his right to touch the wonderful source of his spells for three years would have made him a shadow of his former self.

Tecuul took a deep breath as he reached the top of the stairs and opened the door. Two guards stood just outside of the door, one at each side, each dressed just as their prisoner was dressed now. As Tecuul walked past them towards the exit of the building the guard to his left asked, "How's the traitor today?" They always referred to Tecuul as the traitor. When he was done with his work, they would remember his name forever, but he had no time for petty revenge. It would only hurt his escape, and he had more important things to do right now.

Tecuul turned his head slightly to answer him. The helmet he had stolen from his cell's guard tonight obscured most of his face, but he was careful not to turn his head too much in case the guards recognized their prisoner. "He's as weak and pathetic as ever," Tecuul laughed, all in the voice of his dead guard, "but he's sleeping now."

"I wish the king would hurry up and make his judgment," the other guard interjected, joining in the conversation. "We'd be better off if we could be rid of him, and I'm tired of having to guard the fool."

"Our long lives make for long, careful deliberation, my friend," Tecuul replied.

"Besides," the first guard said, "he's harmless to us now with the barrier of his cell. This is easy work."

"I guess it is easy. But sometimes I think he's more dangerous than we…" the second guard's voice cut off as Tecuul shut the door, having made his way out of the building and finally into the open night air. They could continue their discussion with each other all night, Tecuul had much to do.

The stars! Tecuul, despite his rush, took a moment to take in the night sky. The windowless walls of his cell had kept this view from him. He nearly lost himself looking into the dark sky brightened only by scattered stars and the moons, but as the chill from a sudden breeze hit him, he began to move again. There was business to attend to, and he couldn't waste his time. The city hadn't changed while he was imprisoned and he remembered his way around Jeul. The capital was the largest city within the kingdom, and the city and kingdom shared the name.

In the area where Tecuul had been held captive, several of the buildings around the prison housed the other guards who were on duty to watch the city that night. This area was just outside of the castle and within the walls which separated the castle from the rest of the city. He passed by the white, square stone barracks and made his way down the brown brick streets and out of the gates, unquestioned by the guards there, as his disguise granted him easy passage. He headed for the library, located in a more residential area right outside of the castle walls.

After an hour had passed, Tecuul left the library with the book he required. He would need to find a good place to perform the ceremony, but the time he had in Jeul was shorter now since he had to kill the librarian. He would have preferred to avoid it, but she was asking too many questions and acting suspicious. He'd done what he could to cover up the murder, leaving no trace of blood and hiding the body, but there was always someone watching over the library and if it was discovered no one was there they could soon find her corpse.

The elf hastily made his way through the streets and out of the outer city walls, into the freedom of the open country. The kingdom of Jeul had failed to kill him, and he wouldn't let anyone get the chance to kill him again.

*****

"Seven days!" King Kaalen yelled as he stood in front of his golden throne. "Seven days since Tecuul escaped from the city, leaving two murdered! And none of you have been able to find him or any trace of him!"

Aar Kaalen, king of Jeul, was dressed in a fine, long white shirt and pants buckled over with a black leather belt fastened with a large golden buckle in the shape of the head of a battle axe. Over this he wore a red robe, and upon his head rested a large, golden, jeweled crown. The features of his face were framed by his long, white hair, which was pulled back and tied loosely, and his thick blonde beard, which was beginning to go white. His hands were bare, but on his feet he wore black leather boots decorated with intricate golden patterns. The king's normally calm and kind demeanor was quite stern and imposing, and was made more impressive and intimidating from where he stood at the raised dais of his throne.

Some guards and soldiers in the room shifted uneasily at the king's tirade, which had been going on for some time, while others stood unmoving, truly living examples of how the soldiers of Jeul should behave. Two guards present were obviously more affected by the words of their king than the others and had lowered their heads. They blamed themselves for letting Tecuul fool them and escape. Nearly every soldier and guard had been called to the throne room for this audience with their king.

"He must be found," the king continued, his bright blue eyes piercing them as he repeated things he'd already said, "He's not just a danger to our kingdom. The other elven kingdoms and even the human kingdoms could be in danger. If he…" the king was cut off as the doors to the throne room opened.

"Your majesty," the soldier who entered exclaimed, "we have found him! We have found Tecuul!"

"Where?" the king asked, anxious for the news.

"He was seen approaching a farm near the town of Rollins, and he seems to have gathered together a small group following him. One of our beast mages just spotted him and sent in a hawk with the message."

The king exhaled a breath of relief and took a moment to compose himself before giving his command. One of the specializations some of his mages studied in, to communicate with animals of all types, was rare, but often helpful, and had been particularly helpful now. "Captain Soor, gather together a group of twenty soldiers and five of our mages. Tecuul has always had powerful magic at his disposal, and we cannot take any chances. Rollins is to the east, just outside of Jeul, so you should still be able to catch him." Aar didn't know why Tecuul was still so close since he had so much time to have gotten further, but wondering would get him no answers.

The king paused a moment before delivering his last instruction, "He cannot be allowed to live on. When you find him, kill him." Aar Kaalen realized now he had let his idealism cloud his judgment, and he should have had Tecuul executed when his treasonous activities had been discovered. He couldn't admit this mistake in front of his people or allow them to see any weakness in him. But deep within he could admit he was wrong, and his mistake had cost the lives of two members of his kingdom and maybe more to come.

The captain of the soldiers, Caldoon Soor, went about the king's task of gathering the group.

*****

The soothing sound of the waves against the beach could still be heard from inside the cave. Tecuul finished drawing the symbol on the ground and looked over his work to make sure it matched the book correctly. He had long since left behind the stolen clothes from the guard of the prison for simple black pants and a gray shirt, though he had kept the boots, belt, and the sword. He had made it all the way to the eastern coast from Rollins with no trouble.

Deeper in this cave he had discarded corpses that he had drained of blood. During his time out of Jeul he had gathered a small group of ruffians who followed him on the promise of wealth, and he had used them to kidnap a few more people he would need in order to have a good supply of blood for the summoning. Of course, he didn't let the small gang following him know what the kidnappings were for since he needed their blood as well.

Now Tecuul was alone again and the victims and the thugs were dead. It had been simple to hold them all in place with a spell while he drained them of their life. Their fear and weak wills gave him easy control of them. Humans were usually easier to control with magic, in his experience.

The symbol had been simple enough for Tecuul to draw out, and he had been sure to have plenty of blood on hand to make it. The symbol was a large circle with a square inside, with the corners of the square touching the circle. Inside the square was another circle, with room enough to sit or stand, and it touched the sides of the square. Between the outer circle and square was writing in an unknown demonic language which Tecuul could not understand, but he was able to copy the letters. And then between the inner circle and the square were four small star shapes, one at each corner. On the outside of the outer circle at each corner of the square was drawn a small circle with a strange symbol in it. Each of the four circles contained a different symbol. Between these circles were four triangles, also each containing a symbol, each matching the symbol in the circle to its left.

Tecuul took his place sitting in the middle of the inner circle and drew four stars around himself inside the inner circle, each in the same direction as the other stars. "It's finally ready," he whispered to himself as he closed his eyes and began to focus his magic. Finally, he would get what he worked so hard for.

As Tecuul focused his magic and thoughts, the symbol of blood began to glow, and then it began to move. The square remained stationary, but the outer circle began to turn clockwise while the inner circle turned counter-clockwise. Soon, the small circles, triangles, and stars began spinning as well, all clockwise. A deep, low hum filled the air and the small circles, triangles, and stars lifted from the symbol and into the air, forming a doorway. The demonic writing soon rose from the floor as well and surrounded the doorway and a shimmering blue glass appeared in the frame formed by the symbols and writing, leaving Tecuul sitting in a simple looking pattern of two circles and a square.

Tecuul opened his eyes as the circles stopped spinning and looked at the gateway. He waited a moment before calling the demon, apprehensive about how he would appear. Tecuul had heard stories of demons, of their horrible disfigured forms and terrifying faces and voices. He had heard stories of demon summoning gone wrong, how an incorrectly drawn symbol or the wrong magic or words could lead to death or worse for the one performing the summons. He had never before summoned a demon and had never met an elf who had. Human mages had more experience in dealings with demons, and the ones who did work with demons were considered dark and outcast from other human mages. The elves knew the dangers of dealing with demons were never worth the risk. Even Tecuul had held fast to that belief, but now he had nothing to lose.

He steeled his nerves and spoke clearly, "Vel'dulan, come forth! I, Tecuul, summon you!"

The gateway rippled and Tecuul took a deep breath. Gray smoke began to pour out of the gate, filling the cave and blinding Tecuul from seeing anything. Tecuul began to cough and the smoke cleared from the room as if being sucked back into the gateway.

Tecuul opened his eyes and they widened in surprise, not horror, at what he saw before him. A beautiful woman had stepped from the gateway into the cave. She was tall and had ears pointed like an elf's. Her skin was pale, as if having hardly ever been touched by the sun, and her long curly black hair fell loosely around her face. She wore a simple blue dress that hugged her body tightly from the shoulder to the waist and hung loosely to her ankles. The dress was cut low in the top, and her feet were bare. Her eyes were wide in surprise as well when she saw Tecuul before her.

"An elf?" she whispered to herself. Tecuul still wide-eyed had paid no attention to her words, and she composed herself completely before speaking again, getting his attention. "Why have you called me here?" she asked sweetly.

"Who are you?" he responded in question. As he did, he noticed her eyes for the first time. Her iris was a stunning bright blue, but her pupil was white instead of black.

"My name is Vel'dulan. Am I not who you summoned?"

"I didn't expect such beauty. I thought you'd have horns… or a hideous face. Are you an elf?" Tecuul was unsure what to think of this surprise.

"I appear however I want to appear. Now, what do you want of me?" The sweetness of her voice began to turn to annoyance. She was used to dealing with people more knowledgeable of her kind.

Tecuul stood and looked her in the eyes. "I've read that if I called upon you that I could have any request granted."

"Within reason," she replied grumpily. "There are things that I cannot do. Well, what is it you want?"

Tecuul knew what he wanted. "I spent the last few years of my life in a prison expecting death to come for me. Eventually, it will anyway, even elves don't live forever. But I want to. I want to be able to live forever. Can you grant that to me?"

Vel'dulan smiled, and something about it unnerved Tecuul. "I can and I can't. I cannot," she began to explain, "give you complete control over death. I can, however, stop your aging. You can still be killed, but if you can avoid that, then you will live forever."

"Is that the best you can do? There are people even now who are probably plotting to kill me if they find me." Tecuul began to think he had overestimated the powers of the demons and what they could do.

"Although you can be killed," she said, "it won't be an easy task. You will heal from wounds quickly, even wounds that would normally be fatal. Other things, however, are fatal no matter what. For example, if your head was removed. You cannot heal from that. There are…other things that may be able to kill you, but you'd be safer than you are now." She gave him what was intended to be a reassuring smile. Again it alarmed Tecuul.

But he was a desperate man, and this was the best chance he had at immortality. "Then do it," he simply said.

Vel'dulan approached him and reached forward, taking Tecuul's head in her hands and pain shot through his body. Something was wrong and he tried to break free. But it was futile; it was as if he was frozen in place. After a few moments, it was over. Vel'dulan let him go and he collapsed to the floor, convulsing. She looked down at him until the convulsions stopped.

After a few moments had passed, Tecuul looked wearily up to her. "What… what did you do to me?"

"What you asked for," she replied confidently, "from this moment on you will never age. That is what you wanted, is it not?"

"Yes, but that's not all you did, is it." It wasn't a question; Tecuul could feel something was wrong, something different than what he had originally asked for.

"In addition to your newfound longevity, you have been made physically stronger, of course. And I already told you about your improved healing and resistance to harm." Tecuul narrowed his eyes at her, knowing that wasn't what was bothering him. She smiled, "But of course, there were some other changes. You might consider them negative effects, but they don't have to be."

"What? You never told me…"

"I didn't have to tell you. If you had asked me if there would be anything bad to come of this then I would have had to answer you since you are the one who summoned and bound me here, but since you didn't ask…" she shrugged.

"What did you do?" he asked desperately.

"Very well, I will explain. Know this, I honestly could not grant your desire without some negative outcome, and even if I could have, I probably wouldn't," she laughed gaily and continued. "From this moment on, you can never again go in the sunlight. If you do, you will die, so I hope you enjoy the night. But sunlight isn't the only thing besides beheading that can kill or harm you. Wood driven into your heart will end your life as well, but I wouldn't worry too much about that if I were you." She began to walk as she spoke, at least as far as she was allowed. The summoning spell kept her bound to movement from the doorway to the end of the drawn symbols. "As I said, you'll have extraordinary strength and surely can defend against that. There may be other weaknesses I'm unaware of." She listed these things as if they were of no matter, and Tecuul was suffering a bit of shock with each one. After a pause, she continued, as if she'd almost forgotten, "One more thing, you can no longer eat food for nourishment. You can eat food if you like, but it won't sustain you. You will need to drink blood, instead, to keep yourself alive."

"What have you made of me?!" he yelled at her, revealing the fangs he now felt in his mouth.

She just smiled at him with no response to his question as his anger turned to regret. "Now, you will serve me for a time. Did your book not tell you of your

price? Now listen carefully to my instruction." And he
did.

*****

The party that set out from Jeul was closing in
quickly as the sun was rising, the silver armor of Caldoon
Soor shining brightly as it was struck by the morning sun's
rays. The rest of the soldiers with him were dressed in iron
armor, and the mages wore their blue robes with leather
armor underneath. They had discovered the farm and
noticed that no attempt was made to cover up the
kidnapping of its inhabitants.

Tecuul and his companions had been sloppy. From
the farm they had followed the trail through the town of
Rollins and it had eventually led them to the shore of the
continent. Days had passed since they left Jeul and the
group of elves had been riding as hard as they could each
day to catch up to Tecuul.

"This way!" Caldoon exclaimed as he saw that the
trail led to a cave near the beach. They all dismounted
from their horses and made their way to the cave entrance.
A fire towards the back of the cave immediately caught
their attention, so they pressed onward towards the light.
As they reached the fire, they saw Tecuul sitting behind it,
smiling with several corpses on the ground behind him.
Tecuul stood calmly.

"It's over, Tecuul," the captain said in disgust at the
death he saw before him. He drew his sword, "This time
we won't be taking you in." The soldiers with Captain
Soor all followed in drawing their swords and the mages
began to prepare spells against Tecuul's magic, but Tecuul
did not move. And so Caldoon approached Tecuul and
stabbed him through the heart.

Tecuul winced in pain but soon smiled. There was
pain from being stabbed, but Vel'dulan had been true, he

wouldn't die from this. Tecuul pulled the surprised captain close to him, tore off his helmet, and bit him in the neck. The other soldiers and mages were preparing to attack now, but Tecuul's greater strength extended to his magic and he kept the soldiers and mages frozen in place while he finished drinking from the throat of the captain. After dropping the captain's body to the ground, He focused his magic on the five mages first, subduing them easily. They hadn't sent their best mages, or Tecuul might have been in trouble. They had no idea that Tecuul would have become so powerful. He smiled as the mages bodies fell to the ground in sleep.

He now dropped his spell and drew the sword out of his chest to use as a weapon. With his left hand he also drew the short sword he wore at his waist. "Come kill me, now," he spoke with a smile and let the soldiers come to attack him. The small cave made it easy for him to test his new physical abilities against a few of the elves at a time. The soldiers could not move too many in at once or else they risked falling over each other.

The first three who moved to attack him were strong and worked in unison against Tecuul, but he was faster than they were and stronger as well. He deflected a strike from the first soldier and quickly pierced through the chest of the second soldier faster than they could account for. The third soldier tried to attack at once with the first soldier's next strike against Tecuul, but Tecuul calmly dodged the strikes, slitting the throat of the first soldier in the process.

As the first soldier began to fall, two more quickly joined in to take the place of the two who had been killed. As they moved to join in, Tecuul had bitten the third soldier he had been fighting and put him to sleep with a quick spell. The two soldiers who had joined in were disarmed almost immediately by Tecuul, and he followed up by killing them both. The rest of the soldiers charged in as best they could, but Tecuul was growing tired of fighting.

Tecuul had wanted to try out his new strength and speed against armed combatants, and he had been successful. He stabbed another of the soldiers in the stomach and one more through the throat before casting another spell to put all those who remained alive asleep as those two bodies collapsed to the ground. Before his transformation, he wouldn't have been able to affect that many that quickly. He was impressed with what he had been able to accomplish.

While his abilities were great, he realized from this fight that he still could get tired, and while his spells were stronger, they could still exhaust him. He would have to be careful in the future about how much physical and magical ability he expended at one time. As he stood alone with his thoughts, he moved around the cave to those who were still alive and began to drink from each of them at their necks. As he did this, Tecuul also cut his wrist and gave his own blood to the sleeping victims he had bitten, including the captain and the soldier he had bitten in combat.

When all of his work was finished, five soldiers had been killed in the fight and the rest of the soldiers, the captain, and all of the mages had been turned, as Vel'dulan had instructed Tecuul he could now do. They were still unconscious at the moment. When they began to wake, it was mid-day, and each of them warily looked at Tecuul. When all were awake, he spoke to them.

"Brothers! You have now become as I am." He smiled, "Join with me and we will live forever, and make this land our own!" He didn't truly intend to share power with any of them, but if he was to carry out Vel'dulan's wishes, these would work as well as anyone else to be the first turned. And she did tell him to wait for Jeul's soldiers to find him.

"We will not join you," Caldoon said, overcoming his shock of the events and taking charge once more for his soldiers, "What have you done to us?"

"Like I said, you are like me," he responded dryly. "You will never age again. You will live forever, but you will have to drink the blood of others for food."

"I will never drink the blood of my people or any others," one of the soldiers objected, and the captain nodded with approval to his man.

"Yes you will," Tecuul laughed. "You will do unspeakable things eventually, things you would never have done before because you won't be able to help it. Soon, what I have passed to you will corrupt you to your soul." One of Vel'dulan's explanations after her instructions was that anyone Tecuul turned, or anyone turned by those and so on, would be corrupted to follow his dark path and wouldn't be able to help themselves. Tecuul trusted it was true, as everything else she said had been honest, despite what she was. Tecuul was told no such corruption would happen to him, only those that came after, since he had willingly made a pact with her.

"We will fight that corruption, then," the captain stated. Tecuul approached Captain Soor, holding those around him in place with magic, and pushed him with a great unseen force out of the cave and onto the beach. Those in the cave who watched were horrified as they watched Caldoon's body burn in the sunlight. Screams of anguish could be heard as he stumbled in the sand, his flaming body soon after bursting into ash leaving only his bright, silver armor and clothes on the beach.

"Who else wants the same fate?" Tecuul asked with a crooked smile as he let them stand again. And then, something he didn't expect happened that erased the smile from his face. Five of the soldiers, and three of the mages, having accepted their fate and knowing they couldn't fight against Tecuul's new power, walked out of the cave and into the sun to their death. Only two mages and four soldiers remained, and they joined with Tecuul, seeing no other option and not wanting to die. Tecuul would begin changing the world with the help of these six elves.

CHAPTER 1

THE HIRED CREW

Alexander's fist connected with the man's face. As blood began to flow from the angry man's broken nose, two large men that Alex assumed were the man's friends attacked him. Alex dodged a punch from one of the man's friends only to get caught in the gut with a fist from the other. The man with the bloody nose attempted to strike Alex as he was doubled over, but in his fury, the man didn't notice Maria preparing to attack.

Maria swung with both hands together into his jaw, sending the man to the floor before he could lay a hand on Alexander. Behind the bar, the owner's face was stern and angry as he watched on. Within the walls of the rustic barroom, the patrons cheered and encouraged the fight that had broken out.

Matthew and Naaren, who had been sitting with Maria and Alexander, had risen from their table as soon as Alexander had thrown the punch. The two men got involved in the fight to keep the two friends of the broken-nosed man busy. While Naaren and the man who had missed Alex exchanged punches, Matthew had thrown the man who had struck Alex into a table, spilling the drinks of those sitting there. Naturally, this angered the five men at the table and they rose to join in the fight. Fortunately for Alexander, Maria, Matthew, and Naaren, they weren't alone in the bar this day. More of their crewmates from the trading ship, *Salvation*, were present.

Soon Brill, Melzer, Phyra, and Rendal joined in the fight to help. Things continued to escalate, and the barkeep yelled at his patrons to no avail. The *Salvation's* crew led the fight out of the tavern and into the unpaved streets of Sandor. By now they were outnumbered by the people from town who had been pulled into the fight, but some of the locals had just ended up fighting each other.

*****

Loud noises, yelling and screaming woke Zeyn from his nap. He stood slowly from the chair in his cabin, yawning and stretching as he rose. Nearly empty wooden walls made up the interior of the room, though the occasional framed artwork hung in some spaces. Other than his chair, the only other furniture in the cabin was a small table with an unlit lamp and a large bed with a simple wooden frame. Books were scattered around the floor, both on the area covered by the circular red and blue rug and on the uncovered wood.

The tanned man was lean and muscular, and ran a hand through his dirty blonde hair, scratching his head. Zeyn pulled on a long white shirt that hung over his brown pants and then strapped on his leather sandals. He sighed as he made his way onto the wooden deck of his ship, *Salvation*, and looked out across the docks to the coastal town of Sandor. He noticed the fight in the streets, and he realized that was what had woken him.

He frowned at the commotion of the rather large fight. The frown came from his realization that a number of his crew were involved in this particular scuffle. When he saw Maria make her way out of the brawl, he closed his eyes and shook his head. His sister was a few years younger than he was and the long hair that stopped right below her shoulder blades was the same blonde color as his. Her skin was similarly tanned, spending much time on the ship and in the sun, and they shared the same blue eyes. Her black skirt and green blouse were covered with dirt from the fighting. She rushed towards the ship and looked up to Zeyn.

"It wasn't my fault," she said as she cracked a smile, "I promise."

"Just get the crew back to the ship!" he replied, irritated. "We don't need to get held up by the law here; we're expected in Kassa tomorrow!"

Zeyn began getting the crew that had remained on board to prepare the ship to set sail. His sister returned to the fight and began retrieving the crew, sending them back to the ship as he had ordered. When she had finished, the only ones left fighting each other in the streets of Sandor were the locals.

*****

Horace happily whistled as he exited the horse-drawn carriage and began to walk the dirt streets of Kassa. The others he had been traveling with also began to leave the carriage and enter the busy town. They had been pleasant to travel with, but Horace Finch doubted he'd ever see any of them again. He did stop and turn to wave farewell as one of them, a child, yelled out, "Goodbye, sir!"

Years of waiting for the project to be complete were finally at an end. His white hair and pale, wrinkled skin showed the signs of his age, and he didn't think he had many years left that he could have waited. His walking stick gently pressed the ground beside his feet as he walked through the town towards his destination, carrying his traveling bag slung over his right shoulder. The carriage had emptied in front of the town's inn, and he passed by other small stores and houses as he traveled along on foot.

When he arrived at Gallen's home he knocked twice and waited patiently. The door was soon opened by a brown-skinned young man of twenty-three years who Horace knew quite well. Caleb Highfall smiled as soon as he saw that it was Horace who had arrived. Horace thought to himself that the young man must have recently gotten home from the smithy since he was wearing a black leather apron over his clothes and appeared filthy from work. "We finished it!" Caleb exclaimed, "After all this time, it is finally done."

"Excellent!" Horace replied, "I have the rest of the payment for Gallen. Is he here?"

"No, he's still down at the docks. My father expected you to arrive any day now, so he's been making sure it's perfect." Gallen smiled brightly. "It's the finest thing we've ever built. Would you like to come in? Or are you ready to head out and see it now?"

"I want to see it, of course," Horace said, seeming more alive, as if the news had brought back his youth. But this renewed vigor came not from what they had built, but from where it was going to take them.

*****

Gallen heard Caleb calling to him as he exited the shed on the docks where he had been doing his work. He wiped the sweat from his brow and smiled, waving to his son and to Horace. The day was approaching fast when they would finally get to use his newest creation and all the testing was now done.

Gallen was a little taller than six feet with skin slightly darker than Caleb's. He was solidly built and muscular from years of working hard with hammer and metal, though he did carry some weight in his belly. In his fifty-four years, he had crafted many tools and weapons, but nothing had prepared him for Horace's task. After working on the project with his apprentice and several other workers, and getting input from ship captains and their crews, the vessel was finally complete. It had taken five years of trial and error.

"Gallen!" Horace reached to shake his hand as he approached, "How have you been, my friend?"

"I've been well, despite the work you've kept me on," he laughed in reply, wiping his hands on a towel from his apron's pocket before he shook Horace's hand. "Caleb, check behind me."

As their welcomes finished and Caleb went into the shed to work, Horace retrieved a pouch from his pocket and gave it to Gallen. "That's everything else I owe you."

"You don't even know if it works yet."

"I trust you."

"Ha! Come; see the results of the job you gave us."

Gallen led Horace into the large shed built around a dock at the shore that housed the ship that Gallen had built. There were several workers around the vessel putting up their tools while Caleb was rechecking everything Gallen had already checked. The dock inside the shed split into two paths along the sides with the ship resting in the water in the middle of the split. The two large open doors at the back gave an entrance for the ship to leave the dock and head out into the ocean. The ship was a large, metal cylinder and was unlike anything Horace had seen before. He smiled brightly, realizing in his search for history he had helped to make important history happen.

"So, it will travel under water?" Horace asked.

"Yes," Gallen replied, "but… we've had some issues."

Horace looked to Gallen with concern. He didn't want to have to wait too much longer and had thought it was ready to travel. "Don't worry," Gallen assured him, "we've found a solution. I just want to eventually find a more permanent one."

"What's the problem?"

"Breathing. When we go under the water, there isn't air in the ship for us to breathe. Not for long, anyway. But like I said, we found a solution. For our trip, we have already gotten some elves interested in this journey and they have agreed to come along and use their magic to keep us breathing while we are deep in the ocean. They already came up with a spell for it."

"Do you trust them?" Horace's excitement was beginning to turn to worry.

"I've known them for years and they are friends," Gallen smiled. "Yes, I trust them. They are already in town and ready to depart when we are."

"Excellent!" Horace beamed. Gallen was a much trusted and valued friend, and if he trusted these elves and their magic, Horace accepted his judgment and was put at ease. "We should set out early tomorrow then."

Gallen frowned, "We can't do that. We'll have to wait."

"Why?" Horace had waited so long already and was getting impatient with the idea of having to wait any longer.

"Well, Caleb and I have built this, but it takes more than the two of us to run this ship. We tried to get some of those who helped to build it to come, but these workers are afraid of traveling so deep underwater with nothing but magic keeping them alive."

Horace sighed dejectedly.

"Don't worry," Gallen reassured him, "I already have a ship captain and some of his crew hired to work with us, and I've already given them some knowledge of how it works. Unfortunately, they haven't arrived yet. But as soon as they get here, we will be all ready to leave. I promise."

*****

Salvation sped across the ocean, long gone from the docks of Sandor. Waves crashed against the shape of a carved winged mermaid with long, loose flowing hair, her arms raised at the bowsprit and her blue-scaled tail leading down beneath the water, attached to the bottom of the bow. The rest of the *Salvation's* hull wasn't as decorative, and the unpainted oak matched the body of the mermaid. The ship's name was painted in black near the stern on the port and starboard sides. The sails that billowed from the masts of the ship were striped diagonally in blue and white.

Captain Zeyn Clarke stood on the bridge at the wheel of his ship, looking out over the sea. The waters were calm and the weather conditions were good; if this kept up, they would reach Kassa the next day on time. Maria made her way across the deck to the Captain.

"I'm sorry," she said, apologizing for the commotion the crew had caused in Kassa.

He sighed and turned to his sister, "Apology accepted. I would like to know what happened, though."

"Well," Maria began, "The crew and I were just having a drink after making the delivery. I have the money, by the way. I didn't lose it or spend it." She handed a purse of coins to him. "Anyway," she continued, "some man at the bar starting sending me drinks. I told him I wasn't interested and thought that would be it."

"So you refused him and he got mad?"

"Um, no, that's not how it went. But he wouldn't give up! Soon he sent another drink. Well, Alexander knew I refused him once, and he went to go have a talk with this stranger at the bar. Turns out this guy sending me drinks wasn't alone and before you know it things just got out of hand."

"And Alexander didn't start it?" Zeyn was pretty sure he knew what had happened now.

"Of course not. At least, if you're counting the fact that this guy wouldn't give up when I said I didn't want his attention. Alex did throw the first punch, but…"

"That's all I wanted to know. Take the wheel; I'm going to have a quick word with Alex. You're in charge, first mate."

Maria nodded and took control of the ship as Zeyn walked down the stairs from the bridge to the main deck. He stopped a moment, searching until his eyes finally fell upon the tall, freckled man with the dark hair near the main mast. "Alex!" Zeyn called as he approached him, causing Alex to whip his head towards the Captain in surprise. "In the future, please be more careful in confronting people in bars. We need to keep up good business relations in these towns and starting large fights does us no good." Hearing the captain speaking angrily to Alex about the fight, Matthew, a dark brown-skinned man with close-cut dark hair, made his way away from Alex, whom he had been speaking with.

"I'm sorry, Captain," he replied, frowning, "but you didn't hear what he said about her. She didn't hear it! I'd do it again to keep some lowlife from bothering Maria."

"I know you would, just… be more careful about it. That's all I ask."

"Yes, sir," Alex looked down, "I'll try to be more careful."

"Thanks for looking after my sister." Zeyn clasped him on the shoulder and then turned to make his way to his cabin.

He passed by the crew members working on the ship and entered in through the double doors that led to his cabin. On the table was a list of all of his crew, and Zeyn took it and sat in his chair, looking over the list one last time. He needed to be sure of which members he would bring with him to help run the underwater vessel Gallen had built. While he had already made the selections and the crew members knew who they were, he still could change his mind and wanted to be sure of his decision.

After some deliberation, when he was absolutely sure of his choices, Zeyn stood from his chair and headed back out onto the main deck, to gather together those he had chosen. He had decided on seven men and two women of his crew to join him on the coming underwater voyage.

The captain began to make his way around the main deck and found them one by one until he brought them all together. Annah Freeman was a tall, brown-skinned woman with long, dark hair and dark brown eyes. Like Matthew, she came from the northwest of the continent, from Nadara, and had been with Clarke's crew nearly as long as Alex, almost eight years.

Zeyn spotted her first of the crew that would be coming with him, and she was working at the main mast. "Annah, I want to meet with all the crew that will be going with me. If you would, please get Brill, Melzer, Phyra and Rendal for me. I'll go gather the others and meet you back here."

"I'll go get them, Captain," she replied with a smile, passing on her work to another crewmate before seeking them out.

The four human members of the crew Zeyn sent her to find were Brill Smyte, Melzer Rite, Phyra Brand, and Rendal Traverse. Brill, Melzer, and Phyra were close friends who had worked together before they ever met Clarke and joined the crew, and they had been with him for nearly five years. Brill had freckled skin, light brown hair to his shoulders, and blue eyes. Melzer's skin was tanned, his eyes were brown, his hair was short, and he kept a well-trimmed mustache and goatee. Phyra was also tanned and had short blonde hair and bright blue eyes. Rendal had traveled with Zeyn for over ten years and had joined up with the captain to get his life on a better path than the one he once followed. He had fair, freckled skin and green eyes. His long, red hair was pulled back in a ponytail and he also had a thick mustache.

Shim Lett and Bail Kan were two dwarves from a continent that Clarke and his crew had happened upon during their travels. Both men were short but very strong, and both dwarves had green eyes, thick brows, and dark hair. Shim was clean-shaven with long hair in a ponytail, and Bail had short hair and a thick, curled mustache. Both were supposed to be swabbing the deck, but he found them wrapped up in an argument near the mizzen mast. Zeyn interrupted them before finding out what they disagreed about this time, but he imagined it wasn't anything important. The two were always getting into worthless squabbles.

When he finished talking to the dwarves, he glanced around the deck, but Gor was nowhere to be seen. Gor was from the same land as Shim and Bail, but he was not a dwarf and no ordinary human either. He came from an unknown race of that continent who kept themselves hidden, but he had yearned to seek out travel and adventure. He stood eight and a half feet tall with blue eyes and very smooth, tan skin and grew no hair, like all of his people. He was not only tall, but quite muscular and strong, and very kindhearted.

Like Shim and Bail, Gor had been with Clarke's crew for three years. Zeyn made his way below deck to the galley and found Gor there, trying to get something to eat from the cook. "We're going to have a meeting," Zeyn said, getting his attention. "Get up to the deck." The Captain left the galley and took the stairs back to the main deck.

The last member of the crew joining their underwater adventure was Naaren Soor, who was looking out from the crow's nest. Naaren was an elf from Leef, a group of small villages of elves who had separated themselves from any of the elven kingdoms. Like all elves, he had light skin and pointed ears. His long brown hair was loose and his eyes were bright and blue, and he'd been with the crew from the beginning. At his left side, Naaren wore a sword that he had never used or unsheathed, yet he never went anywhere without. As Zeyn yelled up at Naaren to let him know they were meeting before heading to shore, *Salvation* was pulling into the dock in Kassa and Naaren climbed his way down from the nest.

Zeyn began to address them when the ship was secured to the dock and the crew members he had chosen gathered before him. "You've all done well preparing for this, and you all know your jobs once we set sail on this strange journey in this new kind of ship. We've been able to study the workings of this vessel on previous visits, but this will be our first time actually using it, so we'll have a trial run tomorrow before the actual voyage."

"Captain, do you think we'll be seeing any sea monsters down there?" Bail asked.

Zeyn replied, "I doubt it, Bail."

"I was hoping we might get to fight one."

"With what, dummy?" Shim said, "We can't get out of that metal boat once we're underwater. Not unless you want to drown." Gor laughed as Bail frowned, thinking.

"Just be ready for tomorrow, crew," Zeyn said, "Maria and I are going to meet with Gallen now. Stay on the ship until we get back. We shouldn't be long, and then we'll see about getting some lodging for the night. Annah, come with me." The crew separated and went back to getting prepared for the night.

Zeyn and Annah found Maria as she made her way down from the bridge, and then the three of them walked over to Alex. "Stay with the ship and keep the crew in line," Zeyn told Alex. Alex nodded in reply. "Annah, give him a hand if he needs it."

"Yes, sir," she replied with a smile.

As Zeyn and Maria left the ship Alex frowned, watching them walk into town. "She'll be fine without you for a few minutes," Annah said, elbowing Alex.

"I don't know what you're talking about," he replied, quickly walking away as she laughed.

*****

Horace, Gallen, and Caleb sat around the smooth, black metal table in Gallen's home eating their lunch. Horace's excitement over the past few days had only grown, and he appeared livelier than when he arrived. His excitement was infectious and had rubbed off on Gallen and Caleb as well. As they were finishing their meal, the sound of knocking at the door grabbed their attention. Caleb hopped up and quickly went to answer. He was excited to see Zeyn and Maria as he pulled the door open.

"Hello," Maria said, "We are ready to see this grand thing that you've made."

"Hi, Captain Clarke. Hello, Maria," Caleb replied as Gallen approached and shook the captain's hand.

"Clarke," Gallen said, "we've been anxiously awaiting your arrival." He smiled as Horace approached. "This is Horace, the financer of this project."

"Thank you very much for helping us," Horace said, extending his hand.

"You're welcome, Horace," Zeyn replied as he shook his hand. "I'm Captain Zeyn Clarke and this is my sister and second in command, Maria Clarke."

Maria reached out and shook Horace's hand. "I hope you find what you're looking for."

"Thank you," Horace replied.

"Maria is going to be captain of my ship in my absence," he explained, "and I'll be bringing along part of my crew for the trip. We need some rest, though. After we go look at the finished vessel can we have a day to rest before the journey begins?"

"That's no problem at all," Horace answered. "The ruins I'm searching for will still be there if we wait one more day, I suppose."

"Thanks," Zeyn smiled, "Now, Gallen, let's go see your finished work if you don't mind."

"Follow me," Gallen said and led them back to the docks.

Soon they were all inside of the shed on the dock, looking at the large metal object floating in the water as they stood around it. The gray metal of the vessel was dull in color. Although the ship for underwater travel was mostly cylindrical, the top was flat and had a sealable metal hatch door to allow entrance. The front of the vessel was round in shape, and the back end appeared to taper off until it was flat.

Gallen and Caleb were looking down with pride at their creation, and Maria was fascinated with how the large metal vessel was able to stay afloat. Zeyn knelt down and placed a hand against the cold, metallic side. A grin spread across his face as he looked over the finished ship. "Wonderful." He stood and turned, facing Gallen. "This really is amazing work. Everything still works like you instructed us on our last visit?"

"Yes, it does," Gallen answered with a smile.

Maria got down to her knees and reached out to touch the surface of the vessel as her brother had. "I still wish I could come."

"If you did, who would take care of the ship?" her brother asked rhetorically. "I'd leave Alex in charge but I'd have to tie him to the mast to get him to stay if you were coming with us."

Maria laughed. "I suppose that's true. Well, it looks like I'm Captain Clarke, now."

"Maybe you can come with us tomorrow to take a quick test trip to make sure we know how to operate things?"

She smiled brightly. "Oh, that would be wonderful! Tomorrow then. For now, I'll head back and check on the crew."

Captain Clarke continued to look over the ship that could travel underwater as Maria left. "We'll find a place to stay in town for the night and then we'll be ready. Who else is coming with us?"

"Well, the three of us of course," Gallen said, referring to himself, Caleb and Horace, "you and your crew, and two elf friends of mine, Olii and Noon."

CHAPTER 2

VAMPIRE HUNTER

Kari ran with a hauntingly unnatural speed just beside the main road as she focused on making it to her next destination. Her journey had gone on for several weeks now and despite her strength, she was beginning to feel the toll from her travels. If she had known who to see from the start, she could have possibly found him much sooner, but at least tonight she would finally arrive and get the help she needed. That is if the man she was looking for wasn't on the move again. With his help, she hoped everything could be made right.

As she saw the town from a distance, she slowed her run to a walk and moved onto the road. She smiled, looking around at the night and to the stars in the sky. After all of the terrible things that had happened, she could still smile. A carriage passed by her leaving the town as she reached the gates and entered Langston.

*****

Roland had just put out his lamp and was about to go to sleep when a knock came at the door. He didn't know why anyone would have a need for him at this hour. "I've only been here two days," he muttered to himself as he stepped out of bed. His journey had recently brought him to Langston to follow up on some news, but so far it had led nowhere.

The knock came once again. "Just a moment," he said, putting on pants and a shirt. He lit the lamp by his bedside and made his way to the door, glancing in the small mirror on the wall with his bright blue eyes as he passed by. His brown hair was longer than usual and he hadn't shaved in weeks. He was starting to look a little rough, though his skin wasn't as pale as it usually was.

He opened the door to see a young girl in front of him. She was short and thin with blonde hair to her shoulders and dark blue eyes. Her clothing was filthy and she looked quite unkempt. Roland didn't recognize her. "I'm sorry, you must have the wrong room," he said and began to shut the door.

"No wait!" she yelled out, "Are you Roland Lam? The innkeeper told me you were in this room."

He pulled the door open and replied, "I am. But who are you? Why are you looking for me?" Roland was irritated that his location was given so freely and that irritation shone in his expression and his voice.

"My name is Kari. Kari Sleyn. I'm sorry to disturb you, but I heard that you might be able to help me. I was told you'd probably know what to do. My village is in trouble and we need your help!" she pleaded.

"My help? Slow down." He let out a yawn and took a moment to keep his ill temper in check. The girl appeared to genuinely need assistance. "Why me?" He asked and then frowned with a realization. "Does this have something to do with vampires?" It wouldn't be the first time he'd been approached about a vampire problem, but it had been many years since anyone had needed him to kill one.

She nodded in reply. He opened the door and moved to a chair in his room at a small table. Roland was known as a vampire killer throughout the southeast kingdoms and if someone was coming to him for help he knew that was likely the reason. He looked at her as she stood in the doorway. "Well," he gestured to the other chair at the table, "what are you waiting for?"

"I can't come in."

"Look, you came to me," Roland said, becoming irritated, "I didn't invite you here to wake me up in the middle of the night. If we're going to discuss your problem..." He trailed off and narrowed his eyes, frowning as he moved to the wall and pulled the small mirror from it, facing the glass towards Kari.

Looking into the glass of the mirror, all Roland could see was the hallway, as if Kari wasn't even there. He went to the bed and drew his sword from its sheath from where it was propped against the wall. "Let me see your teeth," he said as he approached her.

"Please," she said, tears in her eyes, "I'm just here to explain and see if you'll help." She raised her upper lip with her thumbs to fully reveal her fangs. "Yes, I am a vampire, but please let me come in."

Roland sighed. "Fine. I suppose you look easy enough to handle if you get out of hand. You may come in." It was a lie. Any vampire would be stronger and faster than he was. Certainly, none he had killed had ever been easy to face, but he had learned methods of dealing with those who he had fought, and his skills had always worked before. He didn't think she would try to attack him.

She smiled as she entered the room and moved closer to the table, drying tears from her eyes with her hand. "Thank you."

"I'm surprised I had to invite you in, I thought that only worked with actual homes. I suppose I'm always bound to learn something new. Since I paid for the room it must act as a temporary home to the curse…" He trailed off with his musings and got back to the matter at hand. "So when you say you have a vampire problem, you're referring to your condition?"

"It's not just me, it's my whole village."

Roland frowned. "There hasn't been a vampire sighted in years. Let me see the bite." He stood and approached her. "Do you have any idea of how many vampires attacked your village to turn everyone?" he asked as he began looking around her neck.

"You won't find a bite. There isn't one," she said. He looked at her questioningly, as her words seemed to be correct. Her neck was perfectly clear of any fang marks. The bite of a vampire was the only wound that never healed when a person was transformed. "And we never saw a single vampire attack."

"The neck is most common, but it's not the only place they'll bite. I'll take your word, though, for now. No one in your town was bitten?"

"No. We all just woke up one day and… we were like this."

"Hmm," Roland placed the sword back in the sheath and returned to his chair. "Tell me everything. Start from the beginning." This curious case intrigued him. It was something new, and he hadn't found anything new with vampires over his searching for the past ten years.

She remembered it all very well and didn't think she'd ever forget. "It started a month ago in Menton. That first night everything was normal. Everyone was in their homes at night. My family had just eaten a late supper and we all had lain down to sleep. No one slept long." She rubbed her eyes a moment and continued. "When we woke up in the middle of the night, my parents and I thought it was strange that we all woke up at the same time when there had been no noise or any other thing to wake us. At first, we thought it an odd coincidence, but then we saw lights in nearby homes.

"My father was about to go to our neighbors to see if something was going on, but then… my mother was the first to notice that our teeth were different. We all did our best not to panic. We had heard of vampires, but we'd never seen one. No one from our village had even been involved in the war, but we knew what we had become. None of us handled it well, but we knew to stay out of the sun and did our best to survive. We'd heard stories." Kari moved to the chair across from Roland and sat.

"We didn't eat for three days. When we were awake, at night, we'd try to eat food as normal, but it didn't fill us, although it still had taste. We knew we'd have to eat blood to survive, but we didn't want to kill anyone. We began to feed on the blood of animals, and it worked. It kept us going, but we were killing off all of the cattle and sheep and everything. After a week we learned how to drink from them without draining them dry.

"Eventually the mayor decided that some of us should be sent out to find help. Those of us chosen all went separate ways with instructions to return in a month, whether we find help or not."

Roland frowned at this. "So, you mean to say that there are other vampires loose in the world again, just wandering around?"

"Yes, but they're like me. They have control of themselves… the people chosen to seek help were carefully decided on. I promise."

"We'll see if they control themselves. I haven't had a vampire to kill in a long time, but if it turns out one of these vampires from Menton starts killing, I will have to again." He thought about what she had said, about them being carefully chosen. "Why were you chosen? You look very young to be out on your own."

"I'm sixteen. Besides, with the powers I have right now, I can safely travel alone."

Roland shook his head. "They sent out a teenager?"

She looked down sheepishly. "I wasn't selected. I volunteered, but they didn't want to let me go. I left anyway, but I let my parents know. This was my chance to explore some of the world and to help my friends and family."

"So how is it you found out about me and where I am? And why do you think I'll help you?"

"When I started traveling, I intended to seek out the elves in Jeul. A... friend I met convinced me that wasn't a smart decision."

"I don't know. The elves in Jeul may have helped you, but there are others who would refuse or worse. Some of them are particularly touchy about vampires."

"Well, this friend, he told me I should find you. He didn't say why you'd be interested in helping, only that he knew of you, and knew you'd likely help." She leaned forward and grabbed his hands. "Please say you'll help us."

"I can try, but that's the most I can offer. Your problem does interest me and may give me some insight into something I've been working on. Stay here and I'll go get some things together. The sooner we get out of town the better. Did anyone notice you in the street? Did anyone see you come in the inn?"

"I don't think so, why?"

"Because if someone noticed..." A loud knock at the door cut him off. "Get out of sight of the door," he whispered cautiously. Kari moved around the bed and hid behind it on the floor as Roland put out the light and removed his pants and shirt to appear as if he'd just been woken, then opened the door. "May I help you?"

A young man with two other men behind him answered him, "We heard someone came in here looking for you tonight."

"Was it some girl?" Roland asked in return. "About this tall," he said gesturing her height with his hand, "with blonde hair?" Kari began to worry.

"Yes, that's her."

"Well, she was the first person to wake me up from my sleep tonight and I sent her away. I'll say the same to you. Leave me alone." He began to shut the door in the man's face, but the man stopped the door with his hand.

"Now wait just a minute, I want some answers."

"First tell me something, who are you?" Roland yawned.

"My name's Darel."

Roland took a moment to look Darel and his friends over and assess them, in appearance and ability as best he could. Darel and one of the men both stood about Roland's height, but the other man was taller. Darel and the tall one had brown hair, Darel's cut short and the tall man's shaggy to his neck, and the other kept his head shaved bald. Darel's eyes were green and the other two had brown eyes, their faces were all smooth and gave away their youthfulness.

Roland knew that he had at least ten years on the three men, and with those years he knew he had much more experience than them. But they were all in good shape, and all were armed with swords at their hips and perhaps other weapons that weren't visible, so they could be a problem if Roland had to fight all three at once. Of course, Kari could overpower them, but if there was a disturbance, someone else in the inn would take note of Roland and the girl as they were fleeing.

When his seconds of analyzing were done, Roland continued with more questions. "And why are you looking for this girl? Did she steal something from you?"

"No," Darel answered, with a shake of his head. "She's a vampire."

Roland sighed and shook his head, "There are no vampires anymore; they were all killed off. I should know." Roland had been afraid they must know her true nature. He began to plan things out in his head. If he could get these men to leave, they could escape and make good distance.

"That's what we thought, too. But we saw this girl leave Arndell two days ago, in the night. She got here awfully fast for someone with no mount or carriage. And we had confirmed reports from two witnesses there that she had no reflection in the mirror in the tavern there, and another witness noticed her teeth."

"I see. Well, she told me she'd be coming back to see me tomorrow, earlier at night before I go to sleep. Come back then and you can kill her or whatever you're after."

"You are Roland the vampire killer, correct? I thought you'd want to kill her yourself," Darel said, puzzled. "I hear you've got a grudge against them." Roland held in his surprise. He wasn't sure how they knew who he was. Maybe they'd asked the innkeeper who was staying there when they heard the girl had visited the room. If he ever came back to Langston, he'd be having a talk with this innkeeper.

"That was a long time ago. Now, I'm just tired and want to be left alone." Roland looked tired and unhappy with the man. Neither expression was an act.

"Fine. We'll be staying here and keep an eye out for her return, then. Come on, men." And with that, Darel and his small group left and went off to rent a couple of their own rooms for the night.

When the door shut, Roland began to get dressed again, this time putting his boots on, too. "Kari, time to get out of here," he said as she rose from her hiding place.

"I thought I was careful," she said with a frown.

"It doesn't matter, the sooner we get out the better, I suppose. Hopefully, we'll be long gone before they can do anything about it." He put on his sword belt and grabbed his pack, then looked at her quizzically, "Did you bring anything with you on your trip?"

"No, I left in a hurry and didn't think to pack anything. There is plenty of food in the forests and I wasn't worried about changing clothes... None of us have cared too much about our appearances, we've had other worries."

"Alright, well then, we don't have anything else to pack, let's get going." Kari began walking towards the door and Roland stopped her, grabbing her by the right shoulder with his left hand and pointing behind her towards the window with his right. "Out the window, don't be seen."

Kari turned and hurried over and looked out the window before leaping from the room on the second floor to the ground below. Roland slung his pack over his shoulder and moved to the window, carefully climbing down to the ground. "Follow me." Roland walked on stealthily and Kari followed him on to the stables.

*****

"You didn't have to buy this carriage from that man," Kari said as she sat in the front of the carriage with Roland as he drove the horses. They had been out of the town of Langston for a couple of hours. "Couldn't we travel faster on horseback? I can travel just as fast without it really."

"Yes, you can, but I can't," he said, "And when daylight comes you can't travel at all. This way we can cover more ground and you can sleep in the carriage with the curtains closed to keep the sun out. Speaking of which, how did you manage to travel to find me and stay out of the sun?"

"I stayed at inns during the day, like the one in Arndell. Other times I'd find dark places in the forests to sleep during the day or in caves if I could find them. When are you going to sleep on this trip?"

"When night comes again, we'll switch. I'll tell you which way to take us."

"I know how to get back home, Roland," she replied.

"We're not going to your village just yet, Kari. I told you I will help you if I can, but I need to get back to my home, first. If that's not alright, then you are free to go back on your own."

"That's fine, I can wait. But my parents do expect me back by the end of this week."

"We will make it back before then." Roland's stomach began to growl. "You may want to go ahead and get inside; I don't want anyone to notice you and it will be daylight when we get to Freyg. I have a friend there who will watch the carriage for me while I get some supplies and a bite to eat. He won't ask any questions and won't look inside."

"I'm trusting you with my life, Roland. I hope your friend is as reliable as you say he is."

Roland stopped and Kari got out of the front and moved around to get inside the carriage, pulling all of the curtains closed. Roland was relieved to be alone in the front. He'd gotten used to traveling alone since most of his companions had abandoned the quest they had undertaken and accepted the fate they were suffering through. Roland kept to the roads and they avoided trouble along the way. Their carriage arrived in Freyg shortly after the sun rose.

*****

Darel had received word from one of his friends, the tall one, that he hadn't seen Roland leave his room at all after morning came. "Maybe he's just sleeping in," Darel said, "we did wake him up, and he was disturbed before us by that vampire girl."

"Maybe that's all it is, Darel," his friend, Will, replied, "But if I don't see him come out in the next hour or so I'm going to check on him."

"Fine," Darel said, "that sounds like a good idea."

When the hour had passed Will knocked on the door twice to no reply. Will and Darel broke in to find that Roland wasn't there. He quickly went to check with the innkeeper only to find out from him that he'd never seen Roland that morning. When their other companion, Tras, returned to the inn, the three packed up their things and began to go to work seeing if they could discover which way Roland had taken out of town.

CHAPTER 3

ELLINE

The metal vessel emerged from the waters inside the shack on the docks at Kassa. The test voyage had been short but successful in making sure everyone could do their jobs. Propelling the craft through the water required much strength, and the job was shared by Gor, Shim, Bail, Brill, Melzer, and Rendal. They each alternated the job of manually turning the crank which moved the vessel in order to save strength. Gor worked it by himself, then the job went to Shim and Bail, and lastly the task was performed by Brill, Melzer, and Rendal, before going back around to Gor. In this way, the underwater ship could continue to move without stopping.

Annah and Phyra worked on the lower deck of the ship with the ballast tanks to submerge the ship. The two women would use the levers to fill the main tanks and the forward and rear tanks. Naaren worked with them to expel the water from the tanks so the vessel could emerge from the sea. Annah and Phyra would again open the tanks and Naaren would use his magic to expel the water out of the ballast tanks.

Naaren also had another important job on the journey. He had put a magic window in place on the main deck so the captain could see where he was steering the ship and to allow the crew to look out into the waters. He also, along with Olii and Noon, placed light spells around the vessel to allow them to see into the distance of the sea while underwater. Lanterns were used by the crew for their inside light. For the duration of the voyage, Olii and Noon used the spell they had devised to keep breathable air inside of the metal ship.

Horace was the first to exit as the hatch along the flat top of the vessel opened. "That was amazing!" he remarked when he was on the docks again. "That magical window was ingenious. I was wondering how we would see outside so we could actually observe the ruins if we find them."

"What are we looking for, anyway?" Brill asked as he exited out behind Horace, followed by Phyra.

Horace smiled to him, "I discovered an old book in the library in Jeul that mentioned an elven kingdom named Moora. But the area on the map where it should be doesn't exist on any current maps we have. The people of Jeul denied its existence, but I believe they were trying to hide something. As I continued my studies, I think I've discovered where it once was. Since there is no land where it should be, I think it might have sunk into the ocean. That is where we are going."

"How is it possible that such a large part of the land would sink?" Phyra asked as the last of the group made it to the docks from inside.

"I don't know," Horace said, "but if we find something there, then I'll know I was right. If we find nothing, then perhaps the book I found was nothing more than a story."

"And this will have been a waste of time," Brill muttered.

"We get paid either way, Brill," Phyra reminded him. "Don't you think it's fascinating anyway? Seeing what could be down there, even if there isn't some old city?"

"I suppose…"

"Think of the adventure, man!" Bail exclaimed and clapped his hand on Brill's back.

"You're still not going to get to fight anything," Shim laughed to Bail.

"Alright, everyone," Zeyn said, "go back to the ship and get any supplies or food you think you might need. We shouldn't be under more than half a day, but relieve yourselves now before we depart. We leave in an hour! Say your farewell to your shipmates while you're there."

The crew replied with "Yes, Captain!" and "Aye aye!" before heading back to the *Salvation*. Horace left as well to rest up before traveling.

As the crew headed back to the ship, Maria approached her brother and spoke, "Thanks for letting me come on the test trip."

"You're welcome," he replied, "Take good care of my ship while I'm gone."

"Don't worry; I'll be a great captain in your absence." She smiled.

"I know you will," Zeyn looked sternly at her. "No fighting."

"Me? I'll try to keep Alexander from trying to defend me. Besides, you won't be gone long. What could happen in a day?" She laughed and turned to head back to the ship.

Zeyn sighed and looked at the ship, then looked to Gallen, who was looking over the hull with his son. "Does this thing have a name yet?"

Gallen frowned, "You know, I'm not quite sure what I want to call it. Caleb and I have talked about it but we never came to a decision."

"He wanted to call it a whale boat," Caleb laughed. "My father is a genius with metal but not very creative with names."

"I could understand that... but I didn't mean the type of vessel. What I mean is something very personal, a name that deeply connects you with your boat. You know my ship is called *Salvation*, and all the other ship captains have names for their ships. Even the pirates... Some are named after people, places, things..."

Caleb shrugged, "We haven't really thought about that at all."

"Well, let me know if you do. I think Gallen should give it a name since it's his creation. I'll be back with my crew in an hour." With that thought, the captain left to return to the *Salvation* and get some things of his own.

A name, Gallen thought to himself as he looked over the ship. *She needs a name.*

When the hour had passed, Captain Clarke returned to the shed on the docks with his crew and supplies for the journey. As he entered through the door he saw that Horace, Gallen, and Caleb were already there. "You're all ready to go?" he asked.

"Yes," Gallen answered, "and I have decided on a name."

"Really?" Caleb asked, surprised his father hadn't told him yet.

"Elline," Gallen said, looking to his son with a smile, "This metal boat will be named *Elline*." Caleb nodded and smiled as his father spoke the name. It had been his mother's.

"A good name," Horace said, being familiar with their family and knowing its meaning.

"Very well then. Let's be off," Clarke said and his crew boarded the diving boat, *Elline*. The crew reported to their positions and began their voyage.

*****

Aboard the *Salvation*, Maria looked out across the ocean. Somewhere down there, her brother was going on an extraordinary voyage. While it's possible it could be boring, discovering a lost city would be exciting if they actually found it. And the adventure of underwater travel was so new and exciting! If Alexander couldn't stay on the *Salvation* without her, then surely Matthew could have been left in charge.

Maria thought her brother must be worried about the worst that could happen, and all of them drowning from a terrible accident under the sea. Sometimes he was too overprotective. It was a wonder he even let her be his first mate and work with him. She let out a sigh.

"He'll be fine, Captain," Alexander said as he walked up beside her and watched some of the seagulls flying over the water.

"I'm not worried," Maria replied, "Well, not too much anyway. I just wish I could have gone, too."

Alex turned to her and smiled. "I understand. Is the crew to stay on the ship for the evening?"

"No, we don't have to. Tell the crew they can go ashore; just make sure they know to report back here in the morning. My brother should be back by then."

"Yes, Captain." Alexander left to gather the remaining crew and give them Maria's orders. Maria watched him go with a smile and something caught her eye in the town. She crossed the ship and pulled out her spyglass, extending it and looking through to get a closer look.

There was a strange procession of what appeared to be soldiers entering Kassa. Soon she could see that they were elves, and they were from the kingdom of Jeul. The soldiers were escorting a carriage along the streets. She closed the spyglass and put it back into the pouch she kept at her side. Kassa wasn't within the realm of Jeul, so why would they be here now? She smiled. Maybe they'd get to have an adventure of their own. *Which crewmates would be the best spies?* she thought to herself as she grinned.

*****

"Thank you for giving us a window down here, too, Naaren," Phyra said with a smile. They had been underwater for quite a while now and the view was beautiful. They had never seen things below the seas in this way before. Phyra, Naaren, and Annah were on the lower deck, and their work with the ballast tanks had been going well.

"You're welcome," Naaren replied, "It's really something."

Annah watched as a shark swam by in their view. "All this time sailing," she said, "and I've never thought about how deep the seas ran and what it was like down here." This trip had been eye-opening for everyone on board.

"I don't think anyone has thought much about it," Naaren said, "Not even my people."

"Well, I'm sure the Captain has," Phyra suggested with a knowing grin, and they laughed.

On the upper deck above them, Brill, Melzer, and Rendal were having their turn at propelling the vessel. Captain Clarke was navigating and steering while Gor, Bail, and Shim were resting in a side room on the deck. Horace, Gallen, and Caleb were all looking out of the magical window that Naaren had set on the upper deck for viewing out into the sea. Caleb was excited by all that he saw in the sea. While he and his father had been building the metal vessel, he had thought much about what they would find when they finally went on this voyage.

"Do you think we'll see any mermaids down here?" Caleb asked to no one in particular. "I've heard stories that they live deep in the oceans."

Olii and Noon both laughed. They were both above deck and were controlling the breathable air throughout both decks of *Elline* together. "There's no such thing as a mermaid," Olii said.

"They are just stories," Noon added, "a tale spread by humans who've spent too much time at sea and gone crazy."

Caleb frowned. "Don't worry, son," Gallen said, "there are plenty of things down here to marvel at without mermaids." Caleb nodded and looked back outside. They had at least seen many fish and other creatures they had never seen before.

Horace remained silent during the exchange, his focus on the waters. Soon he may discover the truth about Moora if it ever really existed. Deep down, he believed that it had existed and that the elves of Jeul were hiding something from him when he had asked them about what he had found in the book. Horace took a seat on one of the stools set near the window, his nerves about the trip relaxed in the view. Soon the bottom of the sea was in view as they traveled along.

"Caleb, would you check on the lower deck for me?" Zeyn asked. "Just see how they are doing."

"Sure thing, Captain," Caleb responded.

"Just Zeyn is fine, I'm not your captain. But thank you."

Caleb nodded and headed down the ladder into the lower deck of the vessel. As he entered the room he saw Annah and Phyra checking the ballast tanks while Naaren was watching the window. "Annah," Caleb said, "Zeyn wanted me to check and make sure everything was going alright down here."

"Everything is fine," she replied, "the boat is moving steadily on the bottom now."

"Do any of you need anything?"

"We're fine for now, Caleb," Phyra said pleasantly. "Thank you."

"Thankfully none of us need to use the head," Naaren said and Annah and Phyra both laughed. Caleb assumed it was a joke, but he didn't know what head the elf was talking about.

"I'll let him know you're alright," Caleb said. He began to turn to climb up the ladder but stopped as he heard Naaren speak.

"Look at that!" Naaren exclaimed. Annah and Phyra turned to look out the window and were surprised as well. There were remains of a city on the ocean floor. Not much seemed to be left, but there was enough to see what may once have been foundations for large structures.

On the upper deck, Horace stood to look through the window, his face bright with excitement at all he saw. This must be what he was searching for! The sunken elven kingdom of Moora. He had no idea how long this had all been underwater, but he saw that a lot of it had deteriorated and broken away. Nothing appeared to be intact. He wondered if perhaps there were any remains of the castle of this kingdom.

"This is what you've been looking for?" Gallen asked Horace, smiling.

"Yes, I'm not crazy," he replied. "It is real. But why does no one seem to know about this?"

"Did you see?!" Caleb asked excitedly as he rushed onto the upper deck from the ladder. "Did you see the mermaid?"

He was followed onto the deck by Naaren. Zeyn looked to him, "What did you see?"

"There wasn't a mermaid," Naaren replied, "but there was something unusual that darted off in the water over there." Naaren gestured to the left near the rocky wall of the continent. Whatever lay beyond was hidden until they rounded the corner. As they did they noticed a large hole, a cave in the side of the wall. "Whatever it was must have gone in there…"

"It looked like a person, it had to be a mermaid," Caleb insisted.

"Caleb, it didn't have any fish parts. Aren't mermaids supposed to be half-fish?" Naaren said. Caleb nodded in response and Naaren continued, "It was something I don't know how to identify, though. I didn't get a good enough look."

Zeyn grinned. "Well, let's follow it in."

"What are we following?" Bail asked, coming out of the side room having heard the commotion. "Did we find a sea monster, Captain?" He had his sword drawn and was followed by Shim, who was shaking his head.

"I don't know yet, but put that away. Naaren, tell the girls we're going into the cave… if that's alright with you, Horace?"

"By all means," Horace replied, "I'm intrigued."

"Very well, then," Zeyn said. Naaren nodded to the Captain and headed below to the lower deck. Gor exited from the side room and took over duties of propelling the boat. Brill, Melzer, and Rendal joined in watching out the window as *Elline* began to enter the cave. Soon the cave was dark except for the light provided by Naaren that was included with the windows.

As the boat moved deeper into the cave, the crew noticed light shining down through the water up ahead. "Well, that's interesting," Zeyn observed. He leaned over the hold and yelled down below to Annah and Phyra, "Prepare to emerge. Naaren, I need to see above me, if you could move the window for me. Gor, stop moving forward."

Gor stopped turning the crank and Naaren moved the window from the front of the deck to the ceiling, allowing everyone to see directly above. He had partially climbed the ladder so he could see the upper deck and where he was moving the window, but then returned below to empty the ballast tanks. The captain, crew, and passengers all looked up. There was an external light source and it did look as if they would be able to surface within this cave, despite being deep under the ocean. Soon *Elline* rose and broke through to the surface of the water. Everyone looked to Zeyn.

"Olii, Noon, we need to be careful," Zeyn began, "I don't know if we can breathe down here this far underground. Could you have your magic ready as we exit to help us breathe?"

"I guess," Olii responded, "although this is quite odd…"

"Maybe we'll find some answers here," Noon suggested.

"Everyone, I'm going out first," Zeyn said. "Just to check that everything is alright." The captain moved to the ladder in the middle of the deck and climbed up and opened the hatch. Olii and Noon stood nearby the ladder and kept a bubble of air around the hatch for Zeyn to breathe.

"Captain Clarke," Noon said, "I'm sensing a very similar magic at work already out there. I think we'll be able to breathe."

Zeyn stepped out onto the top of the vessel and hopped over to a landing of rock nearby. *Elline* had come up next to a large open cave within the earth. It seemed to Zeyn that the tunnel and large cave he stood within now had been manmade. There was also artificial light filling the area. Several globes of light hung in the air, magically placed.

There were four tunnels, two to the left and two to the right which led off to unknown areas and double doors straight ahead that Captain Clarke assumed led to another room. As he made these observations, the others were making their way over. Those that couldn't make the jump were tossed over by Gor first, and he made his way over last, carrying Horace with him.

As Gor landed and joined the others, several green figures, all with dark hair, appeared and approached them. All of them were male and weren't concerned with modesty, as they wore small, brown clothes that only covered them from their waist down and around their groin. They wore nothing on their feet and had no armor of any kind, but they were all armed with pikes and formed a line barring any entrance past them.

Bail drew his sword, and Zeyn motioned to him to sheathe the blade. "You're the only one of us with a weapon and we're outnumbered," the Captain said. "Put it away."

One of the figures spoke, "What are you? Why are you here?" Captain Clarke and his crew all understood the elvish language that had just been spoken. Many on the surface were familiar with the language, though all elves knew the human language and tended to use it when dealing with humans.

"Captain," Naaren said, "let me."

"Very well," Zeyn replied.

Naaren began in his language. "I am an elf. Most of the rest of our group are human, and we have two dwarves and… Gor. We came here to find Moora. Do you know of it?"

Naaren was also curious about these green men, for while all the ones who approached now with weapons were male, he was sure the form they had seen while still in the vessel was female. He also noted that other than their skin color, they all appeared to be elves based on their language and pointed ears.

As Naaren asked his question the double doors opened up and an elf stepped through. He had white hair and his skin tone wasn't green but the skin color of surface elves, though quite pale from his time out of the sun. Though his age, like all elves, wasn't certain at a glance, the fact that he was quite old was apparent in the wrinkles of his face. Also notable to the crew of *Elline* was that unlike the green elves, this elf dressed as those of the surface would, at least one of high station. His purple vestment worn over his white robe, tied across with a golden rope belt, was quite decorative and marked him as someone of importance. Unlike the green elves, his feet were covered in fancy purple shoes.

"Perhaps I can answer your questions," he said in the human tongue and then directed his speech to the green elves, "Allow them to enter and speak with me, but keep up your guard." This also was in the human language, which let Captain Clarke and his crew know that these green elves did speak and understand their speech.

"Thank you," Naaren said with a bow, and Zeyn took the lead to head in through the doors, gesturing for everyone to follow.

CHAPTER 4

THE VAMPIRE WAR

At the corner of a wooden building in Freyg, Roland stood by the carriage he had acquired in Langston. He was having a conversation with a sandy-haired man slightly shorter than himself. The blue-eyed man was also thinner than Roland, though was muscular underneath the blue tunic and black pants he wore. "…and that's the story, Auben," Roland finished. "At least, that's all I know. This could be very important to us."

Auben wasn't the friend Roland had intended to watch the carriage when he told Kari someone would watch her, but it was better that it was Auben. Unlike the friends in Freyg he may have had watch Kari, he was able to let Auben know the entire tale she had told him. "Do you mind watching over her while I go get something to eat?" Roland gestured towards the small restaurant across the dirt road.

"Of course I don't," Auben replied, "if I see Bree, I'll tell her where you are."

"She's back as well?" Roland was surprised. The three of them had split up over a week ago, and he himself was in Freyg earlier than he had planned to be. Either they both had found something interesting as well, or more likely, the two of them were beginning to tire of these trips like their other companions who no longer traveled out from their home in search of answers.

"Yes. She got here the day after I did, and we've been waiting a few days."

"I was worried I'd be the first one back and I'd have to head on without the two of you. That's good news. Did either of you find anything?"

"No, you're the only one who found anything of interest." Auben sounded excited about what Roland had told him, and Roland understood his excitement. After all this time, they may have found a lead to a solution for their own people. This did, however, confirm Roland's suspicions that they had both returned early because they were growing tired of all this. "Maybe we can finally save Aalen," Auben grinned.

Roland was hoping the same. "We'll see." He began to walk towards the restaurant. "I shouldn't be long," he turned and told Auben. Roland was trying not to get his hopes up, but it was good to see his friends able to still smile despite their circumstance. Roland continued across the street and entered the building to get something to eat before the journey home.

*****

Bree Maave walked through the door and spotted Roland as he was mopping up the last bit of brown gravy with the end of a roll and putting it in his mouth. He smiled at her as he finished his drink to wash down his food and waved for her to come over and sit down. "Hello, Roland," the elven woman said as she took a seat at his table. "It's good to see you." She pulled her loose, long red hair back as it had fallen in front of her face.

"You too, Bree," he replied, "I do prefer when the three of us travel together."

"Agreed. I'm sorry I came back so soon, but it's all starting to wear on me," she admitted. "So, I hear you found something good this time. Glad one of us finally has. At least, that's what Auben tells me." Her large, green eyes seemed to shine with excitement.

Roland glanced around to make sure no one was sitting near them or could overhear their conversation. He pulled his chair around the square table to sit beside her, leaning in closer to her before he spoke in hushed tones. "A girl came and found me in Langston. If her story is true, then her whole town, Menton, has been transformed into vampires."

Bree was shocked. "There are vampires attacking people again? I didn't think there were any left out roaming and turning people…"

"According to Kari, the girl, none of them were bitten. I'm going to investigate Menton. Maybe we'll finally get some of the answers we've been spending all these years on expeditions searching for."

"So, we are heading there now?" Bree asked disappointedly.

"No. We're going home first." Roland grinned and she smiled happily back to him.

She had missed home and had been looking forward to returning there. Bree rose from the table. "I'll have to clean up and change clothes. See you at the carriage! I'll let Auben know we're heading home." She turned to leave but stopped and looked back at Roland. "You might want to shave that scruff of your face and clean up, too, in case the other groups are back when we get to Aalen." She turned back and quickly headed out of the restaurant with a skip in her step.

Roland left a few coins on his table to cover the cost of his food and drink and made his own way back out to join with Auben and Bree. He, too, was ready to get back home. And she was right, he did need to clean up and shave.

*****

Kari awoke and looked at the curtains pulled tight over the windows of the carriage. She wasn't sure if it was night yet or still day, but she was shocked to find she wasn't alone, noticing the elven woman sitting across from her. "Who are you?" she asked, startled as her body tensed.

"My name is Bree. I'm a friend of Roland," the woman answered, "Don't worry, Kari. Roland has told me everything." Hearing Bree was Roland's friend helped the girl to relax. "It's very nice to meet you."

Kari had seen elves before, some had even come through Menton as they traveled, but she'd never seen an elf with red hair before. She couldn't help but notice how beautiful the elf was, despite the absence of light in the dark carriage. Her vision in the dark was one gift of the vampirism that Kari was glad to have. The blue dress Bree wore seemed quite fancy to Kari, but she noticed some well-worn pants and a shirt on the seat beside Bree, and dirty black boots on the floor. "Are you from Jeul?"

"No," Bree replied with a smile, "I'm not. I was raised in Leef, but I haven't lived there for many years."

"Oh. Do you live with Roland?" She regretted her phrasing of the question as Bree laughed. "I mean, do you live in the same town. I'm sorry."

"It's fine. We do live in the same town, but Roland is just a friend, we do not live together. I live with my husband." Kari took notice of Bree's hands in her lap and saw a silver ring on the third finger of both of her hands.

"Oh. Is he traveling with us, too?"

Bree shook her head. "He should be home when we get back, though. I can't wait to see him." Kari realized why Bree had cleaned up and changed out of her dirty clothes.

The young vampire looked back at the curtains over the window to her left. "Is it still daylight outside?" Bree nodded, and Kari sighed. She wished she hadn't woken up so soon. She felt as if she was trapped in a cage. She hated knowing that the sun outside could kill her in an instant and that the carriage and the black cloth curtains were the only things keeping her safe. She turned away from Bree and looked at the curtain again. "I hope you all can help me. I still don't understand why Roland wants to go to his home first."

"Trust me, there are people back home who would be interested in what has happened to Menton. Some may even want to come along to investigate." Bree smiled brightly to her. "Don't lose hope. We will do all we can to help."

Kari turned back to Bree and offered a weak smile.

*****

The carriage continued to head northwest along the road from Freyg. Auben was driving the carriage now, while Roland sat beside him enjoying the view. The two men had been quiet for about an hour, each hopeful that something about this mysterious change in Menton's population could lead them to answers they had been seeking.

After coming to a stop and making sure there was no one on the road to see them, Auben pulled the carriage off the road to the left and began to journey across the fields of grass, while the road they had been traveling on began to turn east. When half an hour had passed, the horses arrived on a hidden road that continued to the northwest.

"I hate being away from home so much," Auben began, "If the trouble with this girl's village can finally sort all of this out, after ten years of this…"

"Remember, Auben," Roland replied, "it's just a small chance. I don't think we should let the word get out when we get home. I don't want to get everyone's hopes up."

"I'm telling my family, Roland. It could light a fire in my brother, he's starting to get depressed. And my parents could really use some good news."

"That's fine. I just don't want it getting around the entire city, especially if it comes to nothing." Roland laughed. "My opinion might not matter. Jarec may decide that everyone should know. And maybe they do need to know we are accomplishing something out here on these journeys."

"Do you think any of the other groups will have made it back?"

"Maybe. More and more the groups are getting smaller; the people are getting tired of searching and finding nothing. Sometimes we don't even stay out as long ourselves, and we're down to just you, me and Bree. We aren't the only group that comes back quicker. We're all starting to get tired of this, but I have a little hope now."

Auben nodded. "Me, too. You ready to switch?"

"Sure." Roland took the reins from Auben and he began to drive the horses. They both grew quiet again and Auben leaned back as best he could and shut his eyes as they continued towards their home.

*****

As the sun went down and the moons rose, Bree pulled back the curtains to look out from the carriage and see where they were. She smiled, seeing the familiar farms they were approaching. Kari began to watch out of the window and took notice that there were several scattered farms in this area. She hadn't traveled out of her small village much, but she'd never seen so many farms this close together. Each farm seemed to raise a lot of cattle and other animals, more than she was used to seeing. There were fields of vegetables and fruits being grown as well.

"Where are we?" Kari asked Bree, who smiled to her.

"We're home," Bree beamed, excited to be back after her recent outing with Roland and Auben.

"Is there a town or just farms? What is this area called?"

"These are the farms that feed our city. We are headed there now, to Aalen." As Bree spoke the name of the city, the carriage slowed down and came to a stop near some men who were working in the fields of one of the farms. Bree and Kari saw Roland approach the men and begin talking to them.

"Friends of Roland?" Kari asked, noticing the men were all smiling while they spoke with one another.

"This is Roland's farm," Bree replied. "They work with him. He may just be checking on the crops or letting them know he is back home. But they are friendly. Everyone in Aalen knows everyone else. We depend heavily on each other here."

Roland had approached and opened the door to the carriage to stick his head in. "We're going to be heading into the city now," he said to both of them, then turned to Kari, "Right now my plan is to sleep during the day and head to your village as soon as night falls tomorrow." Kari knew they would leave when it was dark out for her sake.

"Who is going with you to Menton?" Bree asked. "Besides you and Kari, of course."

"We'll discuss it tonight. There is still plenty of time to talk and plan things before the sun rises."

"Don't include me in this, Roland." Bree turned to Kari, "Please take no offense, but I've been long from home and need to spend some time with my husband. At home." She smiled.

"That's understandable," Kari replied, almost blushing from what Bree was insinuating.

"Very well," Roland said, "Auben has agreed to come and his brother might want to come along, too. I'm sure I can get a few people together tonight to join us on our journey." With that, Roland smiled and closed the door, heading back up to the front with Auben.

The carriage rolled onwards and Kari kept her eyes on the surrounding area. She hadn't seen any sign of a city yet and wondered how much longer it would take to get there. Soon the carriage began to move downhill. Kari had thought the land looked flat but noticed this pathway they were on was a narrow road that was leading them underground.

"Welcome to Aalen," Bree said.

The carriage was fully underground, but torches along the walls of the road lit the way for them. Soon the narrow road and entrance opened up into a large expanse underground. The city of Aalen stood before them, comprised of several houses and buildings that would usually only be seen above ground. There were magical lights placed around the city so that the inhabitants could see in the darkness underground. Kari wondered why they would have built a city beneath the earth.

As they moved into the streets of Aalen, Kari noticed that many people were out in the streets. Several of them waved to Roland and Auben as they rode by. Soon they stopped outside of a larger building in the center of the city. Roland and Auben came to the door and opened it for Bree and Kari.

"Hello," Auben said to Kari, "Nice to finally meet you, miss. I'm Auben Dale."

"Kari Sleyn," she replied, "I appreciate your help."

"Kari," Roland said, getting her attention, "come with me. There is someone I'd like you to meet, and we'll explain a bit more about our situation, and why I brought you here first."

"I'm going to head on home," Bree said, "my husband isn't expecting me yet and I look forward to surprising him. Kari, if I don't see you before you leave tomorrow, good luck." Bree smiled warmly to her.

"Thank you," Kari replied, smiling back, "I enjoyed talking with you. Have a good night."

"Later, Bree," Auben added. Roland waved goodbye to Bree before he turned to step into the building, followed by Kari. Auben got back on the carriage and headed off to the stables of the town, where the horses could be taken care of.

As Roland shut the door behind them, Kari noticed there were a few people inside that seemed to be discussing important business with a man sitting behind a desk. The room was tidy but very plain and simple. There were two unoccupied desks in the room and on the sides of the room there were two levels of long platforms with chairs lined across them.

The man behind the desk was a human and had dark blonde hair, green eyes, and pale skin. He was thin and quite ordinary. The two men and the woman who had been talking with him turned to leave and smiled to Roland as they began to walk out. They waved farewell as they passed but did not speak, though they seemed quite curious about in the girl they didn't know. Kari noticed that the three of them were also very pale.

"Roland!" the man behind the desk exclaimed, looking to him, "You're back early! How was your journey?" He stood and crossed to the front of the desk, shaking Roland's hand in welcome.

"It was well, Jarec," Roland began, surprised as he always was that Jarec's enthusiasm didn't fade after all this time, "We need to talk. I have some news that will interest you."

"It has to do with this girl, I assume." Jarec looked her over, a surprising realization coming over his face at the stranger.

As the man spoke, Kari came to a realization of her own, and it was something she should have already noticed. This man, Jarec, was a vampire. His fangs were visible to her as he spoke. She was shocked by this revelation. She had believed all the vampires were dead, except the new ones in her village. "What is this, Roland?" she asked, pointing at Jarec. "This man is a vampire!"

"I know," Roland replied. "And so are you. Look, we'll explain, but he needs to know about your village first. Tell him what you told me of Menton. You can trust him, Kari."

"Very well." She had already put her life in Roland's hands and he had helped her so far, so she was willing to tell her story to Jarec. Besides, she thought, what else could they do to her worse than the curse she now bore?

"Welcome to our home," Jarec said, standing and extending a hand to Kari. As she took his hand and shook it he spoke again. "My name is Jarec Drakon. I'm the mayor of Aalen."

"I'm Kari Sleyn, from Menton."

"And you are a vampire, too? That's quite unusual. Please take a seat." Jarec took a chair from the side of the room and set it in front of the desk for her.

"Why is that unusual?" she asked as she sat in the offered seat. "You are a vampire. And those men and that woman that left were, too." She had been so caught up that she didn't notice it until they were gone.

"That is true, Kari, but there hasn't been a new vampire in over six years. At least, not that anyone here is aware of. And I know every vampire that lives here in this city." As he was speaking, he had made his way behind his desk and took his seat.

Roland still stood where he was, close to the desk and to the left of the chair Kari now sat in. "Her entire village, Menton, has been turned into vampires," Roland said, "and not one of them was from a vampire bite."

"What?" Concern crossed Jarec's face. His concern was for the people of Menton, and concern for what it could mean if there were mass curses like this.

"I don't know for sure if this can lead us to answers we need to cure you and the others," he told Jarec, "but it could be a start."

"You're trying to cure yourselves?" Kari asked, understanding now why they would be interested in helping her, and knowing their motives put her mind at ease about trusting them.

"You've probably heard," Jarec began, "that in the vampire war ten years ago nearly all of the vampires were killed by a united spell from the elves of Jeul. You've been told a lie. A lie we wanted told, and a lie the rulers of Jeul were willing to go along with, but a lie nonetheless. Given your current situation, I think you should know the truth, and I would like to know more of the details about what happened to your village."

Two people had entered into the building while he spoke to Kari. As Jarec finished speaking, one of them spoke. "Welcome home, Roland."

As the woman was speaking, Kari noticed the smile appear on Roland's face as he turned. He immediately rushed to the woman and embraced her, picking her up and spinning around. She seemed quite happy to see him as well, and her red dress seemed to dance as she was spun. Kari looked to see who had entered with the woman and, recognizing Auben, smiled to him. She returned her attention to the woman Roland had now put back down and was kissing.

"Kari," Roland began as he and the woman approached her, "I'd like to introduce you to my wife, Areum." Kari had noticed Areum wore rings as Bree had, and was realizing now that she had overlooked Roland's rings when they had met. She returned her eyes to the woman, as her appearance intrigued her.

Kari was taken in by Areum's features that set her apart from anyone else Kari had seen before. Her hair was straight and black and came down just past her shoulders. The eyes of Roland's wife were dark in color, and their shape was smaller than anyone else Kari knew. Even her nose had quite a different appearance, slightly wider, with a narrower tip, and her lips were fuller than the elven women and the women of Norin.

Kari also noticed that the woman had fangs and was a vampire like others in Aalen. Her skin was pale like other vampires, but the skin tone was noticeably different from the people of the north and the south of the continent, though closer to the color of Kari's skin. Was there a kingdom on the continent with a people like this? She wondered where the woman was from.

"Hello," she said, "I'm Kari Sleyn." She was beginning to realize why Roland had an interest in working with the vampires to help them.

"It's nice to meet you, Kari," Areum replied, "Auben has already told me a little about you and the plight of your village while we were on the way here. I hope we can help." Hearing more of her voice, Kari realized Areum had no defining accent, and sounded like everyone else from Norin.

"As soon as she saw me she asked me where you were," Auben explained to Roland. "I told her you would have found her first if you knew she was here."

"I'm glad your group got back early as well," Roland said, turning to his wife.

"We got back much earlier," Areum frowned, "I'll tell you about it later, in private." Roland simply nodded in reply and took her hand.

Kari had become distracted for a moment by the arrival of Areum but turned her attention from Roland and his wife back to Jarec. "You said something about the truth?"

Jarec nodded in reply. "Yes, the truth," he began, "about why the vampires are still alive. The truth of what really happened when the vampires united to attack Jeul."

As Jarec spoke, Roland and Areum moved to sit at the side of the room, while Auben left the building again. "I have been a vampire for a long time, Kari; longer than anyone else here in Aalen. There may be more vampires still, older than me," Jarec shook his head, "but that's not what's important right now. I'll stay on topic.

"The vampire war wasn't much of a war. We couldn't fight Jeul for days since we'd be helpless during the daylight, so the vampires gathered forces to the west away from civilization. We were compelled to gather there, Kari. I tell you this because, for that brief period, we were pushed against our wills to join together and attack Jeul. We weren't in control of ourselves."

"But I thought vampires were never in control of themselves," Kari stated. "In the stories, people talk about how once turned a vampire would become corrupted and lose their mind."

"That is true... in that way, we weren't in control of ourselves before we gathered. But before, we were divided. Although we were corrupt, we had never tried to join together in such a large group. Some vampires worked together, but never on such a scale. We didn't decide to go west; something in our minds pushed us there.

"But all the vampires over the land joining forces wasn't the only change in vampire behavior. We began to turn people to join us, and it no longer took time for them to become corrupt, it was an instant transformation. We didn't even have to feed them our blood first anymore; all it took was a bite. Our army grew fast. We began to move east, and turned entire towns, destroying them and increasing our numbers, as we made our way towards Jeul."

Kari nodded, "Yes, I've heard about it in the stories. Entire towns were turned and so no reports escaped to warn of the coming danger. If not for a bird belonging to one of the beast mages of Jeul spotting what was happening, the vampires would have been successful."

"Jeul did receive advance warning we were unaware of," Jarec continued, "And it cost us our surprise and allowed them time to prepare a spell to annihilate us. But someone else had escaped from us in a town," Jarec looked at Roland, "And he is the reason that we weren't killed off by the elves."

*****

Roland stared in horror at the blood from Areum's throat and the corpse of the vampire he'd decapitated as it bit into his wife's neck. "No…" he whispered, as his wife's countenance began to change.

"Run," Areum said, "I can… I can feel a change taking over me, run before I kill you…"

Roland felt a coward as he did just as she said, rushing out of the back of the inn with nothing but a sword in his hand and the clothes on his back. Areum screamed in agony as her fangs came in and the darkness overcame her. She snapped her head towards the back of the building but was compelled to join the other vampires in the street. Someone had been in the room with her, but she didn't remember who. Areum snarled as she ran out of the front of the inn to join the others.

Roland had been able to mount up on his horse that had been in the stable located behind the inn. They had been away from their farm to deliver goods in town and visit with friends. He began to head to the northeast, hoping to reach the elves in Jeul. Although they lived within the borders of the human kingdom of Norin, he could reach Jeul faster, and the elves may be able to help him.

As he rode and his nerves calmed, the sound of hooves nearby nearly panicked Roland. The vampires had come into town on horses with red eyes, and they were terribly fast. Roland would have to make a stand if these beasts were upon him. He turned and raised his sword, ready to fight and die. But instead of vampires, the group that approached him were on regular horses and were human. He recognized one of the men, Auben. With him were two women and three more men Roland didn't know.

"Roland!" Auben said, "You escaped as well. Where are you headed?"

Roland turned his horse back around. "Ride as we talk," he replied, "We have to get help. I'm heading to Jeul."

"Jeul?" Auben asked as he and the others followed. "Why there? Why not to Norin?"

"It is closer, Auben. And the elves, with all of their magic, might be able to do something to help." They rode on mostly in silence, occasionally speaking and deciding what they say to the leaders of Jeul when they arrived. They didn't stop until they reached the gates of the elven kingdom.

"Halt!" one of the guards spoke as the human party approached, "Why do you come at such a late hour?"

"We need to see the king!" Auben replied, as he stopped his horse and the rest of the group stopped beside him.

Roland added, "Vampires have attacked our town and turned everyone, and look to be seeking out more people to infect."

The guard motioned to another guard and they spoke in hushed tones before turning their attention back to Roland, Auben, and the others. The first guard spoke again, "You may enter the city, but only one of you may go before the king, the rest of you will be under guard. We have heard of the vampire activity and the city is being very careful with our security." The gates to the city began to open as the other guard notified the gatekeepers.

Roland looked to the group who had accompanied him. "If it is alright with all of you," he told them, "I'd like to be the one to go before the king. Is that acceptable?" The others looked at each other and agreed to let Roland be their voice since it was his idea to go to Jeul in the first place. "Thank you all. I will see if our loved ones can be saved."

The entire group was allowed into the city walls, and Roland was separated from the rest. A group of guards came to watch over the humans, while another guard saw to the horses they had brought with them. One of the guards came to Roland's side to accompany him to the throne room. "Hand me your sword," he told Roland, and Roland complied. He needed to see the king and was willing to follow the instructions that would lead him there. The guard led the way through the city.

Roland followed in silence, and the guard didn't speak anything to him as they walked through the streets. Roland's mind was a mess of thoughts. What were the vampires after? Why did this happen to Areum? Would she have to be killed, or could he save her? Would the elves know a way to save the vampires, and if so, why had they never done it before now? If not… he didn't like to think about what would have to be done if not because it only led to thoughts of his wife's death again. Soon the guard led through the gate of the castle, central to the city of Jeul.

After entering the gates, the guard spoke briefly with two guards at the front of the castle, explaining why he had brought Roland there. "These guards will take you from here," the elf explained as he turned back to Roland. He left Roland's sword with the new guards and returned to his post at the front wall.

"Come with us," one of the new guards told Roland, as they both opened the doors to lead him through the castle. Roland gave no verbal response but followed them. The castle was the largest building in the city of Jeul. The floors were white and shone brilliantly, and must have constantly been cleaned and maintained. Purple carpets mapped out the pathways through the halls of the castle, and tapestries of the history of Jeul hung on the gray stone walls. As grand as the castle was, and Roland had never seen it before, his focus was on the matter at hand. He didn't take in the sights and kept his attention on the guards and where they led him.

Soon the guards opened the doors to the throne room and Roland entered. The king, Yuuric Kaalen, stood in front of a table down the steps from his throne, surrounded by many advisors and powerful wizards of Jeul. All eyes turned to face the human who was being escorted into the throne room by the two guards. Roland was unsure how to act, as he had never before come before any king in a throne room, but decided the best course of action was to kneel down on his right knee and lower his head. As he did so, the guard approached the king.

"Your majesty," one of the guards began, "this man has come from a human town that has been attacked by the vampires." The king nodded to the guard and

stepped from around the table and approached the kneeling man.

"Rise," the king spoke, calmly, and Roland did as he was commanded. "We have already been alerted to the threat of vampire hordes on the rise, but if you have survived an attack, maybe you can give us some helpful information. Tell me your story."

*****

"I told him about what had happened, and about the vampire's horses, which was news to them," Roland explained to Kari. "They had already been studying the movement patterns the vampires had been taking, and the elves knew they were coming towards the city and castle of Jeul. I just helped them know the vampires could move even faster. King Kaalen and his advisors had prepared a spell that would have successfully killed all the vampires, and it was going to require nearly all of the elves of Jeul lending their magical strength to their king."

"So why didn't they kill them all?" Kari asked, confused.

"Roland convinced them to try another tactic with their spell," Jarec answered. "Since the elves could join their magic together in such a way to affect so many vampires at once, he asked if they might be able to attempt a cleansing of the vampires instead."

"I had hoped," Roland said, "that they could possibly turn the vampires human again. Cure them."

"In a way, we were cured," Areum said with a smile to Kari, "the spell didn't make us human again, but it did have an effect on us and restored our minds to us completely. Our hearts and souls were freed from the corruption by the spell."

"Unfortunately, they all still have to drink blood to live, and are vulnerable to sunlight and other vampire weaknesses," Roland added.

"So the elves in Jeul know you are all here?" Kari asked. The story was fascinating to her, particularly learning that the world had been told a lie.

"Yes, when the spell cleansed us, we stopped immediately," Jarec replied. "We had just reached the walls of Jeul when the elves cast their cure upon us. Our free will was returned, but we soon realized that was all we had gained. The kingdom of Jeul met with us and helped set us up here in this location while telling everyone else that they had eradicated the vampires that had attacked Jeul with their spell. Unfortunately, only some of us came to this new society that had been set up." He sighed and shook his head.

"Some vampires were terrible people before they were ever bloodsuckers," Roland said, "And they were dealt with over time by groups from Aalen who were sent out to find them, and also to search for anything that might cure the vampires."

"Alright, so I understand what you are all doing here, and why you are interested in my situation," Kari said, "but what about the other humans and elves here? There were only a few others with Roland when he went to Jeul."

"We needed people to run the farms above ground so that we could raise livestock for blood," Jarec said. "Some of the others who hadn't been vampires very long also still had family alive in the world. I worked with King Yuuric Kaalen to reach out and contact those people. They were invited to Jeul and then, if the elves believed them trustworthy, they were told the story of what really happened and given the opportunity to come live here and be reunited with their loved ones."

Roland and Areum stood. "We are going to head home," Roland said. "Kari, Jarec will see to it you have a place to rest after you've told him of your town. Jarec, we will sleep during the day and meet here with you tomorrow before nightfall. We can leave for Menton at dark."

Kari watched as Roland and Areum left the building. It was the first time since she had found Roland that he had been gone. She had grown to feel secure with him around in the short time she had known him. But she also had become comfortable with being around Jarec already and was curious to learn more of the vampires. As she looked back to Jarec she saw that he was patiently waiting to hear her tale. "This all started in Menton about a month ago..."

CHAPTER 5

THE FALL OF MOORA

Zeyn woke up from his sleep on the floor of a stone room, with his arms bound behind him. The members of his crew who shared the room with him were still asleep. They had separated them all into different rooms in this dungeon, and each room was guarded by one of the green elves. He wasn't sure how the others had been separated but knew that Melzer, Rendal, and Horace were with him, and also were all bound with some kind of plant from the ocean.

He stared at the ceiling of the room, which had been carved out in the rock, and his thoughts drifted to the conversation they had at dinner the night before, with the elf that looked like he was from the surface. That conversation had led to their current predicament.

*****

"I am Braal Savuul," the pale, blonde elf introduced himself. "Welcome to my kingdom."

"My name is Zeyn Clarke," the captain replied, "and this is my crew." He gestured to the others seated

with him. They were all seated around a long rectangular table in the room they had followed Braal into. No guards were present in the room but were surely waiting just outside the doors. "We appreciate your hospitality, your majesty."

The stone walls of the room were covered in what appeared to be the remains of the original walls of a once great throne room. There were cracks in the walls where the original walls were pieced together, but the natural white color of the original walls had been cleaned well. There were stairs carved from the stone floor that led to the throne, and a red carpet that had been recovered from the destroyed castle led along the floor and up the stairs to the throne.

Captain Clarke had assumed that Braal was the king because when they had entered, he had placed a crown that had been sitting on the throne upon his head. Now that he had called it his kingdom, Zeyn was sure. But his doubts had only existed because of how different Braal was from his subjects.

"I am very curious to know why you have come here," the king began, "and how you have arrived here." The king looked to the door as food began to be brought in by the guards who had first come across the people from the surface. There were numerous types of fish and sea creatures, as well as different seaweed and underwater flora.

Zeyn wondered if the guards had prepared it as well, or if they simply were delivering the meal. He had also taken note that the king was not asking a question. He was expecting them to tell him. When the food was served, the guards left the throne room.

"A vessel was created that allowed us to travel underwater," Captain Clarke explained honestly with a smile, "My crew was hired to test the vessel, and we were on our maiden voyage and happened to come across this

area. We noticed one of your people swim by and were curious as to who or what it was since we didn't get a good look. And now, here we are."

Zeyn's crew naturally deferred to him in situations like this. Not that they had ever come across an underwater civilization before, but when dealing with leaders of towns and occasionally other kings, they always let their captain or Maria do the talking. At the moment, it seemed that Horace, Gallen, Caleb, Olii, and Noon were more than happy to let Zeyn do all the talking as well. Many in the group had begun to eat their meal while the discussion continued.

"It must've been one of the guards you saw," Braal replied in response to their story. When he spoke, Zeyn felt the king hoped it was one of his guards. He wondered why that would matter.

"You know how we got here," Horace spoke up, "How did you get here?" Zeyn wished he had gotten a chance to tell those who weren't members of his crew to let him do the talking, but it was the next question Zeyn would have asked. He also had begun to believe that no matter what was said at this dinner, the outcome would be the same. Zeyn finally began to eat the meal of fish before him.

The king smiled, and it unsettled Zeyn. "I suppose there is no harm in telling you the truth," he answered, "You are from the surface and must have some idea already of who we are." The king noticed the puzzled looks on some of their faces. "That is unless we've already been forgotten in the short span of twelve hundred years."

Zeyn wasn't sure what he was getting at. Neither was anyone else who had come with him from the surface. The king turned to look at Olii, Noon, and then Naaren. "Surely the elves know the story, for them, it can only have been two generations since the events."

"I know not of what you speak," Naaren said, "but I am very interested to know what you are talking about."

Zeyn had noticed that Naaren had been quite invested in everything that was going on since they found this civilization of strange elves living underwater. Of course, everyone was intrigued, but Naaren showed a particular hunger for the knowledge of where these elves came from. Zeyn wasn't sure it was just because he was also an elf or if it was something else.

"Are you and your people what is left of Moora?" Horace asked.

"So one of you has heard of Moora," Braal replied, "How is it that a human knows of Moora, but none of the elves?"

"That I do not know. All I know of Moora is from a book I found in the library of Jeul. When I discovered the book, it appeared to have been forgotten and ignored for quite a while. I asked elves all around Jeul and even got an audience with King Kaalen, but no one knew anything about a place called Moora. When I brought up the book, they claimed that no such place had ever existed and the book must have been false." When speaking of Moora, Horace was full of excitement. It was clear that history fascinated him. However, they all noticed that the mention of Jeul made King Braal's face tighten, and he frowned at the mention of Kaalen.

"I will tell you all, then, how we came to be here." He took a bite of his fish before continuing. "I have never told this tale, and I'm the only one living here who knows all of the truth of that day, for I was the king of Moora when it was still a part of the surface world. My reign had begun almost one hundred and thirty years before the war that led to the destruction of our land."

"Wait a moment," Naaren interrupted. "You implied earlier that Moora was destroyed twelve hundred years ago."

"That is correct."

"No elf known has lived more than a couple of years beyond a thousand. Most don't even live to their nine hundredth year. Unless they were a vampire, but I don't think that you are. How are you still alive? If what you say is true, you must be over thirteen hundred..."

"I am actually getting close to my fifteenth hundred year. Just listen! I will explain the reason for my longevity." Naaren nodded.

"It all began," the king continued, "with my cousin. He had become a prisoner of Jeul when it was discovered that he had been spying on his own kingdom for me. There were other circumstances of his imprisonment, but that was the only crime I was fully aware of at the time." Zeyn was beginning to realize that if this king had his cousin work as a spy against Jeul, then perhaps their host wasn't the honest kind of person he was hoping he was. "My cousin was held for three years before escaping, and two years after his escape, he came to me for help. I took him in and kept him safe in Moora.

"Aar Kaalen did send a group of soldiers and some of his advisors to meet with me shortly after, but I managed to put them at ease and convince them Tecuul wasn't in Moora. I even gave them a tour of the entire castle and let them search the kingdom."

"Tecuul was your cousin's name?" Zeyn asked. He had noticed that Naaren appeared to tense a little at the mention of the name Tecuul, but quickly relaxed. He'd have to ask Naaren about it later, if there was a later. The name meant nothing to him.

"Yes, Tecuul Boaruun. Later that year, the king somehow discovered my deception; most likely with spies of his own. When I wouldn't give Tecuul up, a war began between Jeul and Moora."

"How could we not know about this war? We have records of battles and wars dating farther back then that."

"I can't answer that question. All I can tell you is that the culmination of the war was a great spell cast by a large group of mages of Jeul. And that led to the events that changed my people forever. We had learned of this mass spell they had been preparing from another spy we had in place in Jeul. He arrived back to report to me the day their spell would be ready and come down upon our kingdom. I gathered my strongest magicians and advisors to devise a protective spell to keep us from being destroyed, but something went wrong.

"Maybe we were rushed, maybe we miscalculated, but the spell didn't protect our great city. When Jeul's large scale attack hit us, it broke us off from the rest of the lands and we sunk fast and deep into the ocean. However, despite not saving the city, the spell did protect all of the people. A large bubble of sorts, a result of the spell, encased us all as we sank and kept the water out of the city until it changed the people. The spell transformed everyone in Moora to adapt to the sea.

"They grew gills to breathe underwater and their eyes adapted to be more comfortable in the oceans. They were gifted with the ability to still be able to breathe out of the water. The odd changes I don't understand were their skin turning green and their life span decreasing to a mere five hundred years, which we learned later. Because I was used to focus the spell, it didn't adapt me but did extend my life. At least, that is my theory of why I've lived so long.

"When the people were changed and the bubble began to let the ocean flood the city, my people used their magic to keep me alive and quickly carved out this area in the nearby rocks so I could be on land. Over time we extended the space here and made more rooms, in an attempt to rebuild the castle as best we could." The king mused to himself, "I sometimes wonder what happened to those we left on the surface, locked in land battles outside

of the kingdom's walls. I imagine they were all killed or captured."

"If you've been here all this time, why haven't you ever returned to the surface?" Horace asked.

"My people are comfortable with this life," the king answered, "and also, they don't know this story. My original advisors and I convinced the people to forget the surface and to live here, and as the generations have died out, they have been told that we came to live here because the surface was destroyed, and nothing exists there."

"You lied to your people…" Gallen said.

"Yes, I did. It was for the best. They never knew that I hid Tecuul here. They never knew why the war really started. And I wanted Aar Kaalen to believe he'd succeeded in wiping us out. It must have eaten at his soul."

"Who is Tecuul Boaruun?" Olii asked. "I can't understand why Jeul would start a war with Moora over one person, or why they'd try to wipe out an entire kingdom to kill him."

"You've never heard?" Braal stood and shook his head. "I may have lied to my people, but somewhere along the way, you have all been lied to as well." He began to walk around the table and looked at them all as he did. "They were trying to kill Tecuul because he was the first vampire. He introduced vampirism into the world and, judging by the fact you've heard of vampires," he looked at Naaren, who mentioned the word before, "his curse still lives above on the surface."

"He survived the destruction of Moora, didn't he," Zeyn said, without question.

The king nodded where he stood in front of the doors. "He has lived with us all this time but wasn't changed at all by the spell, perhaps because of his curse. He has fed on the people of Moora from time to time, with my knowledge, but he disappeared months ago. He claimed something was 'calling him back to the surface.'

He doesn't have to breathe to live, so I assume he just swam back."

"You let him have your people?" Zeyn was disgusted. "Why?"

"He is my cousin. But more than family, he has been my closest friend since childhood. Had our situations been reversed, he would have done the same."

"But he's a monster."

"Perhaps so am I. Besides, explaining away the disappearances is quite easy, with all the sea creatures out there. He was discreet about who he took and how often, so as to not raise alarm, and he only took those I allowed him to eat. He also stayed true to his promise not to spread the curse among Moora. What's one person, here and there, when there are thousands here and the population remains steady?"

Zeyn stood and the others followed his lead. "Those people still mattered to someone."

"But not to me, as long as I still have my kingdom to rule. You already know I can't let you leave here and risk anyone other than myself or my guards seeing you. They may ask too many questions and learn of the lies they've been told."

"So you'll just kill us then?" Bail said as he drew his sword.

"No, I'll keep you prisoner. I have based these caves on the castle of Moora, so we do have a dungeon, though it's unused. You will remain there, and I will learn all I can from you about what has been going on above while I've been away. Then, when I think I've learned all I can, maybe I will kill you. Maybe Tecuul will return and I'll let him have all of you." The king knocked on the doors and the guards entered, armed with some kind of rope.

How did they know they'd be taking them prisoner? Had Braal Savuul let them know the truth? These were the questions that first popped into Zeyn's mind as he and his crew attempted to fight the guards. Even Caleb, Gallen, Olii, and Noon joined in the fight, but there were too many guards and they overpowered them with their numbers and magic. When the fight finished, they were all bound and led off to the dungeon.

*****

Zeyn played with the bonds around his wrists. The plant material used was very strong and well tied. He frowned, knowing he wouldn't be able to break them. He did wonder how Gor was being held. Surely he could escape these ropes, but despite his physical strength, magic could hold him just as well, and a city of elves never lacked magic. "Well, at least so much has happened since this accursed city sunk that we can probably tell stories of the surface well into our old age," Zeyn grumbled.

Rendal laughed. "Now, Captain," he said, "I know you, of all people, aren't going to just accept defeat."

Zeyn grinned. "Of course not." He noticed that Melzer and Horace were awake now as well. "Horace," Zeyn began, "don't worry. We are all getting out of here."

"I'm an old man," Horace replied, "but I'm not going to just give up, either." He did his best to smile in the face of the circumstance.

"Good. Now, when they come to question us, we will answer honestly. We surely have plenty of time before we run out of new things to tell them about. In the meantime, while we are alone, we can come up with a plan. I don't know when we'll see any of the others, but I think it's important for us all to stay calm. Trust me. I believe we can get through this and back home."

Rendal and Melzer trusted the captain, and Zeyn was glad they had so much faith in him. Even Horace seemed more at ease because Zeyn seemed to have some idea of what to do. None of them knew the terrible things going on in Zeyn's head. What if there was no way out? What if the vessel that brought them here had already been destroyed by these elves? If that had happened, there would be no escape. Zeyn kept these thoughts to himself, it was important that his companions keep up their hope. They would all need it.

*****

"At least they put all of us girls in one room," Annah joked to Phyra, Caleb, and Brill.

Caleb shook his head and frowned. "How can you joke around at a time like this," he complained as Phyra finished loosening his bonds, "Not only are we captive, but we are deep in the ocean, in case you've forgotten."

"We haven't forgotten, Caleb," Brill responded, rubbing his wrists, "but we have to keep our spirits up."

"You can't let a little thing like being put in a dungeon keep you down," Annah laughed, still bound.

"We've been in tight spots before and the Captain will get us out of this one if we can't get out ourselves," Phyra added and grasped Caleb's shoulder. "Never give up." She moved over to free Annah's hands. Phyra had great skill in escaping from being tied up. "And everyone remember, if the guards come back in here, make sure you pretend to still have the ropes on." The reminder was more for Caleb's benefit since her crewmates would know what to do, but she didn't want him to feel bad if she singled him out.

Caleb managed to nod, but couldn't bring himself to smile. The only traveling he'd ever done was when he and his father had moved from the north when his mother died, and it was no adventure. The excitement he had when this journey first began had definitely waned. There hadn't even been any mermaids.

*****

"You can't use your magic to free us?" Gallen asked Naaren.

"No, this cell is designed in a similar fashion to the cells of Jeul," Naaren answered. "There were specific spells used while building these cells to block the magic ability in others when they are in this room."

"I see." Gallen continued to look around the room to see if he could find some way for them to possibly get out.

Olii and Noon weren't talking much and were sitting against the wall and resting. They had both felt empty because they couldn't touch their magic. At least, Naaren suspected that was the case, as he felt the same way. But he had been disconnected from magic once before in his youth, so he knew what it felt like. He also was driven and focused by the news he had discovered the night before. He was closer to Tecuul than ever before, and he would not let himself die here in this prison.

*****

Bail looked particularly grumpy. Shim was just glad his hands were no longer bound. At least they had been able to do that much since Gor was with them. They needed a plan, though and weren't going to just rush out and blindly try to find the others when they had no idea if they were even being kept nearby. Gor had decided that if they didn't hear anything after they were fed that they would go ahead and do just that, and Shim knew that when Gor set his mind to something, there was no stopping him. Shim kept trying to do his best to think of a plan.

He looked at Bail again. "Are you still mad about your sword?" Shim asked though he knew the answer.

"You'd feel the same if it had been yours," he answered gruffly. "It was important to me."

"Important? You haven't had that sword more than a month. You can just buy a new one when we're back home."

"I liked that one."

"Quiet," Gor said, "We have our lives. They haven't taken that yet." The giant man stood from where he had been sitting against the wall. Shim liked Gor well enough, but he towered over everyone and sometimes, he couldn't help but feel like Gor could just squash them all if he wanted. But Gor was friendly to them, and part of the crew. Sometimes Shim had to remember that Gor wasn't the same as much of his people in the land they had shared before joining the *Salvation*.

*****

Four guards were in the hallway of the dungeon, watching each door that the captives from the surface were held in. Although they were only four, they believed they were strong enough to deal with the prisoners, and if a crisis arose, they could always call more of the nearby guards just outside of the dungeon. One of these guards, named Bandar, was particularly interested in these prisoners.

Bandar was the youngest of the guards, and while he had always been loyal to his position and to his king, the arrival of these strangers from the surface had reminded him of a story he once heard from his friend, Sola. Her parents had passed the story on to her as her grandparents had passed on to her parents. Her family claimed there was a war caused by their own king that led to their people living in the sea. When Bandar had heard this from her as a child, he called her a liar and they got into a fight.

Everyone knew that the people of Jeul had been evil and had destroyed the entire surface with their magic, and their kind and loving king had saved them by pulling them into the ocean where they could still live on. But for some reason, he knew to never share the story Sola had told him with anyone. He always feared something might happen to Sola and her family if he ever shared the information and it got out to the king.

Now these strangers appeared, proving the surface world still existed. He wanted to go there, to see the surface. But at the same time, he knew that if he swam up to the surface alone, he might be attacked by the people there, or taken prisoner, as these people from the surface were taken prisoner by them. And so, a plan began to form in the mind of Bandar.

He would need to bring Thela and Sola with him, as they were his closest friends, and he and Thela were in love. But they would need the help of these prisoners in order to arrive at the surface and be safely accepted. He also didn't feel that holding these people was right. He just needed to be able to save their vessel and get them all safely to it, and to the surface, without anyone in the kingdom of Moora finding out about the escape.

CHAPTER 6

THE CURSED VILLAGE

As Roland woke and began to attempt to rise from the bed, Areum grabbed him by the back of his head with both hands and pulled him in for a deep kiss. When a moment had passed, Roland pulled back and smiled, stepping out from the disheveled sheets of their mattress. Reaching to the floor, he pulled on his brown pants over his undershorts and walked to the dresser. Areum smiled at him admiringly where she still lay in their bed as he turned back towards her, pulling the white shirt he chose over his head. "Thanks for letting me at least get a little sleep," he said with a grin. "Not that I mind."

"We have been apart too long," she smiled back, "I couldn't waste the opportunity." She slipped from the bed and stood in her shift, crossing over to Roland and he pulled her in for another kiss. "We do have to leave soon," she grinned, "don't distract me." He laughed and sat on the edge of the bed to step into his boots and lace them. Standing again, he fastened his sword belt around his waist and sheathed his blade in the scabbard. Areum had begun to get dressed as well, fastening the black, divided riding skirt around her waist and tucking in her green blouse, Areum leaned in to kiss Roland on the cheek.

"Now that we've had some time alone and gotten some rest, what brought you back so early?" Roland asked as he double checked the bag they had packed for the journey to Menton. They hadn't spoken of it when they arrived at their home. His wife finished putting on her boots before she answered.

"We were discovered before we could pass through Norin by a group of men out hunting for vampires. I felt the news was important enough to bring back to Jarec immediately. The others with me went to find the few vampire groups that had been sent out and warn them. We are always careful, but we never expect to run into anyone actually looking for us when they should all think we are extinct."

"When I was in Langston, I ran into some men who were chasing after Kari, but now that I think about it, the fact that they would even notice a vampire is a little surprising. Most have accepted that you have all been killed." Roland thought a moment. "The men were together in a group when they noticed Kari, and when I think back on how they were equipped… they must have been looking around for vampires before they ever saw her."

"My dear, I'm afraid that somehow, some people have become aware that there are still living vampires." Areum was finished dressing and had outfitted herself with weapons of her own, an axe and daggers. "I'm ready."

"Maybe some of the vampires of Menton who are traveling like Kari have been discovered. They wouldn't be as careful as we are. If any of them have been caught, then the world might think vampires still exist. What did you all do when you were found?"

"There were only four of them. They ran away when they realized they stood no chance against us, so we let them go. We considered giving chase, but we didn't want to kill them if they were willing to leave us alone."

"I'm glad they didn't press things, for their own sake. Let's go." Roland grabbed their pack in his left hand, smiled to his wife and took her hand in his right as they left their home. He remembered when they first began to build a place to live here and the homes were much more temporary. But as time passed, and the realization set in to the people that this would be permanent, they began to plan and build the town of Aalen as it existed now.

The underground town was beautiful, lit by magic lights provided by the elves living there. The lights would glow blue during the night and red during the day so the residents would know the time of day, since many of them could only venture to the surface during the night. At the moment the globes of light still burned red, but soon they would shift to blue and the journey to Menton would begin.

As the happily united couple continued on to the town hall, they ran into Auben along the way, who was waiting along the path he knew they would take. "Hey, Roland," Auben spoke as he fell in line with them, "Bryn said that he would be interested in coming along with us." Auben's brother was the reason he stayed in Aalen, and the reason their parents lived there. His brother, Bryn, had become a vampire in one of the village attacks before the vampire war, and they were the only ones of their family left.

"I thought he'd look forward to getting out of town for a while," Roland said, "I know he hates when he isn't out on the road. We were going to put him in Areum's group for outings since the rest of his group stopped going out."

"Hopefully there will be some answers in Menton," Areum added. "But your brother would be a welcome addition to my group." *Especially now that vampires are being hunted again*, she thought to herself.

"How long are we going to stay in Menton?" Auben asked.

"Maybe a few days, maybe a week," Roland answered, "I'd like to at least find some answers as to what has happened there before we return home." Roland realistically believed at most they'd find out what happened to Menton's community, and nothing to help Aalen. He was hopeful, but he knew after years of looking for a solution and following other good leads, they were most likely to return home empty handed. As they arrived at the council building, Auben opened the door for them before they all entered. Kari and Jarec were already there, sitting in front of Jarec's desk and in the middle of a conversation.

"Is this everyone who is going to Menton?" Jarec asked as he rose from his seat. Kari stood as well and smiled at them.

Auben spoke up, "My brother is on his way."

"We should only take a small group," Roland added, "so when Bryn arrives, we'll have everyone."

"So it's just the six of us?" Kari asked as she counted the room and included Auben's absent brother. "What if someone else sees something that you all wouldn't?" Kari believed they could learn something to help her, but she was hoping for a larger group of experts from Aalen to help. Still, her faith in Roland and the others' ability to save Menton's population was strong.

"A large group has a better chance of being detected along the way," Jarec answered, understanding Roland's reasons, "The vampires in the group have experience and can probably detect things the vampires of Menton can't. Also, Roland and Auben have been working at this a long time. I know they will do everything they can to help." Jarec moved behind his desk and sat down. "And it's five... I'm not coming."

They all wanted to object, but Areum was the first to speak up, "You're the oldest vampire in the city. You are the most powerful of all of us, and maybe there will be something you can sense that we can't." The others all agreed with her, for the same reason. Jarec was older than middle-aged elves and his knowledge would be helpful.

"I have to take care of matters here. Don't argue with me. My trust is in you all to complete this task." He paused and took out a small bottle of blood from his desk drawer, drinking from it. "I have called a council meeting today to tell them about the vampires of Menton, and to let them know you are traveling there. We have other matters to tend to as well."

Roland nodded and they all looked to the door as they heard it open. Bryn walked into the room with a smile on his face. "I cannot wait to get out of here," he proclaimed, clapping his brother on the back. Kari noticed he looked much like his brother, but his hair was darker, longer and shaggy, while Auben kept his closely cut.

"Well, now that you are all here, you better get going to cover as much ground as possible tonight. It should take two days to get there."

"I've been thinking about that," Roland smiled, "We can make it there in one night; with the right horses." Kari smiled, wide-eyed and excited. Ever since she heard briefly about the vampiric horses the night before, she had been interested in seeing them. She was sure that was what Roland was talking about. When she was alone with Jarec the night before, he had told her that the vampires had changed the horses during the war to move quicker over the land in their attack on the towns and villages.

Jarec shook his head. "It isn't up to me. You'll have to ask Elyse, and you know how protective she is of them."

"We should go see her at once then," Areum stated, "Jarec, we will see you when we return from Menton, and we'll be sure to send word to you while we are there if we learn anything."

"Wait just a moment." Jarec took his pen, ink, and paper from his desk drawer and quickly wrote out a note, then folded and sealed it with his ring. "In case she doesn't listen to you, and she won't, give her this so she knows I approve of this. It may sway her decision." He handed the note to Areum. "I would go with you and tell her myself, but the council will be here soon and I shouldn't keep them waiting. You all better get going."

Kari went around the desk and hugged Jarec. Although they had only just met, she had conversed with him for a long time when they were alone and already felt a close friendship with him. "Thank you so much," she said with a smile before kissing him on the cheek and returned to the rest of the group as they said their farewells to Jarec. They headed out quickly to go find Elyse, leaving Jarec alone at his desk as he waited for the council.

*****

A soft hand gently ran through the chestnut horse's mane, and all was quiet in the stable as usual. Elyse liked the quiet of the stables, and she loved all of the horses so. She, among all vampires, seemed to connect deeper with the vampiric horses than any of the others. There were theories among many in Aalen, but no one truly knew why she had such a gift with the horses, not even Elyse herself. At one point some thought it was because of the age when she was turned.

Elyse would have been twenty-five years now, and ten years had passed since she was bitten when the vampires were making their way to attack Jeul. But she wasn't the only one in Aalen who was changed so young, and the horses didn't connect the same to the other vampires who were, so it was a theory that had died out quickly. She hung the brush in her other hand back on the wall of the stable, when suddenly the sound of approaching footsteps reached her.

Bright green eyes turned to see who was coming this evening. She didn't get very many visitors at the stables. Most of the humans and even many of the vampires were unsettled by them. Elyse could understand, it was very unnatural to see a horse biting into another living animal to eat its blood. On the other hand, it was unnatural to see people drinking blood as well. But at least they fed on meat before they were vampires, and they could treat the blood they had to drink now as if it were just wine in a glass.

She recognized everyone except for the young girl with the blonde hair and gave a welcoming wave as they approached. "What brings you all to the stables?" she asked when they had gotten closer. Areum approached her as Roland moved into the stables and began checking on the horses.

"Elyse," Areum answered, "we need the horses." She didn't wait for a response before extending the note from Jarec out to the girl. Like most in Aalen, it was hard for Areum to think of Elyse as a woman and not a girl.

"Why?" Elyse answered suspiciously as she took the note. Jarec had always been careful to keep the horses within Aalen, and he had given Elyse complete control over their care and how much they could travel. She occasionally would take them outside during the night, but only let them stay around the farms and they listened to her and never got into trouble. The seal was Jarec's, and the handwriting was his as well. "This note only tells me that Jarec agrees they should be used, but it doesn't say why. It also says I can say no."

"This is Kari," Bryn said, leading Kari from where they had stood behind Areum to meet Elyse. "She came to us for help because her entire town has been turned, but they don't know how because none of them were bitten."

A confused look crossed Elyse's face. She had never heard of anything like that happening. "We're going to Menton, her town, to see if we can figure out what happened, and maybe we can find a link to our own problems and curing us. I don't know what Jarec is planning to do if we don't find anything. I imagine he'll invite the people there to come live here, but whatever his ideas, he hasn't told us. He's meeting with the council by now."

"Why can't you just take the normal horses?"

Bryn wasn't sure how to answer, so Areum answered her while Bryn was thinking. "It was Roland's idea," she began, "I believe that the idea of finding answers has gotten my husband excited and he wants to get there as soon as possible. I feel the same. With these horses, we can make the trip in one day instead of two. And if we had to stop and camp with the normal horses, we may need a carriage for Bryn and me, and that could slow us down even more. With these horses, we can get there quickly and, after we've learned all we can, our trip home with any information we find will be quick as well."

Elyse frowned and didn't know how to answer. She wanted to keep her horses safe, but she also felt sad for this girl, Kari, who looked to be about the same age she had been when bitten. "Elyse, please," she heard Auben's voice and turned to him, "I promise, we'll take good care of them."

"Ok, Auben," she smiled at him, "you can use the horses. But I'm coming, too, to make sure they are safe."

"We would be happy to have you along," Areum said, relieved they didn't waste too much time.

"If you come with us," Roland began to ask, having finally rejoined them from the stables, "who will watch the horses you have to leave behind?"

"There are other stable hands who work with the horses. I don't spend all my time here, Roland," she said, slightly offended, as she sometimes was, with the way people thought she cared more about the horses than other people. "I will let them know as we are leaving. How long will we be gone?"

"It should only take a night to get there and a night to get back, but I'd like a few days to make sure we don't miss anything in their town, so perhaps a week at most, unless Menton is larger than I think. Everyone go pack and get back quickly so we can saddle the horses and go. We want to leave as soon as the lights change. Meet back here when you have your things."

"Come with me, Kari, while I go to pack and get the others to take care of the stables," Elyse suggested. "Since everyone else knows so much already, you can fill me in with some of the details." She wanted to know more about the things that had happened in Menton, and she felt a connection to this girl, who had been transformed at a young age.

"Okay," Kari smiled. Elyse hoped they could help this girl, so she didn't suffer her own fate. She imagined that the others who were trapped in their adult ages had it much easier than those like her, physically stuck in adolescence, but mentally beyond it. She watched as Auben and Bryn were already off on their way and took Kari with her, asking her questions along the way. Roland and Areum, already packed, waited at the stables.

*****

Auben and Bryn returned to find that Roland and Areum had already saddled two of the horses, both of them brown. "Have you picked out all of our horses already," Bryn laughed. Roland seemed to be in quite a rush, though they still had time before they had to leave.

"No, I haven't," Roland replied, unamused. "Be sure to pick something dark, we'd rather blend into the night."

Bryn nodded and headed into the nearest stable and Auben followed him in. Many of the horses survived through the vampire's attack on Jeul, and the vampires had been sure to keep all the survivors in Aalen with them. While this meant having several stables to hold them all, so far there had never been any issues with feeding or having enough people to care for them all.

"Roland is being a little reckless, don't you think?" Bryn asked Auben as he saddled his horse.

"What do you mean?" Auben asked in reply as he prepared a horse as well.

"He is taking a chance using these horses. If we don't make it to Menton before sunrise, these horses, his wife, this girl, and myself are all going up in flames, unless we can quickly find shelter. Then we must avoid being caught, hiding a whole day before the night again."

"I see your point, but I trust his judgment." Auben had been going out with Roland for the past ten years seeking a cure for vampirism. He knew Roland was driven by this strange occurrence the same way he himself was. This could possibly lead to some answers. And if not, at least it was different than usual, and that was worth exploring.

"Don't misunderstand me, little brother. I'm sure we'll be fine, even if we don't make it there in time. I am just a little surprised. He normally puts much more thought and planning into these things."

Auben couldn't disagree with that statement. Roland did seem to be acting fast, but Auben agreed with the decision. He wanted his brother and all of the people of Aalen he had come to love cured. As he and his brother led their horses out, they saw that Elyse and Kari had returned and already gotten their horses ready from another stable.

"Everyone mount up," he heard Roland say, "it's time to depart."

The glowing red lights of Aalen shifted color to blue as the group rode out of Aalen and into the cool night air. The cloudless sky left the bright stars visible, and the moons shone brightly. Roland and Areum rode just behind Kari, who was leading the group to her home. Auben, Bryn, and Elyse followed the three of them closely.

A large beaming smile was on Kari's face. She had never ridden anything so fast before. Roland had told her to ride the horse as fast as she could, but she never imagined they would be so quick. She had full confidence that they would make it to Menton before daylight as long as the horses could keep up, and she had been given assurance they could keep this pace all night.

The hooves seemed to land lightly against the ground as they sped their way past the farms of Aalen and soon were traveling through grassy lands towards the nearest road. *Maybe my family and town can be saved*, Kari thought to herself. She had begun to feel more and more hopeful ever since she found Roland. *And maybe I can help save the people of Aalen.*

Soon the ground beneath them changed from grass to dirt as they reached the road. It was the same one that Roland, Auben, Kari, and Bree had ridden on when they came to Aalen from Freyg in the carriage. They took the road traveling southeast, back in the direction of Freyg. Kari knew they would have to travel around the town before reaching the crossroads to take them east to Menton. Roland had reminded her several times to be sure to avoid all the towns so they wouldn't draw attention.

*****

"Where did the girl say she was from?" Darel asked the tavern owner as he took a final drink from the glass and set it back on the bar. He had returned to Arndell to see if he could find more information about the girl since he wasn't able to follow Roland's trail from Langston. Will and Tras had returned with him, and they had met up with their other two friends who had stayed behind when they followed the vampire when she had left.

The older man standing behind the bar took the empty glass as he replied, "Well, let me think a moment." He set the glass back behind the counter to clean it later and continued, "I believe she said she came from Menton. It's a small town out east, across the river. You familiar with it?"

"I've never heard of it," Darel replied. "But I will find it." He looked over to the square table where the four men with him were sitting. "Send someone over to our table. We'll get some food before we head out." The coins he placed on the bar to cover the food and drink clinked as he stood and headed to the table.

"So what did you find out?" Weston asked Darel as he sat down and joined them. Weston and his brother, Simeon, who also sat with them at the table, were twins and both had dark skin. They had met Darel, Will, and Tras as children when their family had been traveling from the north. Both kept their hair close cut and shared the same brown eyes.

"We are going to a town called Menton, out east. But first, we are going to eat." Darel wasn't sure they'd find anything in Menton, but these men had trusted him to lead them this long, and he owed it to them to help them get their vengeance however they could, if possible. Any vampire they found would pay.

*****

There were some people out in the streets of Menton as Kari returned with the group from Aalen. Now that they couldn't go outside during the day, they usually would stay out at night, until the day came. Roland took notice of the dark black curtains that covered all of the windows, and that the area of the town they were in was residential. He imagined they learned quickly of several precautions they needed to take with their new condition. They had arrived with time to spare, as there wasn't yet a sign of sunrise.

A woman approached them as Kari dismounted. "Child, did you find any answers?" Roland and the others dismounted and took in the small town from where they stood. The woman seemed wary of the horses and could feel they were different.

"These people might be able to help us," Kari replied. "But we need to rest and get these horses put up before sunlight."

"I can tell some of your companions are vampires. Were more places in the world transformed?"

"Tomorrow I'll let everyone know the things I've learned on my journey. There is a lot to tell, but no, I haven't found any other places that were changed." The woman nodded and headed back to a group of townspeople to tell them what she learned. Kari turned to her newfound friends. "I'll take you to the nearest stables in town so we can keep the horses safe, then we'll go to my house. I need to find out if anyone else has returned yet. We can sleep there, and tomorrow night we'll meet with the mayor, and then you can start studying the town."

"I will stay with the horses," Elyse announced. "I imagine there are other horses in the stables, and I can keep mine from eating them. And I think they will feel more comfortable with me there."

"That's a good idea, Elyse," Roland said. "Also, Auben and I will sleep during some of the day, but we are going to take advantage of our ability to move around in the sunlight. Perhaps we can find something that will be

missed in the night. But let's not get ahead of ourselves.
Lead on to the stables, Kari."

The girl nodded and led them to the stables, where
they made some adjustments to keep the light of day out.
From there, they moved on to Kari's house, where her
parents were quite happy to see her return and very
interested in their new guests. Kari learned she wasn't the
first to return but wasn't the last either. And her parents
learned about Aalen, and about their new guests.

CHAPTER 7

PRISONERS

A week had passed in the dungeon of Moora, and Zeyn and his crew were still captive. They were still separated in different cells of the dungeon, and Gor had been put in a cell of his own after his escape attempt had failed. Zeyn had overheard the guards talking about the events of that day. At least Gor was still alive, since he was of an unknown race to the elves and therefore too valuable for Braal to kill. His thirst for knowledge wouldn't allow him to waste learning what he could of the large man.

Despite being in different cells, Zeyn was allowed to see the others. He had bargained with his knowledge for the opportunity to make sure they were all still doing well. It was how he had discovered the failed escape attempt Gor had made.

The days for the crew consisted of the guards coming in and asking them questions about life on the surface. It was clear to them that the guards truly had believed all this time the surface world was unlivable, but they remained loyal to their king. Still, Zeyn felt sometimes the questions they asked weren't just the ones

Braal wanted them to ask but were things they were interested in themselves. Sometimes it was Braal himself who took the time to come and visit them and ask questions. While this king was responsible for the imprisonment of Clarke's crew, his demeanor usually appeared nice and calm, and Zeyn felt that they could have gotten along under different circumstances.

Everyone was fed three meals a day in their cells, and the guards were going to remove the bonds on everyone shortly after they had been placed within the cells, only to discover the crew already had undone them. Thankfully, this did not bring any wrath down upon them.

His cellmates were still in good spirits, but Zeyn wondered if they were just hiding their fear, the same way he was hiding his fear from them. Even if they got out of the cell and got everyone else out of theirs, they would still have to find their way back to *Elline* without being caught. Then they would have to get away from Moora safely. It was a very high-risk escape, but Captain Clarke was willing to take the chance when the opportunity presented itself. And despite the odds against them, they weren't without their advantages.

They hadn't just been giving away information to the green elves and their king, they had learned a lot about them as well. Perhaps most importantly, they had learned that the green elves had developed the ability to speak to each other with their thoughts. It had been one of the side effects of the spell that had been used to save them in the war between Jeul and Moora. Of course, Braal didn't know they had learned about this, and would probably prefer they hadn't. But after one of the guards questioning them spoke aloud his astonishment that he couldn't hear their minds, it started to become clear how the guards worked together so well without speaking. Zeyn now knew if they were seen by even one guard, he could report their escape before they could take the guard out.

The captain had no plans to attack the guards; Gor
and the dwarves had acted on their own. Zeyn didn't mind
that they made an attempt, but he was thankful the king
only punished the three of them and not everyone. Gor,
Shim, and Bail were kept in strong chains now and only
allowed one free hand while they ate. Knowing about the
mental speech of the green elves and that Gor had failed,
Zeyn knew they certainly weren't going to succeed with a
direct attack on their captors. But one of the guards had
been giving him hints that he wanted to go to the surface,
and Zeyn thought perhaps he had a friend among his
enemies that was going to help them escape. That was their
second advantage. Captain Clarke just had to wait for that
elf to come back to speak with him again so he could learn
if he could use his help to save himself and his crew.

*****

The sound of silence calmed Maria as she reclined
in her brother's chair in the Captain's cabin aboard the
Salvation. Her eyes drifted open and she glanced around at
the interior of his room. A large blue rug now covered the
wooden floor of most of the room. She had bought it as a
gift for her brother and finally put it in to replace the old
ragged red and blue rug, which she had thrown out. She
was sure he'd like it when he returned. The maps of the
world their crew had made on their journeys were strewn
across a table to her right, and to the left, the small bed
Zeyn slept in while they were at sea. Her own room wasn't
quite as large as her brother's, but her bed was more
comfortable. She had been using her own room for sleep
ever since she attempted to sleep in the Captain's cabin the
first night she oversaw this ship.

It had been a week since she had seen her big
brother, and she was getting increasingly worried as the
days went by. At best, she thought maybe they got off

course and surfaced somewhere far away and hadn't been able to make their way back yet. At worst, she thought they all could be dead after a horrible accident while underwater. She held fast to the belief that they were all still alive and well and would return, but couldn't help the negative thoughts from creeping in. And now she had the problem of these elves from Jeul coming to Kassa.

Alex hadn't been able to find out much, except that he knew that the delegation was there on business from their king. Maria had learned their purpose was to find Zeyn when some of them had approached *Salvation* looking for him. She had told them he was away and that she was acting captain, and they left without any further questions. Something bothered her, though, and she felt that their interest in her brother had to do with the journey he and the others had taken under the sea. How did they find out about the vessel, and did they know about the destination? If the king had sent them, then someone had to have given him that information. Even then, what was Yuuric Kaalen's interest in these things?

Her thoughts were interrupted by a knock at the door. "Come in," she said as she sat up in the chair and looked to the door. As she expected, it was Alexander. He had been very helpful in keeping eyes on the elves and had been a shoulder to lean on when she began to dwell too much on her brother's fate. She was sure to keep a strong spirit in front of any of the other crew, though, and assured them all that things were going to turn out ok.

"Captain," Alex said, "the elves have set up some of their soldiers permanently at the docks, in the building where your brother and the others left from."

"They must be waiting for him to return." She hoped her theory that Zeyn had landed elsewhere along the shore was true. "Anything else?"

"Yes. Matthew spotted an elf that seems to be keeping an eye on the ship. The elf doesn't know we are aware of him, we think."

As good as the elves were, Maria wouldn't be surprised if Alex and Matthew were able to keep watch on one without being spotted. They were the best spies aboard the *Salvation*. Maria had come to a decision. She was tired of waiting around for something to happen. "Alex, gather the crew together on the lower deck for a meeting. And then after that, I am going out to talk with the leaders of these visitors. I want to know what they want with my brother and why they feel the need to keep eyes on us."

"Are you sure, Captain?" She knew Alex would question her. He always did when he thought she might be recklessly entering into a dangerous situation. But what was life without some danger?

"Yes, I am. Now get the crew together, I'll be out in a moment."

*****

Bandar, Thela, and Sola sat near the entrance to the water from the castle of Moora. "If you do this, we can never come back to Moora," Thela said. She had already agreed with Bandar that they should take the opportunity to go to the surface but knew as well that they could still change their minds. "We can still just stop all this and return to our normal lives."

"No. I'm sure I want to do this," Bandar replied, gripping his spear.

"And what about you, Sola? Are you still sure you want to do this? You could always stay behind. You don't have to join us in this."

"I want to leave this place," Sola harshly replied. Her tone wasn't directed at her friends, but at the kingdom itself. Her parents had disappeared a few years ago, and she wondered if it was because someone learned about the story they knew about the surface. She had always known that the tale passed down through their family was true, and now the proof had come to Moora itself. "I want to see the surface world that has been kept from us."

"Good," Bandar stood as he spoke. "I will free the prisoners while the two of you bring that thing they came here in." He gestured at the water. "Bring it right here to the edge so we can all get inside. If we follow our plan, we should be able to get out of here before the others know what's happened."

Thela and Sola nodded and both dove into the waters, swimming away to retrieve the vessel. They had already tested their ability to use their magic to help them move the thing around in the water. Bandar was excited about going to the surface but also scared of what might happen to him if something went wrong. He had decided if he failed that he would take all the blame and do his best to hide Sola and Thela's involvement.

Bandar propped his spear across his shoulder and began to walk towards the dungeon. He would enter the cell of the one called Captain Clarke first, and let him know of the escape. Since it was his turn to question the prisoners, no one would have any reason to suspect a thing.

*****

The cell door opened and woke Zeyn from his nap. Rendal and Melzer were talking quietly to each other but stopped speaking to look at which guard was coming in today. Horace was still asleep and snoring. The elf guard entered and shut the door, and Zeyn saw that it was the guard who was particularly interested in the surface. "Hello," Zeyn said, sitting up and crossing his legs. "Do you have more questions for us, today?"

"No more questions," the elf answered, then lowered his voice, "My name is Bandar, and I'm going to free you."

Rendal and Melzer perked up and nudged Horace to wake him. "Why would you do that?" Rendal asked.

"I want to go to the surface. I had heard stories before, but I never dreamed they were true."

"So," Zeyn smiled, "You want us to take you with us in exchange for our freedom. Why don't you just swim up there yourself?"

Bandar knelt down before answering, "Because I might end up in the same situation as you are in now. You told me in one of our previous meetings that there are no green elves on the surface. If I go there alone, I may end up a prisoner. But if I am with you, then you can help introduce me to the world above. Also, I don't think it is right that we are keeping you all captive here when you've done nothing to deserve it."

"I like your answer." Zeyn looked to the others. "If you can really get us out of here, and all of the rest of my crew, then I'll be happy to take you to the surface. What is your plan?"

"There are two others coming with us, my friends Sola and Thela. They are retrieving your vessel as we speak and will move it into place so you may all enter it. I have to go talk to the other prisoners as well and let them in on the plan. When I leave the room, I will leave the door unlocked. There are two guards posted at each door, but if you all take them by surprise at the same time, we should be able to knock them out and get out before we can be discovered. I will give a quick shout that everyone can hear to signal you all to leap out of your cells and grab the guards."

"How do we make sure we knock them all out?" Melzer asked while standing and stretching. Rendal stood as well and helped Horace to his feet.

Bandar smiled and stood. "You have three elves with you, and I can use magic as well. When we catch the guards by surprise, the four of us will use combined magic to put them all to sleep. Since they won't be prepared to defend against it, they should all fall asleep in the arms of whoever is holding them."

"And if that doesn't work?" Zeyn asked. Although he himself was no wizard, Zeyn understood quite a bit about magic. He knew that the likelihood of four elves being able to overtake ten elves with magic was slim. Bandar dropped two crude daggers onto the floor.

"If the magic doesn't work, we'll use these," Bandar answered sadly. "I would prefer not to kill any of them. They are only doing their job; the same job as me, and aren't my enemies. But if it has to be done, I am prepared. I've got more to give to the others."

Zeyn gestured for Melzer and Rendal to get the daggers, and they did. While he could understand Bandar's reluctance to hurt the guards, he knew his crew would have no problem with it, if necessary. "We will be ready to go. Horace, I'll have Gor carry you once the guards are out. I mean no offense."

"Don't worry," Horace replied, "I know I'm an old man. If it gets me out of here quicker, I don't care if I have to be carried."

"Wonderful, then we're all set. Bandar, we'll wait for your sig…" A loud noise erupted from the hallway and all of their heads turned to the door as Bandar immediately moved to look out and see what had happened as yells and screams erupted from the guards in the hall. Zeyn followed Bandar to see Gor struggling against the guards in the hallway. "Well, there goes your plan."

"I can't believe he broke the bonds we put him in this time," Bandar spoke in amazement, seeing the chains he'd been placed in after his first escape attempt swinging from his wrists. "Take the keys and free the others." Zeyn took the keys as Bandar offered them and moved to quickly opening the cells.

As Zeyn freed Annah, Phyra, Caleb, and Brill, Melzer and Rendal ran to join Gor in the fight against the guards. Horace walked out of the cell and stood watching the fight and waiting. Zeyn directed Caleb to go join Horace and sent his newly freed crewmates to join in the fight. The next to be freed were Gallen, Naaren, Olii, and Noon. "Quick, put them to sleep," Zeyn commanded the elves and pushed Gallen towards his son and Horace.

"Captain," Naaren replied, "I don't think that will be necessary."

Zeyn turned to see that his crew, mainly Gor, had knocked out the guards in the tunnel already. "This one's with us," Zeyn said, gesturing to Bandar to keep the others who had just taken notice of the green elf from attacking him. "His name is Bandar. Naaren, Olii, Noon, if you would, please check and make sure none of them are mortally wounded. If any of them might come around soon, make sure they stay knocked out."

They weren't sure why Captain Clarke cared if any of the green elves died, but they did as he said. Zeyn moved and opened the last cell, freeing Bail and Shim. The two dwarves leaped forth to see that the fighting they had heard from in their cell was already finished.

"We missed it," Bail grumbled. But he then noticed Bandar and rushed towards him to attack. Gor sighed and grabbed Bail by the neck, picking him up.

"The captain said he's with us," Gor said, and then set Bail back down.

"We need to get out of here now," Bandar worriedly spoke, "they had enough time to send out a mental alarm…"

"Lead on, then!" Captain Clarke demanded, then turned to his crew, "Stick together, we're going back to *Elline*, and then returning to the surface. If we need to fight as we escape, take care of anyone in our way, and don't get lost. Gor, carry Horace. Naaren, Olii, Noon, have spells ready just in case, and be prepared for your spells to see and breathe when we are in the vessel." Gor nodded to the Captain and knelt, letting Horace climb onto his back. The elves began to each quietly chant, preparing different spells.

Bandar led them out of the dungeon and up to the first hallway. He moved ahead of the rest of the group to scout ahead, and seeing no one present, waved for the group to follow him. They took a left at the next hallway, and again, Bandar went ahead of them to make sure no one was around, before leading them through the second right hallway which led back into the main chamber where the group had first arrived. Things looked clear, and Zeyn looked to see two female green elves waiting for them, and he saw that *Elline* was at the edge and ready to board. Bandar ran to one of the women and embraced her. Across the way, from the other hallway, Zeyn suddenly noticed a group of distant guards rushing towards them.

"Quickly!" Zeyn shouted to his friends. "Everyone get in the ship!" They were outnumbered and unprepared to face such a large group of their captors. His crew and the other companions were quick to move to *Elline* and they all boarded as fast as they could, taking their positions in the vessel. Zeyn waiting for his crew and for their three new elven passengers to enter, all the while he watched the entrance to the hall where he'd seen the guards. As the guards rounded the corner, Zeyn entered into the ship and closed the hatch above him. *Elline* dove and fled from the sunken Kingdom of Moora, and the guards gave chase, swimming after her.

*****

"Let them go," Braal said to all the guards who had gathered before him. "And call back the other guards who followed them," he directed to the captain of his guards, "they have already escaped us, and I do not desire to recapture them." The captain was surprised but obeyed. It had only been minutes since the escape and he could still reach the minds of the guards who were swimming after the vessel. He called them back to Moora at once.

Braal Savuul stood from his throne and looked around the room. His guards knew the surface wasn't destroyed now, and word has most likely spread to some of their families, despite his command that they tell no one. He was going to tell his people the truth. Perhaps he should have never demanded that the truth die out with the first generation to live under the water. While he was willing to tell his people about the war, he would not let anyone know about Tecuul. The guilt upon his heart for letting his cousin survive off the people under his charge had weighed heavy upon his heart through the years, and he was afraid of their reaction if they knew.

He looked to the captain of his guards. "Go, and gather together the council," he commanded. "And let all of Moora know there will be an announcement from their King before the day is through."

*****

A week had almost passed since they had arrived in Menton. With no clues found within the main town, their searches had begun to spread to the outlying farms by the end of the third day. At the beginning of the fourth night, Elyse had left with the horses back to Aalen, since the return trip wasn't going to require them. She would have stayed, but it was becoming increasingly difficult to keep the vampiric horses from biting into the other horses in the stable. The people of Menton had given them permission to use one of their carriages and two of their horses on their eventual return home.

As the daylight of their fifth day in Menton began to fade, Roland and Auben were approaching one of the abandoned farms of the community. Spirits were low, for while they hadn't visited every location of the people of Menton, they were almost out of places to search. "Do you think there is anything to find?" Auben asked as they made their way across a field towards the empty house.

"Maybe there isn't," Roland admitted. "I thought there must be a cause to this, but we don't even know what caused vampires to exist in the first place. Maybe it just happens."

"Well, if things go the way they have, the others may not even get a chance to meet us out here by the time we're done. It seems like a rather small farm." They had arrived at the house, and Auben was right, it was very small. They had been told in town that the farm home had been abandoned when the family died out, and no one had ever claimed the property. There were other homes in Menton that also suffered the same fate, and the Mayor had admitted that something needed to be done about the land and property that wasn't in use. Many of these homes had already been searched.

Looking out on the farm where they stood, Roland thought it was a shame no one had taken charge of it. Though it hadn't been used in years, the land appeared to be fertile and the barn, though old, appeared to be in good condition. They would search it after they were through in the house. Auben opened the door and Roland followed him into the home.

The house was one story and there weren't many walls, so some of the rooms ran together. Although abandoned, it looked as if some things had been taken from the home after it was no longer in use, but there were two chairs and a table still in the main room. Roland stepped into the bedroom to find a simple, single bed that had sat untouched for years and a small table with a lamp. A small bookshelf held several books that were well-read but in good condition. Some clothes were still hung in the closet, but other than that, there was nothing.

"There wasn't anything in the kitchen," Auben said as Roland exited the bedroom back into the main room. "To the barn, then?"

"I suppose that's the only thing left here to check. There wasn't anything in the bedroom either. Nothing has been touched here in years." Roland turned and made his way through the front door and back outside. It was dark now, and he knew his wife and the others would be coming to meet them. As he made his way around the house, he noticed a cellar door at the back of the home. Auben noticed something had caught Roland's eye and then saw the cellar as well. Roland opened the door and started down the stairs.

His eyes widened as he came upon the scene before him. On the ground lay a body, drained of life and decayed. It had been there for quite some time. But the dead went unnoticed by Roland because the thing his eyes were drawn to was the magical floating door and the tall elf-like man who stood in front of it, smiling upon seeing Roland. "You are finally here."

"Who are you?" Auben asked, having just come upon the man as well.

"My name is Mar'vandi," he replied with a grin.

"What are you?" Roland asked.

"A demon."

CHAPTER 8

A DEMON'S GIFT

Areum worried about her husband as she made her way to meet him at an old farm. He had been so hopeful for an answer in Menton, and it appeared as if there would be none. She still held on to the hope, but perhaps their answer would lie elsewhere in the world, even though in their travels abroad, before the war, they had never encountered vampires in another land. She did hope they would at least find an answer to Menton's trouble while they were here, as it troubled her that all the people living here would be cursed like this at once, which she had never heard of and no other vampire had ever mentioned to her. If no answer was found, then all the people of Menton may have to come and join them in Aalen. They were a kind people and had been very accommodating. She believed the two communities would get along well.

Bryn and Kari were the only ones with her. The people of Menton hadn't found anything in their town and none believed Kari's new friends would find anything, but they were willing to let them do their searching. "There it is," Kari said, pointing to the empty farm up ahead. As vampires, they had no problem seeing in the dark. It was one of the gifts their curse gave them. They wouldn't have seen the farm otherwise, as there was no light to be seen coming from it.

"Well, then, let's see if my brother and Roland found anything," Bryn grinned. "I'll race you!" And with that Bryn began to run, as fast as only a vampire can, followed by Kari and Areum. Smiles came to Areum and Kari's faces as well, relishing the powers they all had.

*****

"A demon?!" Roland said questioningly as he drew his sword with Auben following his lead. He had never before been face to face with a demon, though he had heard of them. Only some of the human mages ever dealt with demons, and even then sparingly. It was a dangerous thing. Roland thought that this demon before him would have passed for an elf if he had run into him on the street, though. The demon had the ears for an elf and his clothing was very plain and drab. His hair was short and brown. If he hadn't admitted what he was, Roland and Auben would never have known, though Roland did notice that oddly, the pupils of his blue eyes were white.

Mar'vandi sighed. "Calm down," he said, "and put away your swords. I'm not here to fight; I'm here to help you."

"Help us?" Auben said. "Why would you want to do that?"

"If you would both put your swords away, I will explain. I have answers for you. I know who you are, Roland Lam, and you, Auben Dale. I have a great interest in Aalen." Roland and Auben both put away their weapons. As they did, they heard movement from the stairs of the cellar and turned to see their friends join them. "Ah, I see Areum and Bryn were able to join us as well. And Kari, you have performed excellently."

"What are you talking about? Who are you?" Kari asked. The others looked at Kari questioningly. "I have never seen this man before."

"It's true, she doesn't know me. But just like I know the people of Aalen," Mar'vandi continued, "I have grown to know the people of Menton over the past months. I have had need of them."

"Let's listen to what he has to say. This... demon is named Mar'vandi," Roland explained to his wife, Bryn, and Kari. "He claims he is here to help us."

"You are all here because you want to be rid of your vampiric natures. I can help. First," he looked to Kari, then closed his eyes, chanted in an unknown tongue, and gave a gesture of his hands. "Check your teeth, child."

Kari was stunned to feel her fangs gone. Her eyes adjusted to the darkness. "I'm cured?"

"You and everyone in Menton are now. You have served my purpose and I'm returning you to normal as a sign of good will to Roland, so he will believe me."

Roland looked expectantly to Areum, but she returned his hopeful look with a frown. "Then why not do the same for all the people of Aalen," Roland said to Mar'vandi, "If you really want my trust."

"Because what I want you to trust me about is how to return them to their former selves. I cannot do it because I am not the one who made them what they are."

"You mean you are the one who did this to me?" Kari asked angrily. Areum placed a hand on her shoulder in understanding.

"Be grateful I didn't leave you that way. I could have," the demon said. "The reason I turned this town to vampires was to get the attention of Aalen. I needed to speak to some of the vampires that were already here, and none of them are in the demon summoning business."

"You couldn't be summoned closer? Or just ask someone to bring us to you?" Areum asked.

"I tried, but… do you know how the first human learned how to summon demons?" Mar'vandi asked.

"No."

"The first human learned because a demon entered his dreams and told him how to summon him. A demon can only touch the dreams of those with the weakest of minds, though, so that human was used to give the information to human wizards who we knew would keep records for future generations to bring us to your world. I tried to simply tell someone in Aalen through a dream, but while I could view your dreams from where I was, I couldn't enter them and interact with anyone there. It is rare to find someone that weak, but eventually, I did." He gestured to the dead body on the floor.

"You killed him?" Bryn asked accusingly.

The demon shook his head. "I wanted this to be clean. I wanted him to summon me, and I intended to send him to Aalen to bring someone to me. The man happened to be traveling near Menton and decided to summon me when he found this abandoned farm, even though I told him in his dream to summon me somewhere near Aalen. The reason he died is because he cut himself wrong and couldn't stop his bleeding. It doesn't take a lot of blood to summon one of us, although some of us demand a high blood price if there is a request for us to fulfill. That is the story of how I ended up here, and I am bound to the area in which I am summoned, so I couldn't just leave and go to Aalen.

"Since I was stuck here, I took matters into my own hands. I discovered that, much like Aalen, I couldn't enter the dreams of any in Menton. I decided to cast a spell on Menton, and along with it, a compulsion to lead them to seek out help. With a bit of luck, I believed they would eventually go to Jeul and be sent to Aalen. It took them a few days, but they finally sent people out. Through my spell, I've been following all of their progress, and this girl did amazing in finding her way there quicker than I expected."

"So we know why you did this," Bryn said, "I want to know how I can be rid of this curse."

"It's very simple, really," the demon replied with a smile, "You just have to kill the first vampire. When you do, the curse will leave all of the vampires. He is the source of all of you, and the spell that created him is tied to his very being."

"And where is he?"

"I don't know where he is, the spell that created him also protects him from me, but I have been following some other events in the world. If you go to Kassa, you may be able to find the answers you seek. Roland," the demon turned towards him as he spoke the name, "your friend, Zeyn Clarke is there, and recently he heard of this first vampire, named Tecuul Boaruun. He is an elf, a criminal, and has never been led by compulsion to do evil as a vampire; he has done it of his own free will. He does deserve death for his crimes. But know this; he is the strongest of all vampires. His speed and strength are greater than any of you, but together, I'm sure you can come up with something. I've told you all I know." Mar'vandi turned to go back through the portal.

"Wait!" Roland said. Mar'vandi turned around. "Why do you care about this? You say he deserves to die. Are you seeking some kind of justice?"

The demon laughed. "I don't care about justice, I just need you to know that you shouldn't feel bad about killing him. My reasons need not concern you. They have no effect on you. It is sufficient enough that you know how to carry out this task and to know that it is what you want. I am giving this to you freely, asking nothing in return, which is rare for my kind. Now go, and do what you have longed for." With those words, Mar'vandi left back through the glowing blue doorway, which closed behind him, leaving them all in darkness. The group took a moment to think about the events they had just witnessed, and then made their way back up the stairs and out of the cellar.

"Thank you," Kari said to Roland, throwing her arms around his neck and hugging him tightly. She then turned to Areum, Bryn, and Auben, hugging each of them as well. "Thank you all! You've saved us."

Roland frowned, but Auben answered her. "You're welcome. But I don't think we really did anything."

"No, all we did was discover the cause, and the demon lifted the very curse he cast," Roland said. "He has been there, waiting for us. I just can't help but wonder why."

Areum placed a hand on his arm. "If what he said is true, dear, then we can help the vampires of Aalen now." She smiled at him. "That's more important than why."

"I know. Kari," he looked to the girl who had come to him for help and smiled, "I'm glad you and your town have gotten rid of your vampirism. Thank you for finding us. Without this opportunity, we wouldn't have learned how to save ourselves."

"I'm glad I could help," she replied, though she felt like saying she didn't have much of a choice if the demon was honest about the compulsion he placed on the people of Menton.

"Well, then, I think we won't be going back to Aalen yet," Roland said to his friends. "We need to get to Kassa. Do you think we'll still be able to take that carriage and horses for our journey there, Kari?"

She laughed. "I'm sure they'd let you take whatever you want since they've been cured. Let's hurry back! I can't wait to tell them what's happened!" Kari ran back in the direction of Menton. She wasn't as fast as she had been just moments ago when she was a vampire, but it didn't bother her. The girl was more excited about eating normal food again and being able to feel the sun on her skin.

*****

The streets of Menton were full of people laughing and celebrating when the group returned. Nearly the entire community had gathered, from the people who lived within the main town to those from outlying homes and farms, all who were no longer vampires and had regained their humanity. Kari's parents ran to her as she was running ahead of the group from Aalen. The family's embrace brought a smile to the faces of Kari's new friends.

"Do you know what happened?" Kari's mother asked her, tears of joy in her eyes.

"Yes! We found the source of the problem, and it's been taken care of. I'll explain the whole story later, but we have to get to Kassa right away."

Roland's smile faded. "Kari, we do have to get to Kassa, but you need to stay here, with your family. What we have to do, you aren't prepared for, especially with your powers gone." Areum nodded, agreeing with her husband.

"Don't worry," Bryn said, "We'll come back and let you know when we've taken care of things. We don't forget our friends."

"I… I understand," Kari replied, though she wasn't sad. She was disappointed, but the joy of her returned humanity outweighed any sadness she could have. And she really did understand, but the journey that had brought her away and back had given her a thirst for adventure, and she had hoped to share the rest of this adventure with her new friends. "You're right; I have been away for a while." She had to admit she'd never learned much about fighting and certainly wouldn't be much help against a vampire right now.

"Bryn's right," Roland said, "We'll be back." He looked around to search through the crowd. "Excuse me a moment. When I get back, we'll go ahead and leave. Say your goodbyes." He made his way to the mayor.

Areum smiled to Kari and gave her a hug. "You're a brave girl, and I'm glad we met you. You're welcome to visit us in Aalen any time."

"Thank you," Kari said, happy for the invitation, "but you'll have to let me know where you all go when you've killed this vampire. Surely you won't keep living underground." Areum smiled again but was unsure what the fate of the vampires of Aalen would be if they succeeded.

Kari hugged Auben and Bryn next. "I'll miss you both so much!"

"Take care of yourself," Bryn said.

"It seems like just yesterday we were riding in that carriage from Freyg," Auben said with a smile. "I'm glad everything worked out."

"Please be sure to tell Elyse what's happened," Kari requested, "and tell her to visit me."

"I will." Auben turned to see Roland returning.

"We can use the carriage and horses," Roland said, "And I let him know about the body at the farm. He should get a proper burial, and maybe they can finally do something with that land. Let's grab our things and load the carriage. We can make it to Kassa by mid-day."

"Goodbye, Roland," Kari said as she wrapped her arms around him and he hugged her back. "You've been a good friend to me."

"And you're a good friend, too." Roland smiled and looked to her parents. "Your daughter has been a great help to us all."

With their farewells spoken, they went to gather their belongings and then packed the carriage. Auben sat up front to drive the carriage, while his brother sat inside and closed the curtains on both sides to prepare for when the morning came. Roland opened the door for his wife and kissed her before she entered. Once she was inside, he closed the door and moved to join Auben in the front. Both Roland and Auben waved to the people of Menton and then headed north, to look for answers in Kassa.

*****

"They just broke off and swam away," Olii said, as he looked through the magic window to the outside of the rear of the vessel. "I wonder why?" He was the first person to verbally express the thought since the elves had left them hours ago. He looked to Bandar, expecting an answer.

"I have no idea," he replied to the look. "As they began to leave us I attempted to ask them, but they didn't respond to my thoughts, and kept their minds hidden from me." Thela had stayed with him on the upper deck while Sola had gone below. She nodded to agree with Bandar. Olii looked away after turning his attention to Thela, slightly embarrassed. Thela and Sola dressed the same as the other green elves. While this didn't bother the crew from the *Salvation*, who had traveled all over the world and seen other cultures unknown to their native land, it was a shock for the others on board *Elline*, who were used to more modesty on the surface.

"Just be glad they did," Gor said gruffly as he propelled the vessel. "Wondering won't get you any answers." He and the others who were working the crank had been pushing themselves hard early in the trip, to stay away from their pursuers. They were relieved when they could take a more relaxed approach to their job again.

Olii turned to look through the front window just as they breached the surface of the water. "We're back!" He exclaimed, relieved. He was ready to stop using his magic, as it did take a lot out of him and Noon to keep the breathable air spell working for a long period of time. Looking out through the front of the vessel, all that was visible was ocean waters for as far as the eye could see. He turned to look through the back and was grateful to be able to see the shore in the distance.

Zeyn smiled and used the wheel to turn the ship around, and Gor began to work a little harder, ready to get back to Kassa. The rest of the crew and passengers began to celebrate. "It won't be too much longer," Zeyn announced. "I think I can spot Kassa right there!" He pointed towards a spot at the shore, and everyone could see that it was indeed a town.

As they got closer, they were sure it was the same place they had left a week ago. The view of the town reinvigorated Gor, and as he began to crank quicker to propel the ship, the dwarves joined in to get them moving faster. As they approached the dock from when they first left, *Elline* slowed under Zeyn's command and dove back under the sea to come up again within the large shed. They had finally returned to Kassa.

As Sola, Annah, Phyra and Naaren returned to the upper deck from below, the rest of the crew already began to climb out of the vessel and onto the wooden docks within the shed. Zeyn smiled, watching them leave. The captain was glad he was able to get everyone home safely. "Bandar," Zeyn said to the green elf, who had not yet left with Thela and Sola, "you and your friends might want to stay with me when we leave. No one on the surface has ever seen a green elf, and we don't need you to draw too much attention just yet."

"You're right, of course," Bandar replied. "I'll wait just outside."

Zeyn nodded, and Bandar along with the two green elven women left the ship. Naaren was the only one left with Zeyn, and the elf clearly had something on his mind. "Is everything alright?" Zeyn asked.

"I'm fine, but I need to tell you something that has stayed within my family. It can wait, though. I want to get out of this confined space and into a cozy bar with some drink. We can talk about it in the morning."

Zeyn grinned. "That sounds good." The captain waited and took one last look around the deck as Naaren exited. This had been amazing, and his sister would be incredibly jealous she missed the short adventure. She'd have to take a trip some time, but away from Moora. He longed to be back on *Salvation's* deck, and feel the breeze as they sailed over the waters, but one day maybe he would venture below again. He put the thoughts of the upcoming celebration with his crew in his mind as he began to climb the rungs of the metal ladder and out of the ship. His cheerful mood quickly dropped as he saw what awaited them in the confines of the shed.

There were several elven guards around the docks surrounding *Elline* and at the doors back out into the street of Kassa. By the look of their armor, Zeyn knew they were from Jeul. His crew and their other companions appeared to not be under any duress, as they weren't being physically held by these guards, but he knew that there had obviously been words of some kind exchanged to keep them from attempting to leave. The eyes of his friends all looked to him as he hopped over to the dock from the hatch of *Elline* and stood tall, looking to the highest ranking among the guards.

"How may my crew and I help you?" he asked. It was at this point that he did notice that the three green elves were physically being held by three of the guards.

"We heard about your voyage under the ocean," the guard replied. "We had hoped to stop you beforehand, but now, we are going to need to ask you some questions."

Zeyn gave his crew a nod to let them know that everything would be alright. "Very well, we will be happy to help you with any answers we can provide." He gestured to the three green elves. "You can let them go, they are friends, and they will come along peacefully." The guards holding the elves let go of them with a motion from their commander, but they kept a watchful eye on them. "Since we are willing to comply, I was wondering if you could answer a question for me. How did you know about the trip we just took?"

"Someone who went with you talked, and word spread to the king. I don't know who."

"This is my fault," Noon quickly confessed. Olii looked to Noon with a confused look on his face, and the other members of *Elline's* crew turned to him as well.

"What do you mean?" Olii asked.

"I'm sorry. I was drunk in Jeul a week before we left, and I told some other elves there in a pub about where we were going and how some crackpot wanted to find a lost elven kingdom that surely didn't exist. I didn't mean for this to happen." Noon hung his head in shame.

"I'm sorry, Horace," Gallen said, "I brought him into this."

"It's fine. What's done is done," Horace replied. He was somewhat satisfied that someone who thought him a crackpot had been proven wrong, but still felt a sting of betrayal, though he hadn't known Noon before they set out.

"King Kaalen is anxious to speak with you," the captain of the guards spoke to Zeyn again.

"He's here in Kassa?" Zeyn asked, surprised. Although, after what they had learned of Moora, Zeyn assumed Yuuric Kaalen must know about it to have come out to see them.

"He is, and he is waiting for you now back at the inn. Follow me." And Zeyn and the others did follow, having no choice.

*****

The sun rose and light spread over Menton. The streets were filled with people drinking in the warmth they had missed. The light didn't burn them up, as it would have if their curse still remained, and there was a smile on every face. They had never known how much they had taken the sunlight for granted. Kari Sleyn danced in the street. By now, Roland and the others should be getting close to Kassa, and would hopefully soon be able to save the vampires of Aalen.

As the crowds began to spread to allow five horses and their riders through, Kari noticed they were strangers to Menton. As her eyes met the man in the lead, recognition crossed both of their faces: a grin on his face and wide eyes in disbelief on hers. "You found me here?" she questioned, knowing the answer.

"We'll go to great lengths to hunt your kind, vampire," Darel exclaimed, leaping from his horse and reaching for his sword. He was followed by Tras, but his other three companions had realized two things. First, they noticed that it was daylight and if the girl was a vampire, she should be dead. Second, they saw the local authorities in the street that outnumbered them, and the other people closing in to protect their own. Things happened fast, and before any other words could be exchanged, Darel and Tras were being held down by four men with swords, while the other three on horseback were being watched closely by the crowd and two other men who had already drawn their weapons.

The men on their horses raised their hands in the air and one of them, Simeon, spoke, "We don't want any trouble."

"Off your horses," one of the guards said, pointing his sword towards Simeon. He dismounted along with Weston and Will. Darel and Tras were brought to their feet and the guards began to bind the hands of the five men. "Why did you attack the girl?" the same guard questioned Darel.

"He's been following me," Kari answered, "ever since he saw me in Arndell." She turned to Darel. "You can see that I am no vampire. I am standing in the sunlight without dying, and…" She smiled and pulled her lips apart to reveal her normal teeth. She gestured to a nearby window, too, where her reflection could be seen.

Darel shook his head. "But you had no reflection in that mirror in Arndell, and we saw how fast you could move in the night."

"We'll lock them up," the guard said and they began to get ready to lead them off to the prison.

"Wait!" Kari stopped them. A plan had begun to form in her mind, but she needed to know more from these five men first. "He attacked me, but he thought I was some kind of a monster." She turned to Darel. "Tell me, why are you hunting for vampires?" And Darel told her and the others of Menton his story, and the others with him gave parts of their stories as well. When they had all finished talking, Kari came to a decision. If they wanted to hunt a vampire, she knew where they could go, and she would go with them.

CHAPTER 9

OLD FRIENDS

As Zeyn Clarke was led through the inn, he took notice that staff appeared to be there, but the rest of the building appeared to be completely taken over by the kingdom of Jeul. Elven guards were everywhere he looked, in their bright armor and blue and white tabards representing Jeul, and must have taken up all the rooms. It made sense that they would want to keep their king safe and surrounded, but he definitely wasn't here in secret. The innkeepers knew who their patron was.

While Zeyn was taken for the audience with the king, his crew and the others were being held in the foyer. This wasn't his first meeting Yuuric, and they had done business before, so there shouldn't be any problems. After all, he wasn't bound by these guards, though they were walking one in front and one behind, making sure he went where he was supposed to go. But when the guards talked to them at the docks, they did mention they had wanted to stop the trip before it started, so maybe things wouldn't be quite so nice this time.

"We're here," the guard in the lead said, opening the door and looking in first. "You may enter." The guard

moved to the right side of the room to stand at his post and
the guard behind Zeyn moved to the left side of the door.
Zeyn walked into the room.

He was surprised to see that the king had taken such
a normal room for his quarters while in town. The room
was small, with a single bed, a lampstand with a lamp, and
a small table with seats for two. King Kaalen was seated at
the table and, to Zeyn's surprise, so was Maria. But Zeyn
was careful to honor tradition first and bowed to the king.
"Your majesty," Zeyn said first, before turning to his sister.
"Maria, what are you doing here?"

Maria Clarke stood and rushed to her brother,
hugging him tightly around the neck. "Welcome back,
brother!" she exclaimed. "I was worried you had
drowned."

"I'm fine, little sister." He broke off their embrace
and repeated his question. "What are you doing here?"

"She was suspicious of why the elves of Jeul had
come to Kassa," the king said, standing from his chair.
There were two guards in the room that Zeyn had not
noticed, who were standing near the door. Yuuric Kaalen
dismissed them with a hand gesture. The guards were
hesitant to leave him alone with Zeyn and Maria, so their
king spoke. "You may leave, I command it."

As the guards exited the room, the king stood and
placed a hand on the door and whispered a few words.
Zeyn knew he must be working some kind of magic, but
did not know what it could be. "What are you doing?"

"I'm sealing the room so that anyone outside cannot
hear what is spoken within these walls," the king answered.
"Though I fear what I share with you may no longer be
hidden, and I'm going to have to tell my people the truth."

"So you do know about Moora."

The king nodded. "Please, have a seat." He
gestured towards the table and chairs, for both of them to
sit. "I have told your sister some of the reasons I wanted to

stop your voyage beneath the water, but I was too late. The royal line of Jeul has been tasked with keeping the secret of what happened to Moora. My grandfather was the king who went to war with them. I never knew him, but he told my father of the war, and my father told the story to me."

"You elves live so long, how could no one else in Jeul know?" Maria questioned. Zeyn wondered the same.

"That is the secret we are more concerned with keeping," the king said. "The spell used to destroy Moora was focused through King Aar Kaalen. My grandfather had come to a decision before the elves had prepared the spell. He had known that if successful, Jeul would have to live with what they had done, obliterating an entire kingdom from the land. With so much magic running through him during the spell that destroyed Moora, he had prepared in secret a spell to cast following the attack to erase the memories of Moora from all the people of Jeul as they were lending their magic to him. And he succeeded. No one remembered there was a war, no one remembered that there was a kingdom of Moora, or that its people had ever existed. They were completely forgotten."

"That's terrible!" Maria exclaimed, frowning.

"I have to agree. I don't agree with what my grandfather did, but I understand that he did it to protect his people. I can't blame him for wanting to keep their conscience clear."

"But if he only made Jeul forget," Zeyn said, "surely some of the other kingdoms remembered."

"The human kingdoms to the north and the south were young," Yuuric continued, "and didn't deal with the elves much at the time. Over the years the humans who had known of Moora, in their short lives, did forget. Some information must have survived for Horace to have come to me asking about Moora. I never dreamed he'd find someone to help him find its ruins."

Zeyn began to laugh and stood up, and the king appeared puzzled by his laughter. "We found the ruins, but you don't know what happened to the people, do you? They are still alive! They survived and have been living underwater ever since Jeul attacked them."

"How can that be?" The king appeared to be glad to hear the people of Moora survived, as if it wasn't just the erasing of Jeul's memory he disagreed with.

"A counter spell they used to defend themselves. I also know about Tecuul, now."

"Who?"

"Tecuul Boaruun. The reason for the war between Jeul and Moora."

The king's eyes widened and he grasped Captain Clarke by the shoulders. "I was never told why there was a war. Please, tell me. Who is Tecuul?"

And Zeyn told him the story of the first vampire, and why the war had happened. He explained how the elves of Moora had been transformed, and how their king still lived after all of these years. And he told him how they had been captured and escaped. Yuuric was fascinated by how the kingdom of Moora also had forgotten the past, although through deception instead of magic. When Zeyn was done, the king sent his guards to bring the three green elves to meet with him. Not to hold them captive, but to see them, and to hear about their underwater kingdom. The king had also come to a decision, that he would let his kingdom know the truth. They deserved to know about their history, and how King Aar Kaalen had taken the memories of their ancestors so the guilt wouldn't weigh on them.

*****

The carriage driven by Auben arrived at Kassa while the sun was high in the sky. He glanced at the docks as they rode beside them on their way in, noticing the *Salvation* was there. He nudged Roland with his elbow to wake him from where he'd fallen asleep. "We're here," Auben said as Roland stretched. "Do you want to check there first?" Auben pointed to Captain Clarke's ship in the harbor.

Roland nodded. "I'll go check and see if he's on the *Salvation*. If not, I guess we'll be checking the pub. Stay with the carriage and keep watch over your brother and my wife. I shouldn't be long." With that, Roland climbed down from the passenger seat and began to walk with purpose to see his friend Zeyn. He was closer than ever before to finally ending the journey he'd started long ago, to cure his wife and the others of Aalen.

As Roland headed towards the port, Auben drove the carriage off to the side of the road to keep out of the way of anyone who may come in and out of Kassa. Tired of sitting down, he stepped down from where he sat and stood outside of doors to the carriage to keep watch over his brother and Areum. Roland continued on down the docks and arrived at Zeyn's ship. He climbed up a ladder on the side of the *Salvation* and stepped onto the deck.

"Roland?" he heard a voice say, questioningly. As he turned, he saw that it was Alexander. "It's been quite a while since you've been on *Salvation*, friend." Roland and Alexander clasped hands.

"It's good to see you Alex. Is Zeyn aboard?" Roland would have enjoyed spending more time aboard the ship that had once been a home to him and chatting with old friends, but that could wait. His focus was on the task at hand.

Alexander shook his head. "He's at the inn, and so is Maria. I'm keeping an eye on things for them here."

"I have to see him right away. We'll have to catch up later, my friend." He turned quickly to make his way back to the ladder.

"There's something else you should know." Roland turned back as Alexander spoke. "There are a lot of elves here from Jeul, and the Captain has been with them since he returned from a recent expedition. I haven't heard from any of them since the elves took them into the inn. I'm not saying it is trouble, but it could be."

"Thank you." Roland climbed down and made his way back towards Auben. He was curious about why the elves were there, but not too concerned. While he didn't know everyone from Jeul, they all knew of him, because of the vampire war. They knew Roland was the one that convinced the king to save the vampires, and Jeul occasionally checked on Aalen and even traded with them and bought from the farms.

"That was fast," Auben said seeing Roland approaching. "He wasn't there then?"

"No, he wasn't. We need to go to the inn." Roland climbed into the front of the carriage. "I'll drive."

Auben nodded and hopped in the passenger's seat and they headed down the dirt road. The streets were full of people going about their own business. Occasionally a friendly person would wave to Roland and Auben, and they would return the friendly greeting. Both Roland and Auben had spotted elves around the town, dressed clearly in the armor and colors of Jeul. Roland explained along the drive about the elves at the inn with Zeyn.

*****

The crew who had arrived at the inn with Zeyn were not being held by the guards from Jeul, but they had remained in the common room of the inn as they waited on their captain. Some of them were speaking to each other in hushed tones, speculating on the King Kaalen's interest in their voyage to Moora. Naaren was listening to Phyra when the front door opened and he noticed a familiar face he had not seen in some time.

"Roland Lam!" exclaimed Naaren, who approached Roland and shook his hand. "It's good to see you, friend. It's been too long." The rest of the *Salvation's* crew also perked up at seeing Roland but stayed where they were to let Naaren speak with him alone.

"It's good to see you, too, but what is going on?" Roland asked.

"We're alright." He lowered his voice and continued. "The captain can give you more details when he's done meeting with the king, but we discovered an underwater elven kingdom that had been forgotten. We have quite a story to tell."

Roland's face displayed his shock at the mention of the king of Jeul. He responded to Naaren in a hushed voice in return. "Yuuric is here?" Roland knew that the king wouldn't make this trip unless it was important and he was very curious now about what the crew of the *Salvation* had found.

"He is. What brings you to Kassa?"

"I'm looking for Zeyn."

Naaren furrowed his brow. "How did you know we were in Kassa?"

"I have quite a story to tell myself, but I can explain it all later. I was told Zeyn had learned about the first vampire, and that he is the key to curing the vampires in Aalen."

"I see." Naaren smiled. "I can answer your questions about Tecuul Boaruun. We all learned about him on our voyage." And so Naaren began to tell Roland his story, about their trip below the seas, the forgotten kingdom of Moora, and everything he had learned about Tecuul.

While he was speaking about Tecuul and his possible whereabouts, Zeyn, Maria, the king, and the three green elves, now dressed in surface clothes given to them by the king, entered the room. The guards all stood at attention at the entrance of their king, and the crew of the *Salvation* and Roland, seeing the king, bowed respectfully to him. Zeyn and Maria immediately made their way to Roland as they noticed him in the room, and they both gave him a welcoming hug. "It's been too long," Zeyn said with a smile.

"Yes, we seem to usually miss each other when you visit Aalen," Roland replied. "Naaren has already told me much of what you've been through."

"Unfortunately, I wasn't there," Maria jumped into the conversation. "Did anyone come with you?"

"Yes, Auben, Bryn, and Areum are with me. Auben is watching the carriage outside while Bryn and Areum rest inside it."

"Isn't it unusual for you to travel with humans and," she lowered her voice, noticing some of the inn workers were in the room, "vampires together? Not that I mind," she continued in her normal voice. "I'd enjoy visiting with Areum."

"It is unusual, but we came here with a purpose, and it's no coincidence that we ran into you here. I was looking for you, Zeyn, and I knew you'd be here."

Zeyn looked puzzled. "You knew? I didn't even know we would still be in Kassa now."

"They've learned of a way to cure the people of Aalen," Naaren said.

"Truly?" Zeyn knew Roland and the others in Aalen had quested many years to end the vampirism that cursed so many of them.

"Tecuul Boaruun must be killed since he was the first," Roland continued, "and I came here because I was told you had learned of him."

"How could you know that?"

"I was wondering that myself," Naaren added.

After making sure no one was too close to overhear him, Roland answered them. "We learned this from a demon." He saw the shock on their faces. "I know the dangers, but we didn't summon him, and I believe he was honest with us. He was the one who told us you had knowledge of Tecuul, and he told us we could find you in Kassa. Alexander told us you were here at the inn."

"Well, we still don't know where this vampire is," Zeyn said. "I need to return with the king to Jeul, maybe they can use their magic to help us locate where Tecuul is now?"

Roland nodded. "That would be the best way. I'd like to speak with the king, anyway, so I will ask him. We can talk more on the way to Jeul." Roland left the group and approached the king to discuss the things he'd discovered and to seek Yuuric Kaalen's help.

"Captain," Naaren said to Zeyn, "I'd like to tell you that story now. If we are going to find Tecuul Boaruun, I want you to know that I already knew of him before we went to Moora, and I want you to know that whether his death ends the curse or not, he deserves to die."

Zeyn was intrigued. He remembered how Naaren had seemed to recognize the name when they learned it, and Naaren had said he'd like to tell him a story about his family. He made his way to a table and had a seat, and Naaren moved to the table to join him. Maria left them alone and stepped outside the inn to greet Auben.

Naaren leaned forward with his elbows on the table, his hands folded under his chin. "Over a thousand years ago, when Aar Kaalen was the king of Jeul, my grandfather, Caldoon, served as the captain of his guards. Tecuul was a prisoner of Jeul, like the king of Moora told us. One night, he escaped from his cell, killing his guard. When this was discovered, the king sent my grandfather along with some of the soldiers and mages to find Tecuul and to kill him.

"They found him in a cave on a beach, near a town called Rollins. It no longer exists. When they discovered him, Tecuul had already been transformed. He had murdered several people in the cave, from what I am told. Most likely they were used in a ritual that brought about his change. No one knows for sure how he became what he is. The soldiers and mages stood no chance against him. Perhaps if they were out in an open space or they knew what a vampire was, but how could they? He killed my grandfather and several of the soldiers, convincing those he let live to join him. They helped Tecuul spread the curse.

"But one soldier did not die and did not join them, though he was left for dead in the cave. That was my father, Duuren Soor. He had been stabbed through the stomach, but the wound was not fatal. When the vampires left, he managed to return to Jeul and report what had happened, after he had healed. The events of the cave and the death of his father had disturbed him, and he left Jeul for Leef, where he met my mother and lived a quiet life outside of the kingdoms. When I became an adult, he told me the story of Tecuul, and so that is how I know of him. I've longed for the day to bring justice upon him."

"Did your father mention the war between Jeul and Moora?" Zeyn believed Leef must have been out of range of the spell that erased the memories of Moora from the people of Jeul.

"According to what we learned in Moora, the war had to have taken place after my father had gone to Leef. And you know how the people of Leef are; they stay out of the world's affairs and keep to themselves. My father was the same; he never returned to Jeul or kept up with their kingdom."

Zeyn nodded. "There may be some in Leef who know of Moora, though. I wonder if that is how the knowledge of it survived for Horace to find."

"Perhaps." Naaren stood.

"I'll go see what the king has told Roland," Zeyn said as he also stood. "Tell the crew to return to the ship and rest while they can. Head back with them. I'm taking you all to Jeul with me when we depart." Zeyn turned and went to talk to Roland and the king, while Naaren gathered the crew to return to the *Salvation*.

CHAPTER 10

UNEXPECTED VISITORS

All of the elven guards in Kassa had gathered together near the inn and were preparing their horses and the king's carriage to leave and return to Jeul. The cloudless sky revealed the stars and the full moons of the night. Areum was watching the sky, hoping that soon she would be able to view it during the day. While she had long held on to this hope, for the first time, it seemed to truly be a possibility.

Since leaving the carriage when night had come, Areum and Bryn kept close to the inn but avoided people in the streets to keep from being recognized as vampires. The elves of Jeul all knew the truth about Aalen, so it wasn't necessary to hide from them. The people living in Kassa would probably not suspect anything out of the ordinary, as they believed all vampires dead, but Areum and Bryn would rather be safe. However, they couldn't stay cooped up in the carriage any longer.

Hearing the door of the inn open, both Areum and Bryn turned to see who was coming out. Most of those they knew were on the *Salvation* and should be joining them soon, but some had stayed at the inn. Maria stepped through the door and looked around, a smile reaching her face when she saw Areum and Bryn. "It's so good to see you!" she exclaimed, moving over to join them. "I heard you were here and was hoping you'd be out at nightfall."

Areum gave Maria a hug with a smile, glad to see her friend. It had been a very long time since she and Roland had sailed with Zeyn and his crew aboard the *Salvation*, seeing the world. "I'm very glad you're here. And I'm glad you'll be coming with us to Jeul. It will give us time to catch up."

"Yes, we'll have to ride together. Is Roland with my brother?"

Areum nodded. "They are both on the *Salvation* now but should be here soon. It looks like the royal procession is ready to get home."

"And we're ready to get there and find this vampire," Bryn added. He had met Maria before when she and her brother had visited Aalen in the past. But he didn't know them as well as Roland and Areum. "If you'll excuse me, I think I'll risk going in and finding my brother. I'll leave the two of you to catch up." Bryn left the women and headed into the inn, where his brother had gone in to get something to eat before the journey.

"So I heard that you were the Captain for a few days," Areum said.

Maria let out a short laugh, "Yes, but only while we were here in Kassa. The crew respects me and they listen to me without arguing, which is nice. Not that I ever had any doubts about my ability to lead. Still, I don't think I'd want the responsibility long term."

"When this is over, I think it would be nice to travel aboard the *Salvation* again. I would love to feel the sun on my skin while traveling across the seas."

"I'm sure we can make that happen! I'd love to have you with us. What's wrong?" Maria had noticed a change on Areum's face as she turned away and looked off into the distance. She appeared surprised and slightly irritated.

"There's someone I know coming this way. And she should not be here."

Maria saw nothing yet, but she didn't have the hearing or sight that Areum had as a vampire. For a moment while they had spoken, Maria had forgotten all about Areum's curse. After a couple of minutes had passed, she finally saw the riders approaching, too. "She's brought some people with her. Do you know them, too?"

"Some of them, but not all." She could see that Kari had brought four men from Menton who appeared to be soldiers. The other five men Areum had never seen before. Kari saw Areum and headed straight to her, slowing as she approached before stopping and dismounting. "Kari, you should be at home."

"Please hear me out first," Kari said.

She hadn't meant to sound harsh towards the girl, but she preferred Kari was safe in Menton with her family after they had all been cured. Their suffering was over and they should be celebrating together. Areum softened her tone. "Alright, I'll listen. I shouldn't rush to judgment. But who have you brought with you?" As Areum asked the question, Maria kept an eye on the strangers and kept an attentive ear to the discussion.

"The men in armor are guards of Menton, and they traveled with us for protection on the journey. These other men," she paused a moment, "they are the ones who visited Roland after I met with him. They were the ones who were hunting vampires." Areum became defensive in posture on hearing this, and Maria stood close beside her with a hand on her sword.

"Wait, they are not here to fight. When they found Menton, we talked and they know the truth now, about the people of Menton, and about Tecuul. They want to help." She looked at one of the men and gestured to the vampire with her hand. "This is Roland's wife, Areum. Tell her what you told me, Darel."

A young man dismounted from his horse and began to speak, "Well, the reason the five of us started hunting for vampires was because our towns were destroyed by them in the vampire war. All of us were just kids, then. I was only twelve years old." He turned to his companions who had also left their horses and joined him. "Will here is a year older than me, and we were friends when it happened. When the vampires attacked Burque, we had been out at Tras' family's farm."

"That was one of the first towns attacked," Areum said, realizing these events had happened before she had been turned.

"Yes, it was. Well, we found Simeon and Weston when we searched the town," he motioned to the twins, "who had been successful in hiding away."

"The vampires moved through very quickly," Simeon added. "If they had taken the time, they could have found us. I wish more people had hidden, but everyone tried to run. We don't know what happened to our parents that day. We weren't with them when it happened."

"My father," Tras continued, "was going to take all of them in, and we were heading back to the farm to prepare to leave the area and warn others, but when we were packing, a vampire got into the house. My dad told us to run and attacked him. He was able to injure the vampire enough to slow him down from following us. We don't know how he got in the house. We were always told a vampire can only enter a home if invited in, but that day, no one was safe."

Areum knew that during the attacks, the vampires were compelled somehow beyond the restrictions they usually faced, except for the sun and other things that could kill them. She let the men finish telling their story, as whatever spell had freed them of some of their restraints back then was long gone, and it wouldn't do any good to share what she knew now.

"I led them all the way to Norin, but it took us several days," Darel continued, "but we were too late. When we arrived, they already knew, and we heard the news that the vampires had been killed by the elves of Jeul. The king was kind to us and gave us a place to stay and tradesmen to learn under. But one day almost four years later, Roland Lam came through the kingdom, and we heard he was a vampire hunter, tracking down the few vampires who had survived Jeul's attack against them.

"This sparked a fire in me, and in my friends here. We decided to become hunters ourselves, though we were still kids, despite what we thought of ourselves. We never really found any, despite all the travels we had after that. Not until this year, when we spotted this girl in Arndell. I think you know the rest."

Areum waited a moment, taking in the story, and then looked to Kari. "What all have you told them?"

"I told them how the demon changed Menton, and they know the people of Menton are human again. I also told him that there was a group seeking to kill the first vampire and that it would end the curse for any still afflicted."

Areum turned to Darel and he spoke, "I can tell you are a vampire, she didn't have to tell me that. But you seem to be in control of yourself, and we made a decision to focus our vengeance on this Tecuul we've learned about. We want to work together with you and your husband in this."

"Very well," Areum replied, "you seem trustworthy, but please understand why I'm cautious. We are leaving for Jeul soon, so be prepared to travel again."

"I understand." Darel turned to his friends, "let's get something to drink before we go." With that, he tied up his horse and headed into the inn, followed by his friends.

"That was quite a story," Maria said and smiled to Kari. "Nice to meet you. I look forward to hearing this story about Menton, too. Maybe you can tell me on the way to Jeul."

"You'll have to wait on that story from her, Maria," Areum said, "I have something else for you to do, Kari, and you can take your guards with you." Before continuing, she turned to Maria again. "Could you please go tell Auben and Bryn who the men are who just entered the inn and that they should be trusted for now. I didn't think to warn them." Maria nodded and left them to enter the inn.

"Now then, Kari, I need you to go to Aalen and tell Jarec about everything that happened in Menton, and about..." She turned and saw Roland approaching, returning from his walk around the town he had taken after speaking with King Kaalen. He appeared puzzled seeing Kari there.

"Kari, you should be home," he said.

"We've already been over this," Areum responded to her husband with a smile. "She brought some people to help us against Tecuul. You aren't going to like it at first, but I think if you'll hear them out, you will understand."

"Who is it?"

"The men who found me in Langston," Kari explained. "They followed us and found me in Menton after you had left. But don't worry! They don't mean any harm, and they understand us now.."

"You're right, I don't like it. But if you both have spoken with them, I'll trust you."

"Now," Areum continued, "I was just about to send Kari off to Aalen to tell Jarec everything."

"That's a good idea. These guards will be escorting you there?" Kari nodded and smiled to the four guards with her. "Good, I'm glad you'll be safe on the journey. Where are the other men who came with Kari?"

"They are inside the inn, dear," Areum answered, and Roland left to go talk to them and learn why they wanted to help. Areum looked back to Kari. "When you get to Aalen, tell Jarec about what we learned in Menton, and tell him that we are heading to Jeul to discover where Tecuul is. We should already be there when you speak to him."

Kari was a bit overwhelmed. She didn't expect to have to leave so soon from Kassa, but she also knew that Jarec needed to know what had happened. She did look forward to seeing Aalen again. "I will go, but can I get some rest first before leaving?"

Areum smiled. "Of course you can. I'm sorry if I seemed upset at you, Kari. It is good to see you again so soon. I'm sure Roland is glad to see you, too, but he's a bit preoccupied. Why don't you head inside and say hi to Auben and Bryn? You and your guards can get something to eat, but I'm afraid there may not be time for sleep yet; you need to head to Aalen when we leave for Jeul, and we are leaving soon. But I'm sure Jarec will give you all a place to stay when you arrive."

Kari smiled and hugged Areum. She left her horse with the guards from Menton, who went to stable all of their horses and hers before joining Kari in the inn. Areum remained outside and looked back at the night sky. Soon she saw Zeyn approaching with all the crew who had gone with him to Moora, as well as Alexander.

*****

"You're really going with them?" Caleb asked Horace.

"Yes," he answered. The king had asked them all to go to Jeul, but Gallen and Caleb had declined. Olii and Noon already left to return to their home. They wanted to recover from the adventure. The three of them had left the inn and were at Horace and Caleb's home, where Horace was getting his things together. "Are you sure you don't want to come to see Jeul?"

"One elf kingdom was more than enough for me now," Caleb responded.

"I agree," his father added. "And there isn't any reason for me to go. We aren't going to be any help in finding this vampire they keep talking about, and neither of us is about to do any fighting. Besides, we have work to catch up on here, and we need to decide what we are going to do with *Elline*." Gallen was ready to finally get a good night's sleep in his own bed.

"Very well, my friends," Horace said, "I won't try to convince you to come along." He took up his bag in his right hand and his walking stick in his left and turned to leave but stopped to take the time to hug them both. "I'm an old man, and I'm not sure when I'll see either of you again." He hoped it was when and not if, but he didn't think he had many years left. "We had quite the little adventure, didn't we?"

Caleb smiled. "Yes, we did. Though I hope if we share another it's not as dangerous."

"Goodbye, my friends."

"Farewell, Horace," Gallen said, "I am glad you found what you were looking for. Have a safe trip."

Caleb opened the door for Horace as he departed. "Goodbye," Caleb said as Horace exited their home. He shut the door and began to head to his room.

"Caleb," his father said, making Caleb turn around. "Yes?"

"Are you sure you don't want to go with them? I can look after things at the smithy by myself."

"I'm sure, dad. Right now I just want to sleep. I've had enough adventure."

Gallen nodded and Caleb continued on his way to his room. But Gallen wasn't too sure about his son's answer. Caleb always talked of going places and dreamed of adventures, and he didn't think the trip to Moora dampened Caleb's spirit. His son was old enough to go off on his own, and while he was great at blacksmithing like his father, Gallen believed his son wasn't meant to just stay in the family business. When Caleb was ready, Gallen would be ready to let him go off on his own, but he would greatly miss having Caleb around all the time. As he made his way to his own room to sleep, he continued to think about his son's future.

*****

While the moons still lit the night sky, the large procession departed from Kassa to make their way to Jeul. Zeyn and all of the crew who had gone with him to Moora accompanied the king and his soldiers, and they were joined by Alexander and Maria. Captain Clarke had placed Matthew, a much-trusted member of his crew, in charge of the *Salvation* and the rest of the crew until their return. The king had provided horses for all of Zeyn's crew who needed one to ride. His soldiers who had ridden the horses to Kassa went on foot on the way back, since the group was traveling back at a slow enough pace.

Bandar, Thela, and Sola were allowed to ride with the king in his carriage, as was Horace, who the king requested to come with them to Jeul. Yuuric was fascinated with the green elves and wanted to learn all he could about their kingdom, and he wanted to hear from Horace about his experiences in finding Moora, and what it was like for him to succeed in his quest. Darel and his friends rode their horses behind the elven guards surrounding the king's carriage.

Roland, Areum, Auben, and Bryn also traveled with the group, though Areum and Bryn did not ride within the carriage along the way, preferring to be out while they

could be. Areum rode on horseback beside Maria, and the
two discussed the events that had led them here, while Bryn
drove the carriage they had taken to Kassa. Inside, Roland
and Auben were joined by Naaren and Zeyn, who told them
about the secret kingdom of Moora and how it came to be
at the bottom of the sea. Roland in return told him in detail
about the demon Mar'vandi and all of the events that had
led them to meet. Zeyn was amazed at the coincidence that
led them together in Kassa, but Roland felt that it was less
of a coincidence and more of the manipulation of the
demon, who somehow knew Zeyn had learned of Tecuul.

Kari and her guards left shortly after the others and
headed southwest to find Aalen. While Kari had been once
before, she couldn't remember the way back, especially
since she had been inside of a carriage with the windows
covered when she arrived there. Auben and Bryn had
given her and all of her guards directions as well as
instructions on how to find the farms of Aalen once they
had to travel off of the road. They were also given the
location of the entrance to the city below the earth but were
told to speak to those above the surface first and explain
why they were there, so they wouldn't seem suspicious.
Auben even wrote out a note and sealed it to prove their
legitimacy.

As her group traveled, they kept in good spirits
while focused on their task; Kari on giving the information
to Jarec and her guards on protecting her until she could
return home. They had originally left from Menton to
protect her from any problems that might arise from the
vampire hunters she was taking to Kassa, as they still
weren't completely trusted. But Darel and his friends had
not made any attempts to harm Kari and had in fact proved
to be pleasant company. Now they were traveling on their
own horses to Jeul with the others. Kari actually hoped she
might meet them again one day. Her thoughts turned to the
friends she had made in her time of great need. She hoped

that they could find Tecuul and kill him, and bring healing to the people of Aalen.

CHAPTER 11

JEUL

The cavalcade of King Kaalen arrived at Jeul before sunrise. Maria's eyes were drawn to the top of the large gate that, when opened, would allow ten horses to ride in comfortably side by side. On each side of the gate tall walls stretched around the entire city, protecting from uninvited forces. There were other entrances on each side of the wall, Maria knew, but she'd only ever been through this main gate the times she'd been to Jeul before. Soon they would reach the castle at the center of the largest city in the land.

Two guards approached the company to inspect them and upon verifying it was their king, opened the main gates to let their ruler, his soldiers, and his guests into the city. The group made their way through the city with little fanfare, as most of the people were still sleeping, though there were a few in the streets who saw them coming through. They came to the single gate in the wall surrounding the castle and were allowed through by the guards. This wall was not as tall as the city wall, and the castle loomed high above it. The gate was smaller, allowing in four horses side by side.

Maria and Areum admired the gardens between the castle and the walls as the procession began to thin and take the pathway through the gardens and around the castle. The two were silent now, having spoken quite a bit along the way, and were both beginning to feel tired. Maria had enjoyed catching up with Areum. Most of the soldiers split from the large group and began to make their way out of the castle gate and into the city, returning home or to posts to help with the guard. Other soldiers stayed close to the king's carriage along the pathway.

When they arrived at the castle stables, the riders began to dismount, and those within the carriages exited them as the king led the way, with guards on either side, into the castle halls. While some of the guests of the king had been within the castle before, at one time or another, Areum, the green elves, Darel's group, and some of Captain Clarke's crew were seeing the castle for the first time. The green elves, in particular, appeared to take everything in with great wonder. While they had seen the ruins of Moora and the attempt at the rebuilt castle in the caves, they'd never seen a building so grand before. Everyone followed the king along the purple carpets until they eventually entered into the throne room of Jeul. When the doors of the throne room were shut, the king looked to the group to address them.

"I think we could all do with some rest," Yuuric said, "and tomorrow evening we can meet here again. By then I will have met with my advisors and mages and we can discuss how to find the whereabouts of Tecuul Boaruun." The king was clearly setting the meeting for the evening to accommodate the vampires, which was appreciated by Areum and Bryn.

"My crew and I are going to get something to drink, your majesty," Zeyn said, "We'll stay at an inn and see you back here tomorrow. Thank you."

"That's fine. I don't know what your plans were, Roland," the king turned to Roland and the others from Aalen, "but I'm afraid Areum and Bryn will need to stay here. We can't have anyone in the kingdom discover there are vampires here. Everyone in Jeul knows about Aalen, but they still may react poorly to seeing them. I hope you understand." Although Jeul sent regular groups to Aalen to check up on them, no vampires had ever been allowed to visit Jeul before now.

"Of course," Bryn responded.

Areum nodded, "It's no problem."

"We have rooms here at the castle you can stay in if that is agreeable?" the king offered.

Roland smiled, "I've never stayed in a castle before. That sounds very nice."

"And for you and your men? There are many rooms here." the king asked Darel.

"This is very nice of you, sir, I mean, your majesty," Darel answered, a little nervously, he'd never spoken with a king before, "but I think we'll stay out in the city like they are." Darel pointed to Zeyn's crew, then turned back to the king and gave an awkward bow.

"Alright," the king replied with a smile. The king nodded to two of his guards. "Go and see that a room is prepared for Roland and Areum, and a room is prepared for Bryn. Auben, will you be staying with your brother?"

"Thank you for the offer," Auben answered, "but I'm going to go with Zeyn's crew."

"Very well." The king turned to Bandar, Thela, and Sola. "I plan on letting the kingdom know all about you and about Moora, but we need to approach it carefully. We will provide you with nice rooms as well, and you can join us tomorrow."

The three looked to each other, and Sola answered, "We understand. Thank you for taking us in."

"You're welcome. Horace," the king smiled to him, "you are also welcome to stay here, or go with Captain Clarke's crew."

"I think a room here at the castle sounds delightful," Horace responded. "I am quite tired and I don't want to have to do more walking than I already have."

"Wonderful! You can stay with us as long as you wish." He then addressed them all. "I hope you all have an excellent rest." The king then retired to his own chambers through an exit behind the throne, accompanied by two of his guards.

Roland, Areum, and Bryn were led to rooms within one of the towers, while Bandar, Thela, Sola, and Horace were taken to guest rooms on the ground floor, in a hall below the tower to the king's room. Their hall was watched over by two guards. Auben, Zeyn, and the rest of the *Salvation's* crew went out into the city of Jeul, to drink first and then get some sleep.

*****

The sun had begun to rise on the farms of Aalen as Kari and her guard arrived. They had no trouble finding the hidden town. Smiles lit their faces as they felt the warmth of the sun, and they were glad to be able to stay out in the day again. Relishing the feeling, they began to look at each other and laugh with joy, hardly believing that just two days ago the five of them were vampires.

There were already workers on some of the farms, busy tending to crops or to the animals they were raising. Kari reached into her bag and pulled out the note that Auben had given to her to show at one of the farms. With the letter in hand, she headed over to the nearest farm with her group around her, drawing the attention of a nearby farmhand.

"Excuse me," she began as she spoke to him from horseback, "but I was sent here by Auben Dale. He told me to show this to you."

The man, who had been a bit shocked at the sight of strangers, relaxed at the sound of Auben's name. After breaking the recognized seal of the letter and reading it, he smiled to Kari and handed her the letter back. "I'd be happy to show you the way," he said. "And keep people from questioning you, since they know me. I can go with you all the way to Jarec."

"That would be wonderful!" Kari replied. "Thank you."

"You're welcome, just let me get my horse."

The man set down the hoe he had been using and ran to the stable of his farm. Kari didn't have to wait long for him, and soon they were heading towards the entrance that would lead them underground. The guards with Kari had heard about Aalen from her as they traveled from Kassa, and were surprised that such a town had managed to go undiscovered. But those on the surface did a good job keeping any outsiders who may find them from discovering the hidden city, and it was very rare for strangers to travel off the roads to get to the farms.

Soon the farmer was leading them down the pathway at the hidden cave entrance, beside the torches on the pathway, until they were led out into the large open underground city of Aalen. The magical globes of light which lit the city shone red, and Kari smiled, remembering her previous visit. Her guards were surprised by the city, though they had been told about it in advance. As they headed down the main road they noticed that people in the streets appeared to be heading home, to sleep during the day, as they were accustomed. They were noticed, but no one approached them, though they did wave or welcome them, seeing they were friendly and accompanied by the farmer.

Jarec was leaving the town hall as they approached, and Kari leapt from her horse to run and greet him, throwing her arms around him. As she pulled away, she smiled big to him, showing off her teeth. It took him a moment to realize what she was doing, so she used her fingers to pull back her lips so he'd notice her teeth. "Kari! Are you cured? What happened?"

She smiled brightly. "I have so much to tell you. And I was sent here by Areum to tell you what they are doing now."

"Who are your friends?" Jarec looked towards the four men who had come with her. They had dismounted and made their way with the farmer over to Jarec and Kari while they had been talking.

"They serve as guards in Menton. They volunteered to come with me and keep me safe."

"Well, I was about to head home to sleep," Jarec said, "but I'm much too interested to wait on this news. Please come in, and you can tell me everything."

Kari smiled. "Gladly."

"Where should we take the horses?" one of the guards asked.

"Elyse at the stables can take care of them," Jarec answered.

"I'll show them the way," the farmer offered. "Then make my way back to the surface."

"Thank you for your help," Kari said to him with a smile.

"You're welcome." The farmer mounted up and the guards did likewise, with one holding the reins of Kari's horse to lead it, and they made their way at a trot to stable the horses.

"I'm glad to hear Elyse made it back safely," Kari said, happy to have heard her new friend's name again. She'd have to be sure to see her before she left Aalen.

"She did," Jarec said as he opened the door and they made their way into the town hall. "She has been anxious to hear of what happened in Menton, and anxious for Auben and the others to return."

Kari followed Jarec to the desk where they sat as they had when she'd first met him, he at his desk and her out in front. "As you saw, I am no longer a vampire, nor are the guards who came with me. The curse on Menton was caused by a demon named Mar'vandi." So Kari continued on and Jarec listened as she told him all that had transpired. How Mar'vandi had cursed Menton to lure someone there from Aalen. How the demon cured Menton to get them to listen to him, and how he had told them about the first vampire, Tecuul Boaruun, whose death would cure Aalen.

She then told him how Roland's friend, Zeyn, was supposed to know something about Tecuul, and so Roland, Areum, Bryn, and Auben went to Kassa to find him, leaving her in Menton. She told him about the vampire hunters who found Menton after they'd been cured, and how she took them to meet Roland in Kassa before she was sent to Aalen by Areum.

Jarec took in everything she told him and thought deeply through his past before responding. "I've never heard of Tecuul. He must not have been with us in the vampire war." That thought was very curious to Jarec, as he'd always believed every vampire had been forced to be there. "Did you learn anything about him while you were in Aalen?"

"Not much. Whatever Roland learned from Zeyn I never heard. But I do know that right now, they are on their way to Jeul, which is why they aren't with me. The king agreed to help Roland find the location of Tecuul."

Jarec had not yet asked why the others hadn't returned to Aalen, and now had gotten the answer to that question which had been on his mind. "I need to speak with my council and make them aware of this. You and your men are welcome to stay here in Aalen as long as you'd like before returning home. I know Elyse would like to see you, and Bree has asked me about you, as well."

Kari smiled. "I'd love to see them, and I'd enjoy staying here for a day or two before we head home."

"Good." Jarec stood up and moved around the desk. "There are rooms at my home that you all may use. Let's go find your friends."

When they left the town hall they found the men waiting outside, the farmer had already left to go back to work. After some brief discussion of the decision to stay, they all went to Jarec's home. He indeed had plenty of room for the guests, as the people of Aalen had built Jarec a mansion to live in since he was their leader. Jarec explained it was against his wishes and he didn't really need all the space, but they wouldn't take no for an answer. Kari understood how the people felt, and knew that the home showed their appreciation of Jarec's leadership. After being given rooms, they all slept through the day as the vampires did. It was what they had been used to, and they were tired from the night's travels.

*****

The deep forests to the west of Jeul were very dark, even during the daylight. It was a perfect place to hide from the sun's deadly rays. Tecuul was glad to be out from under the ocean after all of these years. While he had been kept safe from being killed in the war between Jeul and Moora, he did not have much freedom, and his vengeance had never been fully realized against the kingdom of Jeul. A smile crossed his lips as he thought of finally ruining the elves, and then moving on to take over the rest of the land.

He had only spoken to Vel'dulan once after the first time he had been turned, some time after Moora had sunken to the ocean floor. The spell that saved Moora avoided him, which he was glad of, though he wondered why. He assumed it was because the spell knew his vampirism would keep him alive, or maybe even because it knew he didn't belong in Moora or wasn't a normal elf, but he'd never truly know the answer.

What he did know is that it was incredibly uncomfortable for him, surviving the pressure of the seas, and slinking around unseen until the underwater caves were ready. He still took in water despite holding his breath, and it was a chore removing it from his body when he was able. While he couldn't be killed, he could feel pain, and that pain was immense.

When Braal was able to hide Tecuul in the rebuilt castle of Moora, the vampire had summoned Vel'dulan. The demon was quite upset that Tecuul had allowed himself to be trapped underwater. She told him to return to the surface and go to the forests (where he now was) and contact her, but Tecuul didn't listen, biding his time. He tried his best to stay in Moora, but he grew sick of his stationary lifestyle.

Tecuul was prepared now to see her once again, and he looked down upon the familiar symbol he had already drawn out with blood from sacrificial humans he had captured on his way to the forests, their corpses lying silent behind him. The doorway that formed illuminated the area and Vel'dulan stepped out, anger apparent on her face.

"How dare you face me after making me wait so long!" She snapped. She almost issued a threat but knew that it would hold no weight with her first vampire, as he knew she couldn't harm him unless he allowed her to. He had summoned her and was in control.

"My apologies," Tecuul calmly said. "But I'm here now. Where are all the other vampires? I thought surely they would be a blight on the land by now."

Vel'dulan smirked. "They had no one to lead them. When you hid in Moora and then disappeared from the surface, the vampires had no organization. They would attack villages and towns, but never in unison, and while they occasionally would turn a person a two, mostly they just focused on feeding and then would find places to hide from the daylight. Some people even learned of the ways to kill and repel them. I waited on you for a long time, but when I tired of waiting, I took matters into my own hands, because I could control them. I gathered them all here in the west and sent them after Jeul."

"The kingdom is still there. I saw it with my own eyes as I passed in the night while making my way here."

"I wasn't finished." The demon narrowed her eyes at him. "The vampires failed, being discovered by the current king. They were able to prepare, and performed a powerful spell that cut off all control I had over the vampires, and gave them back full control over their actions. Some of them went off to do evil on their own, and they were hunted down and killed. The ones who wanted to be normal again have made a home for themselves, hidden from the rest of the world. You need to prepare, they are looking for you."

"For me?" Tecuul was puzzled. Surely they believed he was dead with the rest of Moora.

"Another demon, working against me, has told them that to cure the vampires, they have to kill you."

"Would that work?" He had never been told of such a thing.

Vel'dulan nodded, her mouth tight. "Are you prepared to fight?"

Tecuul smiled and spread his arms, gesturing around him, and Vel'dulan turned to look around. There were many others there. Tecuul had brought some of the green elves from Moora that he had transformed, and they were loyal to him. They had been at work transforming towns and villages after they had gotten to the outskirts of the kingdom of Jeul's reach. Tecuul was very old now, and his transformations had become powerful enough to instantly change a person's control of their actions when they became a vampire. Vel'dulan was impressed, as the number was near a hundred.

"That's a very good start, Tecuul," the demon smiled. "You'll need more for us to make an attempt on Jeul, but it's a good start."

CHAPTER 12

VAMPIRE'S BLOOD

Roland and Areum were the last to join the king in the throne room of Jeul the next evening. The flickering lights of candles illuminating the room projected shadows on the walls of the many who were in attendance. Zeyn and Maria were standing around a table with the king and his advisors and mages, while Zeyn's crew was gathered near the steps leading to the throne. The three green elves were talking with Horace, apart from the others. Darel and his friends were standing near the table, watching those around it curiously and occasionally looking around at the splendor of the throne room. Auben and Bryn had been waiting by the door for Roland and Areum to join them.

"Ready to find out where this vampire is?" Bryn asked them as they walked in.

"Yes," both Roland and Areum answered at once. They were all ready to be rid of the curse. Roland made his way to the king at the table and the others followed. On the table was a large map of the entire continent.

"Your majesty," Roland began, "have you been able to find anything, yet?"

The king frowned and looked up from the map. "My mages have not been able to locate him with their magic. They tell me if they had something belonging to Tecuul then they might be able to use a location spell to find him."

"Isn't there some other way?"

"Right now we've been looking over this map trying to guess at where he might have gone since his return to the surface. If he really is back, he is keeping safe and not alerting anyone to his presence. There has been no word of any vampire attacks." The king looked back down to the map.

"Maybe it's not Tecuul you should be looking for with a spell," Areum said.

All the eyes around the table turned to her and the king asked, "What do you mean?"

"Instead of trying to look for Tecuul, is it possible to use a spell to locate vampires? Perhaps if you used my blood, or Bryn's, and performed a spell that was less focused, it would find all the vampires."

One of the mages spoke, "That could work, my king. We could modify the spell we had prepared for Tecuul to search for anyone with vampire blood."

The king smiled, "Excellent!" He turned to face Areum and Bryn. "So, which one of you would like to volunteer your blood?"

Areum smiled, "I'll be glad to. It was my idea." She reached to her side and unsheathed a dagger, then looked to the mage who spoke. "How much blood will you need, and where will you need it?"

"Just give us a moment to prepare the spell and cast it," the elf replied, "then we'll need just a few drops, on the corner of the map." The mage turned to consult together with the others.

While they were all waiting for the mages and their spell, the king pulled Roland aside from the others for a moment. "Roland, if they do find him with this spell, what are you going to do?"

"I'm going to find him and make sure he is dead. It makes no difference to me if it's by my hand or another, but I have been committed for the last ten years to saving my wife, and the people of Aalen, and it is finally within my grasp."

"Be careful. I know you have killed vampires before, but he will be very strong. You know how much age increases their power. I assume Zeyn and his crew will be accompanying you?" Roland nodded. "I'll send some of my soldiers with you as well."

"I appreciate that."

"We're ready," the mage said, and Roland and the king made their way back to the table.

The six mages closed their eyes and began to focus their magic together, and a faint blue glow appeared to surround their hands. "Let blood call to blood, and find those alike," the mages spoke in unison, with one voice. The head mage opened his eyes and looked to Areum with a nod. Areum took her dagger and pricked the forefinger of her right hand, then let three drops of her blood fall to the corner of the map. The mages spoke again, "Let blood call to blood, and find those alike."

The mages opened their eyes, and everyone around the table was watching the map and saw the drops of blood gather together and become larger than when they fell. The blood appeared to become part of the map, no longer just a stain upon its surface. And then the blood moved first to the location of Aalen, where it separated into many dots, representing the vampires there. Two dots of blood went to Jeul, representing Areum and Bryn. The group watched as a part of the blood moved off towards the west of Jeul on the map to the forests, but then vanished from sight. The mages appeared puzzled.

"What does this mean?" the king asked.

"The spell worked," the head mage said, "we can all see it found Aalen." He placed his finger on the map where the other blood vanished. "There is some very strong magic here trying to hide the other vampire. While we don't have the exact location, this shows that he is somewhere here in the forests of the west. But my king, whatever blocked our magic must be very powerful. If it wasn't Tecuul's, then he might have someone with him who is very powerful."

The king looked to Roland. "You'll be leading this expedition. What are your thoughts?"

"I hope we can find him before he causes any trouble, but I wouldn't be surprised if he's already made some new vampire friends for himself. We need to leave as soon as possible. It will most likely take a couple of days to get there. We'll need at least one carriage for my wife and Bryn to travel in during the day. With your soldiers and Zeyn and his men, we shouldn't have too much trouble, if we can find him."

Roland looked from the king back down to the map. The large forests and mountains separated the east and west at the southern parts of the continent, though travel on land was possible across the continent to the western coast at certain mountain passes and forest trails. The large forest was still untouched by civilization, and Roland had ventured that way only a few times.

"And if you don't find him?"

"We'll return here and let you know whether we find him or not. Knowing what we do of his history now, if we don't find him, he most likely will make himself known to Jeul eventually, and you'll need to prepare things here."

"I'll supply the horses and carriage you will need and will gather my soldiers that will accompany you. When everyone is ready I will see you off at the city gates."

"Thank you, for everything you've done for us."

The king smiled at Roland and turned to go and speak to the captain of his guards to make arrangements for the soldiers to accompany Roland and the others. Roland looked across the table to Zeyn.

"Well, old friend, is your crew ready for this?" he asked.

Zeyn smiled. "We are all armed and ready," he answered. "Whenever you are ready to go, we will follow."

"Areum and I just need to get our weapons and bags from our room. As soon as the king has gathered the soldiers who are coming with us, we'll leave." Roland turned to Auben and Bryn. "Are you ready?"

Both men nodded and Auben spoke, "We have everything we need." Roland looked to Areum and together they left the throne room and returned to their room.

*****

The council sat in silence as Jarec finished speaking about what Kari had told him. Their expressions were excited and hopeful, which they had not been in a long time. The council was made up of five men and five women. Only four of the men and two of the women were vampires, and two of the male vampires were also elven. Jarec was standing in front of his desk, and the council sat in a half-circle of chairs in front of him. They had been called in when night fell. Many in the streets who had seen the council approach the town hall had been curious about what they had been called for.

"This is incredible news," one of the men spoke, and Jarec smiled to Kari, who was sitting with her guards to the side.

"I'm glad Kari was able to bring this news to us," Jarec replied, turning back to the council.

"Do you know what Roland plans to do?" a vampire, one of the women, asked.

"That I do not know, but knowing him, as soon as they know the location of this vampire named Tecuul they will go after him."

"Then I would like to make a motion that we send out a group to Jeul immediately to help them. Tecuul could have help of his own."

"I second that," one of the men said.

The vote of hands was unanimous. The council was often agreeable, but the quickness of the decision made Jarec chuckle lightly. His job had never been this easy before.

"Very well," Jarec said, "I can organize the group myself. I will lead them to Jeul."

The council was surprised, and some of their eyes went wide. They voiced their objections, but Jarec calmed them down. "I cannot sit idly by any longer," he said, "and they may need my strength. I know who I will recruit for this, but I need all of you to be here in my absence. If the worst happens, it is your job to replace me."

"When will you leave?" one of the elves asked.

"As soon as this meeting is over and I can gather those I can count on to fight, I will depart for Jeul. Our horses will get us there quickly."

The council stood and all approached Jarec, saying farewells. When they were done with handshakes and hugs and goodbyes, the council adjourned and left the town hall. Kari and her men stood and approached Jarec.

"So, will you stay here, go home, or will you ride with us to Jeul?" Jarec asked. "Whatever you wish to do."

She looked to the guards and the one in charge spoke to her, "We will stay with you until you are ready to go home."

"Then I choose to go to Jeul," she said. "I've never seen the city or the castle there, and I'd like to." She also wanted to see her new friends again.

"Very well," Jarec said. "But there is one condition, you must stay in Jeul when we leave to find Tecuul. You are no longer a vampire and haven't learned to fight. We would hate for something terrible to happen to you. Also, you will all need to leave your horses here, for now. Everyone riding with me will need one of our horses. Hopefully, we can get there before Roland leaves."

She laughed. "I had no intention of going into a fight, and I have no problem staying in Jeul. I can't wait to see it!" She grinned. "And I can't wait to ride those horses again." The guards appeared unsure of the horses. They had seen the vampire horses when they stabled their own horses earlier, and the idea of riding one of them was unsettling.

"Wonderful! Well, then, let's go pay Elyse a visit, and then start to gather a strong group to come with us." And with that, they left the town hall and headed to the stables.

*****

"Finally, I might get to fight," Bail said, and Shim gave Bail a disapproving look.

"I like fighting as much as you," Shim told him, "but I'm not excited about dealing with vampires."

Zeyn's crew was standing together, already armed and ready for what was to come. They made up twelve members of the group going after Tecuul. Each of the crew, including Zeyn himself, had been given two armbands, one for each arm so that the king's men could recognize them as friendly if there was a battle to break out. Half of the band was blue and the other half was white, the colors of Jeul. Zeyn and Maria were with the crew, standing in front of them. Auben and Bryn also were nearby, and already wore their armbands as well.

"I know you are all strong, and you can all fight," Zeyn said, addressing his crew. "Despite what we may be facing, I trust you can handle yourselves. However, if any of you wish to stay behind, you may, and you won't be judged for it. There is a possibility that some of us, or none of us, will come back from this."

"There was a chance we wouldn't get back from our trip under the sea," Annah said. "We won't let this stop us now."

"Aye, Captain," Melzer said, "we're with you 'til the end."

The rest of the crew echoed the sentiment and Zeyn smiled. He was glad to have such loyal followers. "Good. We are strong when we stand together," Zeyn said. "I would expect no less from you all, my crew. My friends."

"Remember, everyone," Naaren added, "that what we are dealing with is something different than we've faced together before. If there are in fact more vampires than just Tecuul, they will be faster and stronger than you." He looked to Gor. "Well, maybe not stronger than you, but the rest of us need to be wary of their strength. I will consult the mages and we will devise some spells to help protect us from the advantages they will have, but they will be stronger. Be smart about how you fight, and try to remove their heads."

"They could also stake them," Roland said, approaching the group. Areum and Roland had returned from their room with their bags and their weapons, Roland's sword at his side and Areum's battle-axe slung across her back. They both also wore the blue and white armbands. "I have plenty if everyone would like to carry some. Just make sure that you leave the stake in the heart once you've stuck the vampire."

"But if there are more vampires Tecuul has made, they aren't in control of their actions, right?" Phyra asked. "Couldn't we focus on Tecuul to free them, too?"

"We can," Areum said, "but you all need to be concerned with your own lives as well. If the choice is between you or them, then kill them."

"I will."

"Another problem is that none of us have ever seen Tecuul. We should be able to figure out which vampire he is by his strength, but if we don't know, we will end up fighting against the others he created instead."

"There may not even be any other vampires," Roland said, "but it is best we are prepared for the worst. Perhaps Tecuul will identify himself for us." Roland's eyes moved to find Darel. He had listened to Darel's story, and he believed the man, but he still kept thinking of the first time he met him in Langston. But if Kari was able to trust these men, and they didn't bring any harm to her when they learned the truth, then he could begin to trust them as well. His wife had also vouched for the men, and her judgment was always good. "Are you ready?"

Darel nodded. "We've been ready for this for a long time. I'm sure we can say the same for you." His friends nodded in agreement. Each man wore their swords at their waist and had bags at their sides with their own vampire hunting equipment. Roland had to laugh a bit inside that he had inspired them in their youth.

"I have selected my soldiers to accompany you," the king announced, and Roland turned to face him. There was a large group of soldiers, some armed with swords and others with pikes. There were also mages with them, and all of the elven soldiers wore blue and white tabards over their armor with the crest of Jeul, and the mages wore blue robes over their armor, with white sashes around their waists. "These thirty soldiers will accompany you, as well as five mages." The soldiers were well trained in fighting, and every one of them, as an elf, knew how to perform some magic. The mages were powerful sorcerers who had honed and focused their natural magic beyond what most elves achieved. "It may seem like a lot, but if you really think he has already made more vampires, then you'll need them."

"I appreciate your help, your highness," Roland spoke with a smile. "If we make it back alive, we will be in your debt."

The king shook his head. "If you are successful, fixing the blight of the vampires for good is something that will benefit everyone. You will owe us, and the rest of this land, nothing else. So, is that everyone?"

"No, it's not." Everyone turned at the sound of the woman's voice. It was the green elf, Sola. "I would like to help you," she said. "It was my kingdom's fault for harboring him all these years. They were on the wrong side of the war with Jeul, and most of them probably didn't even know it. If there is going to be a fight, then let me fight with you."

Bandar and Thela looked to one another for a moment, appearing deep in thought. Then they stepped beside Sola. "Sola is right," Thela said, "we want to come, too."

Roland looked at the three of them. "You may come with us," Roland said. "What weapons will you need?"

Bandar pointed to the pikes carried by guards in the throne room. "Those look similar to the weapons we use in Moora," Bandar said.

Roland turned to the king, and the king gestured to three of his guards in the throne room who carried pikes, and they approached him. "Lend your pikes to these new allies," the king said, "then go to the armory and rearm yourselves." The men handed their pikes to the green elves, then left the throne room. "As I said, I will accompany you to the gate. We will have a carriage prepared for Areum and Bryn. Bandar, Thela, and Sola should probably ride with them as well. I assume they can't ride a horse." The king also didn't want anyone in the city to see the green elves until he had as chance to tell them all the truth about Moora.

A smile crossed Roland's face seeing the strength of everyone who was following him to find Tecuul. "Let's make our way to the gate."

*****

The sound of the hammer striking metal rang out again and again as Gallen worked, shaping a blade on the anvil at his smithy. He was working alone this night and thinking of everything they had been through. While he tried to stay focused on his work, his mind did wander and drift away to thoughts of *Elline*, which was still in the harbor. What would he do with the vessel, now that they no longer needed it? It needed too much magic to be a useful tool for anyone to regularly use. He had thought of just destroying it, but it was an impressive piece of work and one that was named after his wife, at that. Maybe he could discover how the vessel could be used without magic.

He returned his thoughts back to the sword. The blade was formed now. While he quenched and tempered the blade he began to think about the hilt and sheath for the sword. He knew some good artisans in town who would be able to make what he wanted for this project to help him complete the sword. Gallen hoped the gift would prove valuable.

*****

At the western gate of Jeul the group of fifty-nine, led by Roland, were prepared to depart. They were all on horseback, except for Areum, Bryn, Bandar, Thela, and Sola, who rode in a carriage with its windows covered, though the moons still stood high in the night sky. Auben sat up front to drive the carriage. The king sat on horseback himself, having ridden with them to the gate. His white horse was ornamented in blue, white and gold, and he had two guards with him on each side. The king pulled his horse up beside Roland's and placed a hand on his shoulder. "This is the end of a very long journey for you," Yuuric said. "How do you feel?"

"It's not quite over yet," Roland began to answer, "but knowing I am this close, it feels like a great weight has been taken from me."

"Return safely, friend of Jeul." The king shook his hand. "You kept us from making an error and killing off so many people ten years ago. I much prefer the outcome we got to what we had prepared before you came to us. Methods had been tried to cure vampires before, and we just reacted to the danger upon us. We were rash and didn't think that the power of the entire population could possibly cure them. And although the intended effect was different, we hadn't even considered trying to save their minds."

"It was hard to have perspective when vampires have been such a curse on the land for so very long. I understand why you planned to kill them, but I am very glad you listened to me. We will return victorious."

"When you return, I will make my announcement, telling my people the truth about Moora and about Tecuul." The king looked concerned. "I know it must be done."

"I believe in your people, they will understand it was not you, it was your grandfather. You are a great ruler, and I think your honesty will mean much to them."

"May Elar watch over you, Roland."

Roland nodded to the king and then began to lead his group out through the gate and towards the forest of the west at a slow trot. Once they were all out, they began to move at a much faster pace. Roland wanted to find Tecuul and end his existence quickly.

CHAPTER 13

THE HUNT

The king watched the group leaving from Jeul until they were no longer visible. He turned and his guards escorted him back to the castle. Yuuric's heart was heavy, as he looked at the buildings along the way back to his castle. He thought of his people living there, and how they would feel about being kept in the dark about Moora, and how they would feel about their ancestors' memories being wiped of the knowledge of what had happened.

As they made their way back, King Kaalen looked to people on the street who were out, greeting them with a "Good evening" or a wave and a smile. They responded back with a bow or curtsy, and "Your majesty." The smiles they returned at seeing their king stung Yuuric's heart, wondering if they would still smile at him after he made his announcement. His soldiers and guards already knew, and so far they had taken it well and understood the reasons for his grandfathers' decision. But some of the people might get angry about what had been done, and some might even leave Jeul to go to Leef or to the human kingdoms, if not all the way to the elven kingdoms in the desert or the mountains. He couldn't blame them, and they were free to leave as they saw fit.

When they arrived at the castle, the king returned to the throne room. His guards thought he'd be retiring to sleep since the king had been awake ever since they returned to Jeul from Kassa, but the king had one more thing to do before he could rest. He took a seat on his throne and looked to one of the guards on his left. "Bring a messenger, quickly," the king ordered. "And I don't care if you have to wake him." Despite the group Roland had taken with him, the king was worried about what could happen, and what kind of force Tecuul might have gathered. He needed to send out a message immediately, and hope it arrived in time.

*****

Teeth tore through the flesh of the cooked rabbit. The group had set up a quick camp to rest a few hours before moving on, and Auben and Bryn had caught themselves a snack. Bryn had already drained the creature of its blood and given the flesh of the animal to his brother, who sat at the fire. Auben had not been able to sleep at all, though he was glad that most of those with them, except the few chosen to stand guard, had been able to get some rest. "The sun will be up soon," Auben told his brother.

"I know," Bryn replied and stood. The dark sky was beginning to become brighter as light crept onto the horizon. He looked over to Areum, who was seated and running her hand through Roland's hair, his head in her lap.

Areum nodded to Bryn and carefully moved her husband, laying his head down on a folded blanket for support, before standing and making her way over to Bryn. "Now we can get our rest," she said, looking to where the sun would soon be rising, "I look forward to seeing it again."

"I think we all do." Bryn had felt the same himself, and it was a common thought among many in Aalen, to feel the sun and see blue skies.

"Auben, let Roland rest another hour before waking him, then we can move on." Areum knew her husband has missed much sleep of late and wanted him to get his rest. She was worried about him having to fight and not being prepared. "And if you can, get someone else to drive the carriage and try and get some sleep yourself."

Auben grinned, finishing chewing the bite in his mouth. "I will check with one of the soldiers or one of Captain Clarke's crew."

"Thank you."

"Rest well, little brother," Bryn added, and then the two vampires went to the carriage. As they entered into it, they saw the three green elves had stayed inside and were sleeping. They closed the door and sat across from the elves, making sure all the curtains were drawn. They both leaned against their side of the carriage and quickly fell asleep.

*****

"Wake up."

Roland's eyes opened and he sat up with a yawn, looking to see it was Auben who spoke. He also noticed that the sun had risen. "You should have woken me sooner," he grumbled, getting to his feet. "I don't want to waste too much time."

"Your wife's orders," Auben replied with a smile. "She wanted to make sure you got enough rest."

"Well, I have now. Make sure everyone is awake and ready to depart." Roland looked around, seeing that most of the people were already awake. "I don't want to make too many stops before nightfall. Be sure to spread the word to everyone that if they need to relieve themselves, they should do it now."

Auben nodded and held out a piece of meat towards Roland. "Rabbit?"

"Thank you," Roland said, taking the small piece of leftover meat and eating it. "Tell everyone that we won't stop to eat, so they should eat from their supplies as we are on the move."

"I will have everyone ready to move shortly."

Roland headed off to the nearby wooded area. A yawn escaped Auben's mouth and he wished to finally get some sleep of his own. He first made his way to the elven soldiers and mages and let them know Roland's orders, and then walked over to Darel and his friends and told them what Roland had said as well. When he finished speaking with Darel's small group, he approached Zeyn and his crew.

"Hello, Captain Clarke," Auben said, getting Zeyn's attention.

"Are we ready to move?" Zeyn asked. All of his crew were awake and looked ready to go.

"We are. Roland wants everyone to know we won't be making many stops before night, so if anyone needs to clean themselves out, do it now. Also, we'll eat while we are moving." Zeyn's crew all nodded at this and those who needed to headed off to take care of their business. Zeyn started to leave, but Auben stopped him. "I'm sorry, Captain, but before you head off, I have a favor to ask. Could one of your crew come and drive the carriage in my place, while I try to get some sleep?"

"I'll send someone over."

"Thank you." Auben left Captain Clarke and made his way back to the carriage. As he returned, he noticed that Roland was back and mounted, watching for everyone to be ready. The elves of Jeul were already there and lined up, ready to move. Auben remembered the green elves, and carefully opened the door of the carriage to check on them.

"I'm sorry, I forgot to ask if any of you needed anything. The camp is getting ready to move."

The three elves looked at him and Thela answered for all three, "We are fine."

"Well, if any of you need to relieve yourselves, you should do it now. Roland wanted me to let everyone know we won't stop for a while."

"That's a good idea," Bandar said.

"Be careful getting out," Auben warned. "You'll burn them if you let the sun in." The three elves soon joined him.

"Where should we go?" Sola asked.

Auben gestured to the woods nearby. "Just find a private spot for yourself and hurry back when you are done. Roland is probably anxious to get going."

Sola nodded and the three elves left Auben there. He noticed Annah from Zeyn's crew approaching him. "Hello. Are you here to drive the carriage?"

"I am. My backside will appreciate it. I don't care much for riding horses."

Auben laughed. "I imagine most of you don't spend much time riding."

"No. Most of our time is spent at sea. I would say I'm beginning to miss it already, but after being trapped beneath it in Moora, I can do with some time on land."

Auben nodded. "The stories you all told me in Jeul were fascinating. I think I can imagine what you mean, though. Being stuck in a prison on the surface, you could maybe escape or be set free and go somewhere, but down there…"

"Well, it's not something I have to worry about anymore." She offered a smile.

"If you want to go ahead and take your seat, I'll wait here for the elves to return and then join you there.

Then I'll let Roland know we're ready." Annah climbed up into the driver's seat of the carriage, and Auben turned to watch the woods, leaning against the wagon as he waited.

Soon Zeyn's crew were all mounted and ready. They weren't following a specific line or formation but were ready to move out. Zeyn brought his horse up beside Roland's to ride with him when they resumed their journey. The group was rejoined soon after by Darel and his friends, and finally, the green elves returned to the carriage.

"Are you all ready?" Auben asked them.

"We are," Thela said, carefully opening the door to return within.

"Auben, may I ride outside of the carriage?" Sola asked. "We are far outside of the city of Jeul now."

He shrugged. "I don't see why not."

She smiled and climbed up in the front while Bandar returned inside. Auben took a quick look at his sleeping brother and Areum before shutting the door and then climbed up after Sola. From where he sat, he looked to Roland and nodded to him, to let him know everyone was ready. Roland turned to lead the group onward, and they all followed.

*****

Clear blue skies were overhead as they proceeded towards the west. "I'm sorry," Sola said to Annah. Their carriage was following directly behind Roland and Zeyn. Auben had climbed onto the top of the carriage and was sleeping on his back as they traveled. Annah turned her attention from the four horses of the carriage in front of her and looked to Sola.

"What are you apologizing for?" she asked, though she thought she might know the answer.

"For your capture in Moora."

Annah was right, she knew what this was about. "I appreciate your apology, but it wasn't your fault, Sola. In fact, if not for you, Bandar, and Thela we would probably still be there."

"I still feel responsible. They are my people. At least, they were my people." Sola turned away from Annah and looked at the horses.

"And now they aren't your people?" Annah asked, turning back to focus on the horses she drove.

"I think we've made a new path, separate from them. We will have to find somewhere here in this new world to belong."

"I wish you all the best," Annah said. "I'm sure you will find a place. And I think the Captain will be willing to help you."

"Thank you." Sola's focus stayed on the horses. "These creatures are so fascinating! I've never seen anything like them in the sea. I have so much to learn about this world."

"We'll help with that, too," Annah said, turning to her with a smile.

"Is that another town?" Sola asked, looking off in the distance. They had stopped at a few as they had progressed westward, though Sola had been within the cabin of the carriage for most of the journey.

"Your eyes are very good, I can barely make it out. Captain!" She looked down in front of her to Zeyn. "There is a town up ahead!"

"What's going on?" Auben asked. He had woken and turned around, now lying face down on the top of the carriage. He was propped on his elbows as he looked at them.

"We are coming up to another town," Sola answered him.

Roland stopped the party and turned to face them all, while Zeyn rode off towards the town. "Alright everyone, we'll do the same as we have in each town we've come across." When they came to other towns along their journey, Zeyn would scout ahead to make sure the town was alright before the rest of the group would enter. Once Zeyn returned, he would let them know what he had observed, and then Roland would decide if they stopped in the town or avoided it.

Many dismounted and took advantage of this moment of reprieve, as they often did any time the group stopped. They rested themselves, took time to eat something or drink some water, though if they went in town they might get some food and drink while there. Some also fed their horses, as Annah had begun to do for the horses of the carriage and Sola helped her. But Zeyn returned quickly, which was unusual. Annah and Sola were close enough to hear and continued feeding the horses as they listened.

"Roland, the town appears to have been attacked but no one is there," Zeyn said. "It was only recently made vacant. I think we all need to go investigate. There may be some survivors, I didn't check everywhere."

"We are getting closer to the forests and are outside the boundaries of Jeul," Roland replied. "This might confirm our fears." He looked around to everyone. "Get mounted and we'll check the town."

Everyone was quick to get on their horses and follow Roland to the apparent ghost town. Annah and Sola returned to the seat of the carriage, where Auben already sat. "I'll drive again if you don't mind," he said. "I'm feeling well rested now."

"That's fine with me," Annah said. She looked towards the town as Auben drove the carriage after Roland and the others.

*****

"Vampires?" Darel asked Roland, as they stood just outside the town. Everyone has once again dismounted and prepared to check out the town.

"I don't know yet, but it's possible," Roland answered. "We'll split up to check out the town. Darel, take your group to the end of town and start looking around. Sola," Roland looked to the green elf, "if you would get Bandar and Thela from the carriage, I'd like the three of you to go with Auben to the other end of town as well. The elf nodded and went to the carriage, and Auben followed. "Zeyn," Roland continued, looking to his friend, "break up your crew into three groups and start searching from this end towards the far end and meet the others in the middle. I'll have the soldiers from Jeul stay here and watch for anything outside, and to keep an eye on the horses." The captain of the soldiers nodded to Roland, hearing him. "Thank you."

When they set about their given tasks, Roland started making his way towards the center of the town, to wait for the groups to meet with him. The town was small. It appeared to be mainly homes around the outside, with buildings in the center being various businesses. They had no idea if there were any outlying farms. As Roland was walking, observing the homes around him, a scent hit his nose and curled his nostrils. It was a familiar fragrance, the scent of death. He followed the smell to a house on his right and opened the door, his mouth dropping in shock. He wasn't surprised they had left the dead behind.

The pile of corpses in the house all belonged to children. Roland shook his head and covered his nose as he entered to observe the bodies. They had been drained of blood through their necks. The mark of vampire teeth was unmistakable. He knew what must have happened. All the adults were turned, and now following Tecuul, and the children were killed and left behind. Tecuul must have only wanted adults. Roland turned around and left the building, continuing to the middle of town to wait for the others to meet him. When the others returned he looked to each group for a report on what they found.

"We didn't find anyone," Darel said, "but we did find some blood and signs of a struggle."

"The same for us," Auben echoed. "He must have turned the entire town."

"Not the entire town," came Phyra's voice behind them, Roland turned to look at her as the groups Zeyn had set searching approached. "My group found a house full of dead children." She tried to sound calm but was clearly shaken. Melzer, who had been one of her group, pulled her close to give comfort.

"We didn't find anyone," said Gor, and the other groups nodded in agreement.

"I also found the building of children when I was on my way here to wait for you all," Roland said. "Come, let's return to the others and move on. We must stop them before they can do more of this."

The walk back was mostly silent. News of the slaughtered children had made those who hadn't seen it somber, and those that had seen it had been hit even harder by the sight. Roland saw their attitude and while they were saddened by what they had witnessed, he did believe this would strengthen their resolve in the upcoming fight. Zeyn approached Roland as they were getting close to the edge of town. "We are going to have a battle on our hands, aren't we?"

Roland nodded and waited a moment to speak. "If any of your people want to return, I won't force them to see this through."

Zeyn turned back to look at his crew. "I don't think that will be an issue. We will want blood for blood."

"Good. But remember this, if we can kill Tecuul, we can free these new vampires of their curse as well. He is the only one responsible for this, not these people who were turned." Zeyn nodded in response as they reached the elves, the horses, and the carriage.

"Everyone mount up!" Roland commanded. He waited for everyone to get ready to leave before he continued. Annah returned to her horse and Sola rejoined Auben in the seat of the carriage. Bandar and Thela stood outside of the carriage to listen to Roland before entering. When everyone had saddled up, Roland hopped onto his saddle and turned his horse to face them all. "We have witnessed the results of an atrocity here, which most likely was carried out by Tecuul." He looked to the elves of Jeul. "You weren't in town with us, but know that all the children were slaughtered, and the adults were most likely turned to vampires and are now following Tecuul. I don't know how many we are to face, but with our skill and magic, I believe we can prevail."

Roland looked around at everyone. "I know we will be outnumbered, but if we kill Tecuul, any power he has over the vampires on his side should be gone. If we get locked into battle with them, try to find him and focus on killing him. It's our only chance against the odds ahead of us. Some of you might wonder why we don't go back and increase our force, and the idea has crossed my mind. However, every moment we let him live, he could be destroying more lives, killing some and turning others. We need to find him and end him now." He turned to the mages of Jeul. "Have your spells ready. We could come across the vampires at any time."

The head mage nodded to Roland. "We have them prepared. You will all be able to keep up with their speed. This effect might not last long, so take advantage of the speed while you have it. They will still be stronger than you, but you will still have some protection from that strength. Strike fast and you will kill them."

"Thank you. This will be dangerous, everyone. Some of us may not come back. But we will win. And when we do, if I'm not here, I want those who survive to return here and give those children a decent burial." Everyone nodded in agreement. "Let's go."

CHAPTER 14

TECUUL'S STAND

Moonlight shone down upon the dark forest, which spread throughout the center of the continent and around the mountains. The scene before them showed what appeared to be a small military installation at the forest's edge that had been attacked by the vampires, and as with the small town they had come across, people were missing. Unlike the town, though, no children had been left behind, as none were probably there to begin with. Zeyn shook his head in disgust. He wasn't sure who the stone structure had belonged to, but he knew it was no one's now. There was no need for everyone to come and look over what remained, Zeyn had time enough to see everything.

There were differences from the town before; the people at this hold had been able to mount a fight against the vampires. However, they had killed none of the monsters. A few armored corpses remained of those who didn't survive to be turned. Another difference that Zeyn noted was that people weren't the only thing that had been taken, the armory had been looted. Not a single weapon remained, even those of the deceased, who surely were armed when they fought back. If they had taken these people, too, then they would be severely outnumbered.

Roland better be right, Zeyn thought to himself. If killing Tecuul stopped the other vampires from fighting, then they would survive. If not, Captain Clarke saw no way they would survive the onslaught of vampires. He mounted and rode back to report what he had seen.

When he had made it to the others, he pulled his horse beside Roland, who was standing by his horse, feeding it while he also ate. "Roland," Zeyn reported, "there were some dead bodies of men who tried to fight, but most of the people are gone. All of the weapons have also been taken. It was the vampires again; the dead I found were drained of blood through their necks."

"How long do you think the bodies have been there?" Roland asked.

"I'm not sure, but I think we are getting close."

"We could go check," Bryn added. He had made his way over with Areum. "Now that the night is here, we can check these bodies and see if we can follow their trail."

Roland nodded. "We will catch up with the two of you there." Bryn ran off towards the hold, the speed his vampire abilities granted him moving him quicker than on horseback. Areum kissed her husband's cheek and followed Bryn. "Everyone get ready to ride!"

Roland mounted and began to lead the way and Zeyn kept his horse at Roland's side. "This fight could be the end of all of our lives," Zeyn said gravely. "But we are with you to the end, my friend."

"Have faith," Roland encouraged. "We can do this, Zeyn. We just have to kill Tecuul as quickly as possible." Zeyn wasn't convinced it was that simple for his old friend. His speech at the town they had found revealed that Roland knew he himself could perish against these vampires. "We have a solid plan."

Zeyn gave a nod and looked to his crew who were following close behind them. He could see that they were all ready to follow him wherever he led. There was no surprise to see that Naaren's eyes appeared to thirst for blood, for justice. Hopefully, Tecuul's death would finally bring closure to Naaren about the death of his grandfather and all Tecuul had done to his people.

He also noticed Maria and Alexander rode close together. Had he finally admitted to her how he felt? The entire crew knew, even Maria herself. Maybe his sister had finally told Alex herself, considering the circumstances. The man couldn't drag his feet forever. Zeyn had thought about telling his sister she should leave to watch the *Salvation* if he didn't make it back, but she wanted to be here. And when Maria really wanted to do something, she was unstoppable.

As Roland stopped in front of the low walls, his wife and Bryn returned from within, their faces grave. "They aren't far from us," Areum said to Roland.

"Which direction?" Roland asked.

Areum replied by pointing into the forest.

"We'll be fighting soon," Bryn said. "I'll get the elves out of the carriage."

"Unhitch the horses," Roland responded. "We can leave the carriage here for now. You and Areum and Auben can ride and each of you can carry one of them. Leave the extra horse here with the carriage." Roland knew that Bandar, Thela, and Sola had no experience riding and wouldn't be able to handle it alone. Bryn and Areum left to get the horses and the others at the carriage.

Roland turned to face everyone following him again. "We are close. Be ready to fight, they could set upon us at any moment. Areum and Bryn will lead us into the forest to their location. If we're lucky, we can surprise them first." He looked to the mages. "Can you perform a spell to keep them from sensing our approach?"

The group of elves talked quietly amongst themselves and then looked back to Roland. "We can. We'll need to draw some magical strength from the other elves here. Our own is being used on the defensive spells we've prepared."

Roland nodded. "How long will it take to cast?"

"It will only take a moment. I have a spell in mind that won't take long to prepare. It can mask us."

"Thank you." Roland looked to Zeyn. "Are you and your crew ready?"

Zeyn turned to his sister. "Is everyone ready?"

"Aye!" exclaimed Maria. "We are ready." The rest of the crew gave their own signs of agreement.

"We're ready," Zeyn said to Roland.

Roland then asked Darel, "Are you and your friends ready?"

"We have been ready for years," Darel answered.

"And soldiers of Jeul, are you ready?" The mages nodded, confirming their masking spell was complete, and the captain of the soldiers gave Roland a nod and a salute of respect, placing his right fist across his breast. As the elves of Jeul replied, Areum and Bryn returned on horseback with Auben. Sola rode with Areum, Bandar with Bryn, and Thela with Auben. The green elves each carefully carrying their pikes.

Roland smiled at his wife. "We are all ready, lead the way." And so, the group entered the dark forest in search of Tecuul and his vampire followers.

*****

The forest had become so dark that some of the elven soldiers had created small balls of light to provide illumination for everyone to see. Areum didn't need the light to see or to follow the trail, but she knew everyone else did. Well, everyone except Bryn. She wished they had more vampires with them, though she knew the new vampires Tecuul had made wouldn't be strong enough yet to match her. Time did equal strength, to a point, when it came to the vampires. Tecuul would be stronger than them all, unfortunately. If they could kill him before any fighting, it would be quick and easy. If a battle did break out, Bryn had already agreed that the two of them should put their focus on Tecuul and try to kill him fast, since they were the strongest among the group. Their strength was even more than Gor.

She came to a stop and dismounted. "It would be best to leave the horses here. They will hinder us further in the forest if we do have to fight. And we could move quieter without them." She still had hope they could take the other vampires completely by surprise. "Naaren, I know the other elves are all using much of their magic, could you use a small spell to keep the horses here for our return?"

"I can," Naaren answered. As everyone dismounted, he moved from horse to horse, seemingly whispering to each one. "It is done. They will await our return. And if we don't return, they will flee."

Areum nodded to him. As they continued on, there was silence among everyone, but they all moved with weapons ready. Much was at stake, and they all knew that surprise was a key to their victory. They soon came upon a stream and Bryn put his hand up to halt everyone. The vampires were staying close to the water. It wouldn't be much further until they would find the vampires camp. Bryn moved to Roland and whispered in his ear. Roland gestured ahead for all to see so that they would know what they were coming upon. Many among them tightened their grips on their weapons, and Roland began to silently lead the way to the vampires.

As they approached the camp that had been set up in a small clearing, they saw no vampires but did find seven humans who had been taken prisoner. They also saw a strange symbol that had been made in the earth, which some recognized was used to summon a demon. All of the prisoners had been tied at hands and feet, but they appeared as if drugged and their eyes could hardly open. Their mouths moved slowly, and no sound escaped their lips.

Upon closer inspection, Roland found they had been bitten by vampires, which he pointed out to the others. Areum saw their state and saw they weren't just bitten once. They had been used as a food source for the vampires. They must have set up near the water to keep the humans hydrated so they could keep feeding. Kneeling beside them, Areum pulled out one of her daggers and cut the ropes that bound them, but they didn't try to move.

"They've been eaten from recently, but no attempt made to turn them," she said to her husband. "And this can't be all of them, this wouldn't be enough to feed all of his vampires, unless…" She started to sniff with her nose. "Oh, no." Everyone watched as she darted off a little north of the camp and they followed, finding a hole that had been dug into the earth. They knew not how deep it went, but could see it was full of bodies that had been completely drained of blood. The smell was wretched. She was amazed everyone didn't smell it from the camp.

"Have we lost track of them?" Bryn asked.

"No, the vampires should be here," she responded.

"They did manage to keep us from seeing exactly where they were on the map. Maybe whatever power hid them there is helping them hide now," Auben suggested.

"Let's head back to the camp," Areum said, "We can try to get those poor people to safety."

"You won't have time for that," a voice said and from all around them, vampires made their ways out of the trees. There appeared to be near two hundred, if not more. Roland and his band were caught by surprise. Bandar, Thela, and Sola were especially surprised to see the green elves who were with Tecuul. They must have been turned during the time Tecuul was kept safe in Moora, but they didn't recognize the faces. No one knew which vampire had spoken, but all eyes searched for the one that was the first, the one who brought this evil to their world in the first place.

"Which one is Tecuul?" Roland asked. Unfortunately, none of them knew what Tecuul looked like, but they did know he would be one of the elves. Fortunately, Tecuul had only found a few elves to turn, it appeared.

"Him," Naaren answered, pointing to one of the elves. The shock in the vampire's face revealed that Naaren was right. Tecuul had long, brown hair, and wore armor that must have been stolen from the armory they had recently attacked.

Roland smiled, despite the overwhelming numbers. "He's the one to kill!" he commanded, pointing to Tecuul, and then the vampire horde moved to crash upon them. The soldiers of Jeul surrounded everyone else as the battle was set to begin. "What are you doing?" Roland was confused by their actions.

"What our king commanded," the Captain spoke. "If it came to this, we are to protect the rest of you and the mages first, if we can."

As the vampire force came upon them, the soldiers held their best against the number. The mages, who stood in the middle of everyone, were chanting and keeping up their protection spells for the fight. The soldiers did well. There clearly wasn't room enough for all the vampires to move against them as a single group, or the heroes sent by King Kaalen would have had no chance. Soon a couple of heads rolled from the bodies of vampires, ending their lives, though the elves didn't want to kill them.

Tecuul had not yet joined the fight, but Areum and Bryn were not going to sit back while the soldiers fended off the vampire army. The two leapt over the soldiers and past them, taking down vampires as they chased towards Tecuul. The First Vampire laughed and began to chant, but his spell seemed to roll over the two vampires approaching him. His laughter turned to a scowl as he drew his sword, prepared to fight the two. "Why can't I control you?!" he growled as the attacks came.

Areum attacked first, but Tecuul seemed to have no problem knocking her axe aside as she swung towards his head. As he sliced towards her neck, Bryn's two swords caught his and knocked him back slightly. They both now knew Tecuul's strength and were stunned. The strength of this vampire would not easily be overcome.

As three soldiers fell to their deaths against the vampires, the others pushed through to get into the fight. Zeyn and his crew were eager to fight and began to do what they could against the terror around them. Gor matched the vampires in strength, and the wide, flat blade he wielded with one hand ended the life of one of the vampires while he held another by the neck with his large gauntleted left hand. The swords of Shim and Bail cut through legs and guts of their enemies, but the wounds were quick to heal. Alexander stuck closely to Maria's side, him fighting with a sword in one hand and stake ready in another while she used her sword and shield.

Rendal and Brill paired off to watch each other while fighting. Though they started well enough, Rendal quickly lost one of his two short axes, and Brill found himself on his back with his cutlass tossed away and an unarmed vampire on top of him. Phyra saved Melzer from the bite of a vampire, throwing a dagger into the temple of the one trying to drink from his veins. She tossed an extra sword to Melzer and he sliced the throat of what used to be a man, probably from the ghost town they had found.

Zeyn, using his sword, was joined by Bandar, Thela, and Sola against a group of green elven vampires from Moora. They were outnumbered but were holding up against them in the fight. Soon Annah came to their side with her spear to lend aid. Naaren deftly made his way past the crew and the vampires, ignoring them and joining Areum and Bryn against Tecuul.

Tecuul had pulled Bryn, Naaren, and Areum down into his army and gotten away from them, making his way towards the mages. Naaren disappeared chasing after Tecuul. As another soldier died, one of the magic lights they had brought went out, which had been created by that soldier. Bryn and Areum found themselves fighting two green elves from Moora, and they realized from their strength that these elves must have been turned long before they were. Areum wondered, as they fought, how long ago. These vampires could be hundreds of years old.

She looked to her husband and found Roland fighting alongside Daryl, Will, Tras, Weston, and Simeon. Like all the others, they were no longer in the circle of soldiers from Jeul. But they still lived and fought, trying to get to Tecuul. Roland defended and attacked with his sword, wielding it with two hands. Weston and Simeon were at each other's back, the twins equally skilled with their daggers. Darel, Will, and Tras all used swords well in their battle. Areum didn't remain distracted from her own fight and, with Bryn's help, they buried a stake into the heart of one of the green vampires, the life leaving her body as it fell to the ground, empty. The other green vampire tried to fight back against them, but Bryn stabbed him through the head, then removed his blade and buried a stake in his heart.

A yell of pain brought Areum's attention then, and she took note of Zeyn's crew. One of the men, Brill, had teeth in his neck as Tecuul took a bite and forced vampiric blood from his wrist into the man's throat. Areum frowned. If they could get to Tecuul and kill him, Brill could still be saved. She could see Tecuul return to his original path.

"Protect the mages!" Areum cried out, hoping her voice could carry over the sound of metal on metal and the screams of those who died. Only twenty soldiers of Jeul still stood. As she ran towards the mages, she saw them throw their hands up, expending much of their energy to drop balls of fire on some of the vampires. They managed to take out almost twenty, but the numbers were still too high. Bryn had left her to join his brother, Auben, who had been fighting off many vampires alone.

Her eyes searched for her husband again and saw the body of Weston dead on the ground. His twin yelling with every blow he struck against the vampires around him, tears in his eyes. A vampire bit into Tras and pulled him to the ground, drinking from him before tearing his throat out with his teeth. The vampire smiled but had her head removed quickly by Daryl and Will, whose faces were angry and grief-stricken at the same time.

"Pull together!" Roland yelled, trying to rally everyone. She had found him, standing from staking a vampire, then swinging his sword to the left through the neck of an elven vampire. Daryl, Will, and Simeon started rushing back to the numbers that remained near the mages while Roland defended their flight. There were two vampires on him, but she would make it soon to help him. Roland cut through the gut of one of them, bringing him down until he could heal from the extreme wound. As he turned to face the other vampire, Areum cried out watching the vampire's sword enter Roland's body.

CHAPTER 15

SALVATION

The battle raged around Zeyn and his crew and
while they still stood, he worried that soon they'd grow too
tired to keep up the fight. They had done their best to push
after Tecuul, but there were just too many vampires around
them, and they had to kill some. A sword slashed across
Zeyn's right leg, bringing him to the ground, and, if not for
Gor, his life would have ended. As the vampire attempted
to stab down into the Captain, Gor snatched the fiend up by
the throat and crushed it with his hand before tossing the
body to the side. It would take the vampire some moments
to recover. He then punched another vampire hard in the
face with his gauntlet, crushing the enemy's skull and
taking him out of the fight for a few minutes.

"Captain," Gor said. "We have to end this soon, or
we are all going to die. There are too many."

"I know," Zeyn responded as Gor helped him to his
feet. He looked around for his sister and spotted her and
Alexander helping Melzer, Rendal, and Phyra fend off
Brill, who had apparently been turned into a vampire
during the fight. "Oh, no."

"I saw it happen, but was too far away to stop it." Gor was looking at the scene as Brill buried his sword in Melzer's heart and tried to bite Phyra, but was stopped by Rendal.

Suddenly they both heard a voice over the battle. "Pull together!" It was Roland, and Zeyn knew that he was right. They had all gotten too spread out and needed to gather their force.

"Help my sister and the others and try to get back to the mages," Zeyn ordered. They would mourn for Melzer later. Another light went out, another soldier dead. Zeyn's mouth grew tight. Gor nodded and fought his way across. "Follow me!" Zeyn shouted to Shim, Bail, Bandar, Thela, Sola, and Annah. He could not find Naaren. They fell back to him, fighting the whole way.

They all had taken damage in the fight. All had at least been cut once, and Annah was bruised on her left leg, though it didn't slow her down. Shim and Bail had been doing well cutting down the masses around them and appeared to have taken the least amount of wounds, being easily overlooked. The three green elves had been focusing their attention on the vampires that had come from Moora.

A sound of a scream reached their ears as they were following Gor's path to get the crew together. Zeyn looked in the direction it came and saw Areum but did not see Roland anywhere. As he began to worry about what must have happened, a large group of vampires was upon them, and Zeyn was tackled to the ground.

*****

As the vampire looked down at his handiwork and prepared to leap onto Roland's body and feed, Areum's axe swung in an arc upwards to remove the monster's head. The axe cut through in one clean strike and the head flew to the ground. As the body fell, she kicked it away so that it wouldn't fall on the body of her beloved. Tears were in her eyes as she looked down at Roland, dropping to her knees by his side.

"Don't cry, love," Roland said weakly, blood in his mouth as he was slumped against a tree.

He still lived! If her heart could beat, it would have leapt. She ripped open his shirt and looked at the wound. The blade must have missed his heart, and so she still had some time. "Shh," she said softly, "Save your strength a moment." She had put down her axe and drew one of her daggers. Vampires approached them, but Bryn and Auben had made their way over and were defending the two of them.

Areum cut her wrist and put it into Roland's mouth as she leaned across to bite into his neck at the same time. Tecuul still lived, and so she could save her husband's life. She hadn't turned anyone in many years, not since she had no control of herself in the vampire war, but the vampires of Aalen still had the ability to turn people, though they didn't use it. She left her wrist in his mouth to drink as she pulled away from the bite. Auben and Bryn turned to check on them while they fought, as they worried about their friend.

Roland's eyes widened, then remained open normally as his body relaxed against the tree. Tears stained her face while she waited, and then Roland's wound began to heal. When the flesh from his stab wound looked closed and normal again, she wiped away the blood stains and kissed his cheek. The transformation would not be as quick as it was for the vampires Tecuul created, but it had saved his life. Roland closed his eyes and slept.

"Areum, there are too many," Auben said, the corpses of two vampires lay at the feet of him and his brother. For now, the vampires were ignoring them as they fought near Tecuul against the remaining forces from Jeul and Zeyn and his crew.

"We are lost if we don't kill Tecuul. I have to protect my husband until he wakes." She stood and picked up her axe.

"I'll get him this time," Bryn said. "Stay here brother, and help watch Roland."

"I will," Auben replied and his brother ran off towards the enemy.

As vampires drew in, Auben worked to injure most, to the point they would need time to heal. Areum did the same. Despite being overwhelmed, they knew these vampires had no control of what they were now doing, and they deserved a chance to survive this. However, when they couldn't be slowed by injury, they were killed. Areum proved most deadly with her weapon, and Auben, though not as strong as his opponents, was a skilled warrior and could deliver the killing blows. As a large group began to push towards them and they prepared for their last stand, a large number of allies from deep in the forest pushed through and began to take the vampires to the ground.

Auben stopped and stared, as did Areum. The people of Aalen had arrived and had evened the odds against what they faced now. They spotted Jarec leading them. "How did they know to come?" Auben asked Areum as if she would have an answer.

"King Kaalen sent a message," Bree answered, hearing his question as she stepped up beside them.

"We were on our way to meet you all in Jeul," Nolan, her husband, added, "but a messenger met us along the way who told us you'd already left." His short hair looked like fire, like his wife's, though unlike her he had been human before being bitten. The last time Areum saw Nolan he looked defeated, as if he had given up on ever being cured, but she could see a bright light in his blue eyes that shone like crystal. He definitely had a renewed vigor since hearing they had finally found a cure.

"You must tell Jarec to go after Tecuul," Areum stressed, skipping pleasantries. "If he dies, these other vampires will be freed from his control and we will all be cured! He is an elf with long dark hair and dark eyes. He was wearing dark iron armor over a blue shirt and had no helmet. But he is very strong! Be careful."

"I'll tell him," Nolan said, dashing off quickly.

"How is he?" Bree asked, looked down at Roland.

"He will survive," Areum said, reassuring herself.

"Well, I'm off to join this fight while there is still a fight to be had!" The elf ran off into the thick of the battle, long red hair flowing behind her.

*****

The dwarves were knocking back the vampires after Zeyn had been knocked down, protecting him. Bandar, Thela, and Annah were still fighting as well while Sola helped him back to his feet. "Thank you," Zeyn said and then shouted, "Keep moving!" Shim took the front while Bail took the back, helping them to push quicker. Gor soon joined them with Maria and Alexander. "Are you alright?" Zeyn asked his sister.

"I am," she answered, "and so is Alex."

"We're here," Phyra said with Rendal behind her. "Brill?"

"He lives, fighting on their side."

"We are almost back to the others..." Zeyn trailed off as he noticed the reinforcements from Aalen. A smile made its way onto his face and he began to get a second wind. "We won't die here!" he said, holding his sword tight. "Fight hard, and let's get to Tecuul!" Gor knocked a vampire off his feet with a strong left backhand and took the lead, charging through to make a pathway. Everyone fell in line with the dwarves in the rear and pushed towards Tecuul, who was fighting with the elves from Jeul.

*****

Darel, Will, and Simeon had made it to the mages. The circle of soldiers had broken, and now, while only seventeen soldiers remained, they only made a half circle of protection. One mage had been killed, but once Darel and his friends arrived they had been able to protect the open area to save the others. More grieving would come later, but for now, they were strengthened by their loss and determined to make it through, for the sake of those who had died for them.

Tecuul had been pressing against the main force of soldiers, surrounded by his vampires, and when they had a moment of rest from fighting, they observed him. "He's toying with them!" Simeon exclaimed.

"You're right," Will confirmed. "He could probably have ended us all by now."

"I don't think so," Darel said. "He might not be giving it his all right now against Jeul, but he has a personal hatred for them. All these other vampires, the ones we have injured or killed? They were trying to fight us. Stay strong, we can win!"

"Why don't we take a charge at Tecuul?" Simeon asked as he prepared himself to fight an incoming vampire.

"You've seen how he takes out the elves. He's too strong for us. Let's focus on protecting these mages so they can keep their magic on us." Darel held his sword ready for attack and watched as another vampire pulled the incoming vampire down and hacked its head off. She looked at them and smiled and he noted it wasn't Areum or Bryn. In fact, she looked like a teenager. He saw others coming that were joining in to fight Tecuul's forces. As he looked around, he saw one approach with raised hands.

"Hello," the man said, "My name is Jarec, and we're here from Aalen to help. Do you know which one of these vampires is Tecuul?"

The three men felt a great weight lift off them and pointed past the mages, where Tecuul was fighting with four of the soldiers at once.

*****

Naaren was quick and had been avoiding as much fighting as possible. Although he wanted revenge on Tecuul, he was not blinded by it and wanted to save as many people as possible. He did find himself having to fight occasionally, but he was able to avoid killing blows. With the added forces from Aalen, he would have an easier time getting to Tecuul. His left hand occasionally hovered over the sword at his left side as he grew closer to his prey. Suddenly he was stopped in his tracks.

Before him stood Brill, one of his crewmates and friends, but Naaren knew something was wrong. "I don't want to fight you," Naaren said, shaking his head. He knew Brill had been turned. The man said nothing but leapt at the elf with bared fangs, and Naaren had to respond to the attack in kind. He drew his sword from his right side and struck his friend across the face with the hilt.

Brill growled and stood, but Naaren was already upon him and slashed him down the back and then across the stomach. "I'm sorry. I do hope you heal before Tecuul dies." Naaren turned and hurried on his way, while Brill winced in pain, holding his guts inside his abdomen as the wounds began to heal.

*****

"Fall back, soldiers of Jeul!" Jarec's voice boomed as he approached them. "You've fought well today."

Tecuul stopped fighting and spoke. "You can't beat me. You are an old one, to be sure, but I'm far older and stronger still. I am the FIRST!"

Jarec didn't waste time with words and went to action in the fight, swinging straight for the head. Tecuul dodged quickly and stabbed towards Jarec with his blade, but Jarec was quick as well and parried the blow. The mages and the soldiers, relieved of their battle, lent what magic they had left to Jarec to make the match more even. Tecuul's strength was still almost more than Jarec could bare, and Jarec knew that he might not last.

As their battle went on, others from Aalen protected Jarec and fought against Tecuul as well, but the first vampire's magic was stronger than any they'd ever felt, and he'd had millennia to perfect it. Jarec thought of his people and all they had endured through the years. This was their moment, their chance to break free of their curse, and they couldn't afford to lose. As Tecuul's blade pierced Jarec's side, Jarec grunted and wondered if the killing blow Tecuul had planned next would succeed. As Tecuul swung at Jarec's throat, another blade knocked the sword away and Naaren stood between them.

Tecuul was take off guard and was almost too slow as the elf's sword moved across his throat. A line of blood formed on the vampire's neck, but the cut had not been very deep, certainly not deep enough to remove his head. For the first time, Tecuul looked worried about the outcome. He leapt back from his opponents and yelled out, "Everyone attack!" All the vampires still in his command began to focus on one point as Tecuul retreated.

*****

This can't be happening, Tecuul thought as he fled, making his way to his camp. His eye caught two of his vampires piling on a short man and cutting off his left arm before another short man cut the head off one of the vampires and a giant crushed the head of the second between his hands. Tecuul did not stay to watch the rest of the outcome. As he ran, some humans who had come with the reinforcements tried to stop him, but he killed them both quickly. The last sight he caught before he left the battle and made it to his camp was a woman, a vampire, standing beside a man, while another man lay on the ground near them. He tried to take control of her mind, but like the new vampires that appeared, he could get no control over them.

As he got to the camp, he pulled the captives, who had not fled though their bonds were cut, to him with compulsion. He killed each of them over the symbol, filling it with blood until the door opened, and Vel'dulan appeared. "I need your help!" he cried. "Get me somewhere safe."

"Safe?" She scoffed. "You've threatened my own safety bringing me here when this battle is raging." As she finished talking, the elf he had been fighting and some others filled the camp. Most were still fighting the other vampires in the area they came from.

Tecuul turned just as he was about to be struck, but Vel'dulan stopped the elf's hand, freezing it in place. "What is this?!" the elf asked. Vel'dulan froze everyone else in the camp before they could attack, too.

"If the rest of them come here I won't be able to stop them all," she explained to Tecuul.

"So you do have limits," he observed.

Before she could answer, shock covered her face as a hand reached through the doorway and grabbed her by the hair, dragging her back to their realm. The door sealed shut and vanished.

As Tecuul looked on astonished at what had happened, he felt something enter through his back and out of his chest. Looking down, he saw a wooden blade. The vampire fell to his knees. He turned to see the elf behind him. "Your legacy is over," the elf said. As life began to leave Tecuul's body, he felt anger and frustration. He wasn't ever supposed to die, that was his bargain. His eyes remained on the elf a moment and he remembered the captain of Jeul he killed all those years ago when this first began. He wondered why he had that thought as his sight began to fade away until all he saw was white.

*****

Roland's eyes opened; his head cradled in his wife's lap. "What happened?" he asked. "The last thing I remember was…" He moved his hand to where the wound should be. It wasn't there.

A tear from Areum's eye hit his face. "I saved you," she smiled, "I had to turn you, but I saved you." Roland felt his teeth with his left hand. "Tecuul died before your teeth changed."

"He's dead? But what about your teeth?" he asked, having noticed that she still had fangs.

"I don't know. Jarec thinks that it's just something we are stuck with." She helped him to his feet. "We are no longer vampires, though. Watch."

He looked at her as she reached down to pick up her axe. She struggled, unable to lift the weapon easily as she once had. He noticed she appeared sad at that fact. She then put his hand to her heart, and he could feel it beating. He smiled at his wife and pulled her in close, kissing her. After all these years, they had finally found what they had been searching for. As he pulled back from the kiss, he remembered something she had said. "Jarec is here?"

"Yes, King Kaalen sent for them right after we left Jeul. They were already on the way to Jeul when the message reached them."

Roland looked around at all the living and dead, still illuminated by the light orbs that were left. Many of the soldiers from Jeul had died and one of the mages. Weston and Tras had died while he still fought by their side. He watched as Darel, Will, and Simeon retrieved their bodies. Zeyn's crew had all suffered some injuries, and one of the dwarves was missing an arm, begging for the mages to try and reattach it. Roland wasn't sure if that was possible or not. Zeyn had found Melzer's body and Gor carried it over to the other dead. Phyra cried over him while Brill stood near but looked away. Roland knew the three were very close.

The scene was full of many who were rejoicing in their humanity. There were also those confused about the short time they were vampires and part of Tecuul's army. Roland saw that Bandar, Thela, and Sola were trying to explain all that had happened to a group of five green elves from Moora, the only ones who had survived the fighting. Emotions were mixed, but there would be celebration later, after the mourning.

"Roland," Jarec said, as he approached. "How are you feeling?"

"I am feeling better," he replied, his arm around Areum. "And I am very happy we've succeeded."

"As are we all. I spoke with the survivors from the town of Lind. While they appreciate our help, they want to bury their own dead. They plan to take the bodies of their deceased back home from the battlefield. They'll take care of the children's bodies, too."

"So Lind was its name. I didn't know."

"Yes. We'll head to Jeul before returning to Aalen. It will be interesting moving at a normal pace again."

Auben made his way over as he looked around. "Did Elyse come?" he asked Jarec.

"Yes, she's with the horses now, but she was helping in the fight earlier."

"Good, so she's safe. I don't think anyone from Aalen fell in battle."

Roland noticed it was true as he looked around. The former vampires of Aalen were all much stronger than those recently created. "So, Jarec, do you know what the future holds for us now?"

"I'm not sure," Jarec replied, "but it won't be easy to rejoin with society. Especially because we still have fangs." Roland was curious about that. When Menton was cured, so were their fangs. But he assumed it had to do with different demons being involved and the way they became vampires. He put the thought from his head. "I told the people of Lind that they may want to come join us in Aalen when they've buried their dead, but it's their choice."

"Thank you for coming, Jarec. I need to have a word with Zeyn."

Roland walked over to Zeyn and his crew and noticed Naaren holding a sword with a wooden blade in his hand. The hilt was familiar, and then Roland remembered the sword Naaren always kept with him but never used. "So, that was what you've been hiding all this time."

Naaren looked to Roland with a smile. "The hilt actually came from my grandfather's sword. I was the one who killed Tecuul, Roland. I feel that I've completed my family's mission."

Roland smiled at him. "Thank you. You've done more than that. You've given all of the vampires their lives back. Are you still staying with Zeyn's crew?"

"Of course. They are my family, too."

"It's good to see you alive," Zeyn said, approaching Roland and Naaren.

"I'm sorry for your loss," Roland said.

"Melzer was a great man and a strong member of my crew. He will be missed. But most of all by his closest friends. Brill is taking it the hardest. It was by his own blade. They had turned him during the fight."

"He wasn't in control of himself," Naaren added, "I know, I fought him before getting to Tecuul."

Suddenly, everyone realized the sun had risen. The light streamed through the treetops, and those who were once vampires realized they could stand in the rays of the sun without burning. Some stood reaching up to the sun, others fell and began to cry. Roland, hand in hand with Areum, looked at his wife's face. Her eyes were closed and she smiled, beaming at the feeling of the sun on her face. Tecuul had been ended, and the curse of the vampire was gone from the world for good.

EPILOGUE

BEGINNINGS

"How dare you interfere with me!" Vel'dulan's voice echoed through the dark halls of their domain.

"I was trying to save you," Mar'vandi replied harshly, "but it may not matter after all. The others meet even now as we speak, and they are not happy with the extent of your interference in the world this time. It could have set back their plans."

She laughed. Their plans, as if they were all united. "Oh, Mar, trying to save me?" she asked, mockingly. "Are you feeling sentimental?" He hadn't shown any feelings towards her almost as long as they'd been banished to this awful place, separated from the world. In recent years he'd only shown contempt and loathing.

He shook his head. "I have no love for you anymore, Vel. The only reason I want you alive is because you have much power and knowledge, and it will take all we have to walk in the world again and to conquer it. But you had to try to conquer it alone, and they won't like that. They are jealous of you. If you had just worked with me as we originally planned…"

"Worked with you? And split the world with you when we conquered it? Why would I want to share."

"You are too greedy, woman, and your greed may have cost you too much, this time."

Suddenly, a woman appeared before them. Her ears, as all of them, were pointed as an elf's. Long, curly blonde hair spilt down the back of her green dress. Her eyes, also green, were bright, with a white iris. "Vel'dulan, you are summoned," she said, with no hint of the decision they had come to.

She had no choice, and she knew this. Like the other *demons*, she was stuck in this place, and the others had more than enough magical power to force her to appear before them. Vel'dulan bowed and approached her. The other demon, Sha'lura, snapped her fingers and the two vanished, appearing in another room, where a group of eleven stood circled around them.

As Sha'lura moved to take a place in the circle, Vel'dulan noticed Mar'vandi appear in the room to observe. She observed some others standing around to watch the events that were to proceed, but there were many not present. She had thought she might be important enough to warrant more attention.

"You know why you're here," Sha'lura began. "We've already come to a decision, but if you'd like to sway us, now if the time to speak."

Vel'dulan remained silent for a moment and thought. She'd only witnessed these events a few times in the long time they had been banished, and while they had no true governing body and the ones passing judgment were always chosen at random, the outcome had always been the same. She would have to serve time imprisoned. The most anyone had ever been forced to be chained was a century, and Vel'dulan knew they'd force her to stay chained that same length, if not longer. She finally spoke. "I know nothing that will change your minds. Know that I did what I did to conquer the world for myself, and I'd have left the rest of you here to rot."

Sha'lura smiled. "You cannot remain here any longer. We will soon set things in motion to bring us into the world once again, and you've proven you can't work with us. You won't be a part of our new plans."

"Then death?" She became desperate. "Please, I beg of you, let me live, chain me up and leave me here, but don't extinguish my life! We are better than any of them, we are all supposed to live forever!"

"Not you," she responded, smiling again. "We will make it painless."

Vel'dulan attempted to move, but the circle had already held her in place with magic, and she'd been too blind to notice. She struggled against it, but she could do nothing. He eyes searched for Mar'vandi and her expression pleaded with him, but he just looked away. Was that regret she saw on his face? Remorse? She knew it didn't matter, that this was the end.

The group all bathed Vel'dulan in magical power, and she began to feel sleepy, but she couldn't close her eyes. Soon all that was left was her lifeless body, still standing from the magic holding her in place. They released their hold, and her body went limp to the floor. They left her there, and all went their separate ways. Once the room had emptied, Mar'vandi approached, closed the eyes of her corpse, and set the body ablaze with a magical fire that consumed even the ashes.

*****

The throne room of King Kaalen was filled with light from the midday sun. The king had given his speech the day after Roland and the others had left, and his kingdom's reaction differed from person to person. The day found him sitting on his throne, contemplating the results of what he had shared. Surprisingly, though some were angry, most were not, their reasons generally being that the spell was cast on their ancestors who were long passed away. Some were happy their king had decided to tell them the truth, though some of them felt he only came forward because the green elves had been discovered. Others didn't care at all, and a small number were very excited about meeting the green elves of Moora or even finding the opportunity to visit their kingdom.

Horace had been a great help in explaining Moora, as everyone had been curious about what the underwater kingdom was like. He had given a first-hand account from the king's platform and had personal discussions with any who wanted to talk to him when the announcement was over. He also helped the elves keep their perspective about the secret, as the entire kingdom of Jeul knew about the vampires of Aalen, but kept the secret from the world. Horace had been offered a chance to stay in Jeul but decided to leave with Zeyn and return to Kassa.

When the heroes returned from killing Tecuul, they had only stayed in Jeul for a night. Roland reported all that happened to the king, and though he regretted the loss of his soldiers, he knew they died stopping a threat that would have built and cost the lives of many more. Their bodies had been burned, as was tradition, at the field of the battle where they fell. It was an old tradition and was once believed their spirits would remain to protect those on the side of right in future battles of the area. Though that belief was long gone, they still held to tradition. The king had heard that two of the young men who had died were buried there in the field, and the body of one of Zeyn's crew was brought back to be burned so his ashes could be spread at sea. The vampires who'd been killed, including Tecuul, were burned up to ash, and would never return again.

One surprise was that five new elves from Moora, three female and two male, who had been vampires under

Tecuul's control had come to Jeul with the others. These five, along with Bandar and Thela, decided to stay in Jeul, and the king was happy to have them. Several elves in Jeul had met these green elves of Moora and heard their stories, and the elves of Moora were very glad to share. Sola left to join the crew of the *Salvation* but promised to return for Bandar and Thela's wedding.

Kari had been waiting in Jeul for the return of Roland and the others from Aalen. When the messenger had reached Jarec, he had sent Kari and her guards on to Jeul with the messenger while they rushed to go help Roland. While Roland and the others had all returned to Aalen, Kari had said her goodbyes and returned home to Menton. Something told Yuuric he'd see that girl again one day, and that her thirst for adventure wouldn't let her stay in her town, but time would tell.

Before Roland had left, the king had sent out a proclamation to be spread in all the towns and villages of the kingdom of Jeul. The purpose was to let everyone know about Moora, and about the vampires of Aalen, if they hadn't known. The messengers also were to tell everyone how the vampires were fully cured and human again. In order to prove the change of the vampires, he sent along a volunteer from Aalen with each messenger to prove they were no longer affected by sunlight and they had no powers.

In addition to spreading this throughout his land, he sent messengers to all the kingdoms to the north, west, and south, each messenger with a former vampire, to speak with the kings and queens. From there, the rulers could spread the word around their kingdoms. Everyone would know of Moora, and everyone would know of Aalen. The hope was this could help the former vampires return to normal lives.

When Roland left Jeul, all of the people of Aalen did as well, including Darel, Will, and Simeon. The king, now knowing their story, was saddened to know their lives had been so damaged during the vampire war when they were just children. They planned to help in Aalen until Jarec decided what would happen to the underground city. Jarec had admitted to the king that they were all unsure. King Kaalen knew that Jarec would weigh his options and be cautious moving forward. He was wise and not one to rush.

"Sire?"

The king looked up from his thoughts and sat tall, looking to the servant who had just entered the room. The man had knelt to his right knee, holding out both hands, palm up, by his sides. "You may rise," Yuuric said. "Do you have news?"

"There is a guest seeking audience, sir." The man rose, and his facial expression appeared surprised. "A guest from Moora."

*****

"Are you sure about this? I don't mind staying here and continuing to learn." Caleb had asked his father this several times since Gallen told him that he'd gotten Captain Clarke's crew to take him on.

"Yes, son," Gallen answered. "Like I said before, I am sure. You are old enough to set out on your own, and you already know the craft as well as I did when we first came here to Kassa."

Caleb would miss his father. He knew the *Salvation* stopped often in Kassa, but he and his father had been together every day for as long as he could remember. He knew his father had already arranged a job aboard the ship maintaining the tools and weapons of the crew. The adventure of travel and seeing other lands, as he knew Zeyn's crew visited, was very enticing, but he couldn't help but feel like he was somehow betraying his father by leaving him alone. But if this is what his father wanted, he wouldn't question it anymore.

"Alright. I will go with them." It wouldn't be too bad, he did have lots of friends on board. "I'd better pack some things before I join them. They are setting out tomorrow, and I'd like to get my things on the ship. Can I still sleep here one more night?"

"Of course, Caleb. You always have a room here in our home." Gallen hugged his son. "I have something for you."

Caleb watched as his father left the room and returned with a long, wrapped box. He set the box on the table and Caleb approached the table, carefully removing the wrapping paper. As he opened the lid of the box, he saw within it a sword. The sheath of the weapon was blue and plain, but the handle and hilt were not as subdued.

The handle of the sword was in the shape of a beautiful mermaid with a blue tail, and the hilt appeared as waves of the ocean. Caleb smiled and picked up the weapon, drawing it and observing the blade. The double edged sword had amazing balance, and Caleb would expect no less from his father's work. He swung the sword twice, before sheathing it and admiring it again.

"It is a bit decorative in appearance, but trust me, son, it's ready for use if you ever have need of it." He knew his father hoped he wouldn't need to use it, but believed in his son being prepared. "I know you have learned some things about sword fighting, but take the time you can on the ship to train with anyone who will teach you."

"Thank you, dad," Caleb responded and wrapped his arms around his father's neck. He fought back the tears as best he could. He would miss his father.

*****

Things in Aalen had been interesting. Some of the people had only returned to gather their belongings and were planning on leaving soon. They didn't want to wait for the messages to get out in all of the kingdoms, they just wanted to get back in the world. Another group had been waiting so long as vampires they didn't mind spending a little longer in Aalen, but they, too, planned to leave. Yet a third group wanted to stay in Aalen and make it an official part of the kingdom of Jeul, and their claims about how abandoning the farms would be a waste couldn't be argued with.

One very strange occurrence came with how everyone was dealing with their fangs. Many were fine to keep them, as if a badge of honor, for the rest of their lives. But some, a small number, decided to file their fangs down, which proved a painful process but made re-entering the normal world very easy. Jarec himself had been living with his fangs so long, he was actually glad he was able to keep them. While he was happy to be able to walk in the day again, it would take some time to get used to sleeping at night again. He also would miss the benefits of being a vampire, his fast speed and increased strength. There had been rare cases of people in Aalen becoming depressed from the loss, but the good outweighed the bad. Especially the food.

Jarec was walking around the farms and found himself approaching Roland's. Areum and Roland waved to him from their fields and walked over. "How are you today," Areum asked. Jarec could see how happy she was to be outside in the day.

"I am well, and yourself?"

"Very good."

"Jarec, thank you for your leadership all this time," Roland said. "Have you given any more thought to the council's request?"

He had put it away from his mind. The council had met with Jarec when they'd returned, attempting to convince Jarec to start a new kingdom, with himself as the king. While they had been away fighting, the council had been meeting with the people of Aalen who had remained. The majority of them, who made up a fourth group, wished to not only stay in Aalen but wanted Jarec to lead them as their king. "I am not sure. I know they have come to that decision, and if I don't lead them, they will most likely find a suitable replacement. If we did set up a kingdom of our own here, we would be the smallest kingdom in the land."

"Perhaps, but you would be a good king. Your years have brought you much wisdom. I'm sure you'll make the right decision, whatever that might be."

"I see that Darel and his friends are helping work the fields here." Jarec looked over to where the three men worked.

"Yes," Areum replied. "If you do become king, those three need a place in this world, and I think they would serve you well in your guard, or as soldiers or knights, if they'll accept such a position."

Jarec agreed. "Even if there is no kingdom formed here, they are welcome to live here and be a part of Aalen." After a moment, Jarec spoke again. "I've heard a rumor the two of you are leaving."

"It's true," Roland said, "but this is our home now, we will return. We just thought we could do with some travel that doesn't involve hunting down demons or vampires."

Jarec laughed. "Yes, you deserve it. We all do. I suppose everyone will be finding time to relax in their own way. Where will you go?"

"Well, we will probably try and find our old home first," Areum answered, "and after a short stop in Kassa, we are going to head north."

"Well, have a good trip, my friends, and be safe. I look forward to your return."

"Thank you."

"We look forward to seeing if there are any changes when we get back," Roland added.

*****

"All of that really happened?" the girl asked melodiously. Her voice was sweet and innocent, and Zeyn had missed it very much. Almost a year had passed since he last heard it.

"Oh yes, all of it," he answered. "The great battle ended the menace of the vampires. We suffered the loss of a crewmate, but we won." Zeyn and his crew had shipped out weeks ago from Kassa with their new crew members, Sola and Caleb, and were delivering shipments to the western coastal towns. He was glad he found Serah. The last few times he'd been here, he had missed her.

"Are you going to swim with me?"

Zeyn sat on the rocks at the shoreline smiling down at the girl in the sea, not too far below him. Her wet, slick hair was golden and her eyes were blue and bright. Her bare shoulders peeked out from the surface of the water, and by her smile, she was clearly smitten with the man. "Not today, dear. I need to get back to my crew soon. We are going to be shipping out and moving north tomorrow and I'll need to get back to town and get some rest."

Her smile turned to a pout. "Not even a short one?"

"I'm sorry." Even her pout was cute. But he really did need to get his rest.

"Thank you for seeing me. I've missed you, Zeyn."

"And I've missed you." A sound behind him caught his attention. Someone had been trying to sneak up on him, and it wouldn't be his crew. "Hide," he whispered, but she had already vanished under the water. He stood and turned to confront those approaching but they were upon him too fast and knocked him out before covering his head with a bag. They carried him far up the coast to where they had a canoe waiting to take them out to their ship. And all along the way, Serah followed them under the water by the coastline, the blue scales of her mermaid tail never once splashing above the water.

*****

Deep in a forest, in another land, a woman awoke on the grass. She lay on her back and squinted her eyes as the sun hit her face. As she attempted to rise to her feet, her legs nearly gave out, as if she was trying to stand for the first time. A nearby tree lent support to bring her to standing.

As she brushed light green hair back with her left hand, revealing her elven ear, she thought to herself for a moment. *What is my name? Where am I? How did I get here?* So many questions filled her head, as she took careful steps from the tree, getting used to walking. She knew how to walk, but at the same time felt she had never done this before.

The sound of nearby people made her cautious, and she looked up a nearby tree. She felt power well up within her and used it to leap high to the nearest branch, then climb up further. *Magic.* The word popped into her mind. She had just used magic, though she didn't know how, and wasn't sure if she could reproduce the effect. Soon she saw the group approaching.

She knew they were elves. That was something she remembered, but she couldn't remember elves with pale, snow white skin and hair that matched. They looked around as if hunting. Their weapons and tools looked very primitive. From what she could recall, elves were far more advanced than this. She waited in the tree until they passed and decided to stay safely in the branches until a little more of her memory returned.

THE END

GLOSSARY

Aalen (AY-len): Hidden city.

Arndell (AHRN-del): Town to the south in Norin.

Astor (as-TOR): Eastern human kingdom.

Bandar (ban-DAHR): *Elf.* Bandar is a guard from Moora. He is a friend of Sola and engaged to Thela.

Boaruun, Tecuul (BO-roon, te-KYOOL): *Elf, Vampire.* Tecuul made a deal with a demon that turned him into the first vampire.

Brand, Phyra (BRAND, FI-rah): *Human.* Phyra is a member of *Salvation's* crew and close friend of Brill and Melzer.

Burque (BURK): Town attacked during the Vampire War.

Clarke, Maria (KLAHRK, MUH-ree-UH): *Human.* Maria is the First Mate of *Salvation.* Zeyn is her brother.

Clarke, Zeyn (KLAHRK, ZAYN): *Human.* Captain of the merchant ship, *Salvation.* Maria is his sister.

Crane, Nolan (KRAYN, NO-lehn): *Human, Vampire.* Nolan lives in Aalen. He is Bree's husband.

Dale, Auben (DAYL, AH-ben): *Human.* Auben is a friend of Roland who travels with Roland and Bree. He is Bryn's brother.

Dale, Bryn (DAYL, bren): *Human, Vampire.* Bryn lives in Aalen. He is Auben's brother.

Darel (DAIR-ull): *Human.* Darel is a young man with a deep hatred of vampires traveling with his friends, Will, Tras, Weston, and Simeon.

Drakon, Jarec (DRAK-un, JAIR-ek): *Human, Vampire.* Jarec is the mayor of Aalen. He is the oldest living human vampire.

Elar (EH-larr): Elar is the Creator.

Elline (EL-een): Underwater vessel commissioned by Horace Finch and created by Gallen Highfall. Named after Gallen's wife.

Elyse (EH-leese): *Human, Vampire.* Elyse is a woman with the appearance of a teenager since she was turned into a vampire at the age of fifteen. She keeps the stables in Aalen.

Finch, Horace (FENCH, HOAR-us): *Human.* Horace is an old man who commissions the voyage to Moora. He is friends with Horace and Caleb.

Freeman, Annah (FREE-man, ANN-uh): *Human.* Annah is a member of *Salvation's* crew. She grew up in the capital of Nadara.

Freyg (FRAYG): Town to the North in Norin.

Gor (GORE): *Unknown race.* Gor comes from the same land as Shim and Bail, far from Maruun. His people are hairless and have extraordinary strength. He is a member of *Salvation's* crew.

Highfall, Caleb (HI-fahl, KAY-lehb): *Human.* Caleb works as apprentice to his father, Gallen, in blacksmithing in the town of Kassa.

Highfall, Gallen (HI-fahl, GAL-enn): *Human.* Gallen is the blacksmith in the town of Kassa and a friend of Horace. Caleb is his son.

Jeul (JOOL): Elven kingdom. The first kingdom established in Maruun.

Kaalen, Aar (KAY-len, ahr): *Elf.* Aar was a former king of Jeul.

Kaalen, Yuuric (KAY-len, yuhr-ICK): *Elf.* Yuuric is the current king of Jeul. Yuuric is a descendant of Aar.

Kan, Bail (kahn, BAYL): *Dwarf.* Bail is a dwarf from the same land as Gor. Shim is his best friend.

Kassa (KASS-uh): Harbor town in the Northeastern part of Norin.

Lam, Areum (lam, AH-rum): *Human, Vampire.* Areum is not native to Maruun, but came to Maruun on the *Salvation* from another land that was not her own, either. She is Roland's wife.

Lam, Roland (lam, ROW-lahnd): *Human.* Roland is a well-known vampire hunter throughout the kingdoms. He is Areum's husband.

Langston (LANG-stun): Town in Norin, east of the capital.

Leef (LEEF): A town of elves who left their kingdoms to get away from the rest of the world.

Lett, Shim (leht, SHIM): *Dwarf.* Shim is a dwarf from the same land as Gor. Bail is his best friend, though he irritates him sometimes.

Lind (LEND): A town far to the west in Maruun.

Maave, Bree (mave, BRE): *Elf.* Bree travels with Roland and Auben. She is Nolan's wife.

Maruun (MAHR-oon): A continent on the Northern part of the world.

Maruun Ocean (MAHR-oon O-shun): Ocean to the East of Maruun.

Mar'vandi (MAHR-vahn-DEE): *Demon.* Mar'vandi is one of the demons people have summoned, though he hasn't been brought between worlds in many years.

Matthew (MATH-yoo): *Human.* Matthew is a member of *Salvation's* crew.

Menton (MEN-ton): Small town in the North in Astor.

Moora (MOOR-uh): Lost kingdom of elves.

Nadara (nuh-DAHR-uh): Northern human kingdom.

Noon (newn): *Elf.* Noon is a friend of Gallen and best friends with Olii.

Norin (NOHR-en): Human kingdom to the west of Astor.

Olii (AHL-ee): *Elf.* Olii is a friend of Gallen and best friends with Noon.

Rite, Melzer (RITE, MEHL-zuhr): *Human.* Melzer is a member of *Salvation's* crew and close friend of Brill and Phyra.

Rollins (RAWL-ens): Town that no longer exists.

Salvation (sal-VAE-shun): Merchant ship captained by Zeyn Clarke.

Sandor (SAN-dor): Harbor town in Astor, east of the capital.

Savuul, Braal (sahv-OOL, brail): *Elf.* Braal is the king of Moora.

Sha'lura (shah-LOOR-uh): *Demon.* Sha'lura considers herself leader of the demons, though the others do not see it that way.

Simeon (SIM-e-UN): *Human.* Simeon travels with Darel. Weston is his twin brother.

Sleyn, Kari (SLANE, carr-E): *Human, Vampire.* Kari is a teenage girl from Menton whose entire town was mysteriously turned into vampires.

Smyte, Brill (SMITE, bril): *Human.* Brill is a member of Salvation's crew and close friend of Melzer and Phyra.

Sola (SOH-lah): *Elf.* Sola is a citizen of Moora. She is a friend of Bandar and Thela.

Soor, Caldoon (SEWR, kal-DUNE): *Elf.* Caldoon was the captain of the soldier in Jeul under the reign of Aar Kaalen.

Soor, Naaren (SEWR, nay-REN): *Elf.* Naaren is a close friend of Zeyn and member of *Salvation's* crew. He always carries a sword at his left side that has never been unsheathed.

Tentrees, Alexander (TEN-trees, AL-ex-ZAN-dur):

Thela (THEE-lah): *Elf.* Thela is a citizen of Moora. She is a friend of Sola and engaged to Bandar.

Tras (TRACE): *Human.* Tras travels with Darel.

Traverse, Rendal (traa-VURS, REN-dahl): *Human.* Rendal is a member of *Salvation's* crew.

Vel'dulan (VELL-dool-AN): *Demon.* Vel'dulan is the demon that Tecuul made a deal with that turned him into the first vampire.

Weston (WEST-un): *Human.* Weston travels with Darel. Simeon is his twin brother.

Will (WIL): *Human.* Will travels with Darel.

And now a sneak peek at the sequel,
Mermaids' Hope!

Coming soon!

PROLOGUE

ORIGINS

"Before any of us were created and swam the oceans, and before man and even the elves walked the surface, there was a time of nothing," the mermaid Raella explained to her granddaughter as they sat on rocks jutting out of the water near a small, uninhabited island in the sea. At the age of 10, Serah was old enough now to hear the story that all mermaids passed on to their children, and since her mother had died prematurely due to an illness, the task was left to her grandmother. "But there was one being in existence, and he began to create the world we live in and all of the rest of the universe. Then he created all the creatures in the sea and on land, and the first people he made were the elves of Maruun."

"Why did he do that?" the inquisitive young mermaid asked as she brushed some blonde hair out of her eyes.

"I don't know. The elves might, if they haven't forgotten him. Maybe he was lonely, or perhaps just bored."

"Does he have a name?"

Raella nodded to the child. "Yes, his name is Elar." She flipped the fins of her bright blue scaled tail against the water. To those of the surface, she could be mistaken for Serah's mother, since mermaids physical aging would stop between the ages of twenty and thirty. While their lives would last for up to 200 years like a human's, they remained forever young in their appearance.

"Have you ever met Elar?" Serah pushed off her rock with her hands and swam closer to her grandmother, treading the water and waiting intently for an answer.

"No, dear one, no one has seen him for a very long time. But he is always watching over us." Raella smiled. "Now I will continue with the forgotten history of the elves."

*****

Duren Kalen, the leader of the elves, walked through the streets of the great city his people had created. The name chosen for the city was Jeul, and it was decided by Duren and his council that this city would be the main center linking the other elven cities together into a great kingdom. The elves had grown much since their primitive infancy, learning how to live in harmony with the world around them. Since their creation by Elar, they learned how to make tools, how to hunt, and how to farm. They took these early skills and expanded them greatly, learning more advance methods for everything. They built homes and communities and made many towns and cities. Elar, pleased with their growth, gave the elves the gift of magic. He also put Duren in charge of the elves thousands of years ago.

The people lived in peace, though there was occasionally an incident which needed the council's attention. Sometimes it was as simple as solving arguments between neighbors. The worse crime committed was theft, and the council was quick to judge and sentence those who deserved it. After serving their time, no criminal was ever a repeat offender. The systems they had in place worked, and everyone did their part to live harmoniously.

Duren turned to look at the center of the city, where a great castle was being built. A king had not yet been appointed for the kingdom, but Duren was confident that when the time came, Elar would come to the city and appoint the right ruler. After a king was crowned, the council would remain to help serve the people as they always had and to guide the king to the best decisions. He had more important things to think about today, though. As soon as he had finished his rounds checking around the city, he could get back home to his wife. She was due any day now, and it would be the first child they had together.

As he turned the corner by one of the buildings into an alleyway, suddenly a woman appeared in front of him. "Velan!" he said, surprised. "You frightened me. Is there some trouble for the council to take care of?"

"No, this is nothing that needs the council's attention," she answered. "But Shala is very upset."

His quizzical expression at her response quickly contorted into pain as a woman who had snuck behind him drove a knife into his back. Duren turned around as he fell, then looked up at her face. "Why...why?" he asked, losing blood quickly.

"You chose Jera over me," she said coldly, "Also, I know Elar will make you king. I would have been happy to rule at your side, but since that won't happen now, I've had to make other arrangements to take power. The council will back me, so when Elar does come, we'll tell him of your accident, and they will suggest to him that I become the ruler of Jeul."

"You're wasting your breath," came the voice of a man, Mar, who was behind Velan. "He's dead." Velan

turned to Mar and wrapped her arms around her husband. She wasn't ready to see a man die.

Shala looked down at Duren's corpse. "Oh. I…" She looked into the open, empty eyes of the man she once loved. Shock began to come over her in the realization that she had committed the first murder. She almost regretted her action, but her heart had become filled with hate and jealousy watching Duren's wife grow larger with child all these months. There was no room left in Shala for remorse.

"We need to go," Mar said, "We should leave the body. When it's discovered we, as the council, can place the blame on someone else. We are trusted above all."

"Very well. I'll see you two tomorrow at the meeting."

After the three left, another man walked into the alley and picked the body up, carrying it away.

*****

"Has anyone heard anyone mention finding Duren?" Shala asked the other eleven members of the council. There was no answer.

Mar stood from his chair at the square table. "Jera hasn't even shown any concern about his disappearance last night."

As the council continued to talk about the events of the previous night and a few began to question if they'd made the right decision to get rid of Duren, Velan's mind began to race about what had happened. If Duren had survived, then that would be awful for the council. Despite their power and the supporters they had set up throughout the cities for the takeover, Duren would have more support from the entirety of the elves than they would. The entire council would lose that fight, and all be imprisoned. Or would Duren seek retribution and kill them all?

"Are you alright?" Mar asked. "Velan?"

"What? Yes, I'm fine."

"I had called your name several times and you weren't responding. You look like you might be getting sick."

"I'm just worried."

As Mar reached down to comfort her where she sat beside him, his attention, and the attention of everyone, was drawn to the doorway. Elar had come and they all felt his presence before they saw him. He appeared to them the way he always had, looking much like the elves themselves, with short dark hair and pointed ears, and his clothing was similar to their fashion. He wore a white tunic that hung loosely over gray pants. A black rope belt was tied across the tunic at his waist, and over his clothing he wore a gray cloak. Unlike the elves, his feet were bare, as they always were. All the council who were seated stood, and all of them bowed together in respect. Their creator walked to the empty chair at the table that was left open for him, should he visit, and removed his cloak, draping it over the back of the chair before he sat down.

"Elar," Cal, one of the more voluminous elves said, *"you honor us with your presence today."*

"You haven't been with us in nearly four months," Shala added. *"We have missed you."*

Elar looked into Shala's eyes and a sense of dread filled her. *"I am always in your presence. How could you forget?"* Velan and Mar looked to each other as silence overcame the room. Sadness came upon Elar's face as he looked over each one of the elves seated before him at the council table. *"How could you all forget that I am always with you, and I know what you are doing? I've been making plans throughout the rest of Maruun, and across the oceans to other lands, and in places you will never know, but wherever I was, I was also here. You could not hide from me what you had planned, and what you have done."*

The council stood, and Elar stood in response, pointing to the door. Shala's eyes widened in terror at the sight of Duren as he walked into the room and made his way to Elar's side. Velan fell back into her chair in shock and slumped down, unconscious. Others in the room showed surprise at Duren's appearance, and others tried to act is if it wasn't out of the ordinary

"Duren, you've finally made it!" Cal said with a forced smile.

"Do not attempt to lie," Elar spoke harshly as he pointed at Cal. "All of you are guilty, each of you! Duren has faithfully led you all as I asked of him. He has never done any less and often has done more. He was a friend to you all, and yet you let Shala poison all of you against him. In her lust for power, she wormed her way into all your hearts and minds, convincing you she should be the ruler of Jeul."

"If you know all of this, then you know we have one more plan," Shala said. The council members had moved across the room from Elar and Duren. "Now!" Shala exclaimed as she reached out to the elves beside her and they all joined their magic together, sending a large blast of energy towards Elar. It was a fruitless effort, as the energy washed over Elar and Duren, touching neither.

"Enough." With that word, spoken in a hushed, saddened tone, all the council froze in place as if made of stone, though they could all still see and hear. "You all knew that I was going to appoint a king or queen soon, but you were wrong in your assumption. Duren has led for so long, and I was going to give him rest. The ruler of the kingdom could have been any of you, but when your evil intentions first began to surface, I knew that couldn't be. You will not get to stay in Jeul or in this world at all. Where I send you now, you will have to make your own path." As he finished speaking, the council vanished from sight.

"Where are they?" Duren asked.

"I've sent them, and their conspirators in Jeul and the other cities who weren't on the council, to another plane of existence where only they will live. What they do now is up to them."

"Will you still know what they are doing? Can they find a way back?"

"Yes, Duren, I will know, and they may find a way. After I've finished my work in the rest of the world, I will leave it up to you and the others yet to come to take care of things. This is my charge to you."

"I don't want to be king."

Elar sat back in his chair and Duren sat beside him. "I know, and you won't be king, but I need you to keep leading the elves. I have given life to you again for a short time. You have 20 years. In that time, I need you to teach your son everything I've shown you and that you've learned, and show him how to lead the people well. After those years, I will return and will announce him as the first king of Jeul, and your family line will rule the kingdom as long as it exists. After he is made king, I will take you with me. You will not have to die again."

"Will I have other children before you take me away?"

Elar smiled. "That is up to you and Jera. Cherish the time you have left with her." Elar stood and put his cloak back on and Duren looked up at him. "There is something else, very important, you need to know. While I was away, I created men and women in the north and the south. They are not elves but are called humans. Their lives will not last as long as an elf's, but they have the capacity to build great kingdoms and are intelligent. They look slightly different from elves and do not have the magic you all have. You should send some trusted people to check on them from time to time and report back, but don't interfere with their advancement. If any of them come here to Jeul, welcome them. Tell your son if they have not found Jeul within 200 years, then he should send a group from Jeul to the humans of the north and a group to the humans of the south to make contact."

"How do they look different?"

"Their ears are not pointed but are rounded here." Elar traced along his ear to show where the human ear differed. "Other than that, they are the same physically."

"A rounded ear? That's so strange."

Elar laughed. "There are so many things to come that you will find strange. One day you will see them all. Thank you for the work you've done, I know you will continue to do as I've asked. Now, you may want to rush home. Your son will be born very soon."

Duren stood in surprise and bowed quickly before rushing out of the door to be with his wife. Elar vanished and the candles in the room blew out.

*****

Serah thought on what her grandmother had just told her before responding. "Elar put the elves in charge of the future of Maruun. And after he made the elves, he made the humans. When did Elar make us?"

Raella smiled. "After he made the humans, he made more elves west of Jeul. Then he made the mermaids in the oceans east of Maruun before coming here and making the mermaids we descended from."

"Why don't we have men like the elves and the humans?"

Raella frowned. "There were mermen once. But one of the mermen, Mikal, began to see the banished elves of Jeul in his dreams, and they corrupted him and showed him how to summon them back into this world. When he did, it was Shala, now calling herself Sha'lura, who came through. Although she was powerful, she was ignorant of how the summoning would work, and learned that the summoning symbol kept her trapped from moving freely in our world. Mikal, in a moment of clarity, refused to break the seal and help her to escape. Before he sent her back, she was able to place a curse on him and on all the other mermen of the seas."

It seemed like such a sad tale, and Serah could feel the pain of her ancestors in it. "What did she do to the men?"

"Her curse made the men only produce female offspring with their mates." Raella took a moment and then continued. "When they realized this was happening, the men and women knew that our race would be doomed when the men died out. But thankfully, their cries were heard. When the mermen were gone, the mermaids of every ocean were drawn to the surface where a man sat upon a raft floating on the water. This was the first time our clan ever saw the mermaids from throughout the world and saw how different, and how similar, we are. They would come to find out that there were different humans and different elves as well."

"Who was the man on the raft?" Serah asked impatiently.

"The man said his name was Duren."

"The elf! This was still before his twenty years had passed?"

"No," Raella laughed. "A thousand years had passed since he had left with Elar."

Serah's eyes were wide with disbelief. "Then how did he come?"

"He was sent back by Elar to help the mermaids. He told them that he could not reverse the curse that had been placed on them by Sha'lura, but he was sent to give us a gift that would keep the mermaids from dying out." Raella pushed off her rock into the water and swam to the island, pulling up onto the beach. Serah watched as her grandmother concentrated and transformed her fins into legs to walk with. She stood and smiled at her granddaughter. "We were given a bit of magic within us so that we could find men of the surface to mate with."

Serah swam over and pulled herself onto the beach, too. She had lain on the beach before, but never grew legs! "How do I do that?" she asked excitedly.

"I will teach you how and teach you how to walk properly. One day, when you are old enough and if you desire, you may go to the surface to find a mate as well. Most mermaids return to us in the ocean once they have mated. Some decide to stay, but that will be your choice to make. However, mankind, human and elf, do not know of our existence and we prefer to keep ourselves hidden. You should never tell anyone on the surface what you truly are."

*****

Serah smiled at the memory. Her grandmother had such a hard time teaching her, but she succeeded, and Serah could still use the ability, though she had only used it before in practice. She sat naked at a small fire she had started for warmth. Her body was dry, but she was still waiting for the blue dress Raella had given her for this trip to dry off. It was too bad they had no way to store it and keep it dry underwater. She wasn't entirely honest with her grandmother about why she had decided to come here. Raella had asked her if it was to find a man, and Serah said yes. It wasn't really a lie.

She wasn't far from where Zeyn had been kidnapped three months ago. She had followed them all the way across the ocean. The men had taken him to the land where she first met him. She would have gone to see Maria first about the abduction if she knew the pirates were going to be taking him so far away. Hopefully, Maria would know why they had taken Zeyn there, if she could find her. The *Salvation* was docked in a nearby town, so Serah knew that was where she should find them. This would be the first time she ever even been to any town, let alone anywhere far on the surface. Once she found Maria and Zeyn's friends she could lead them all to go save him and bring him back home. And then maybe she would have a talk with him about something that had been on her mind.

CHAPTER 1

STOWAWAYS

The green-haired elf didn't know why she was following the strange white elves she had seen in the forest. Something compelled her to continue to watch them, and she had been studying them from a distance for weeks now. She still didn't know who she was and while she remembered knowing elves in the past, she couldn't place any faces or names together. One thing she did know is that these elves were different than the ones she knew.

The first thing that stood out to her after all this time was the lack of magic use among them. Since she had not once seen them use any, her theory was that they had no magic at all. However, what they lacked in magic, they made up for in strength. She had seen several feats of strength, even from the youngest among them. They could leap longer distances than a normal elf could (unassisted by magic, of course) and could easily lift at least three times their weight, by her guess. Even when running their speed seemed abnormally fast. The elves were intelligent, but the language they used sounded harsh to her, even when they appeared to be enjoying each other's company.

They hadn't seemed to notice they were being followed and she had become very adept in her stealth. She wondered if this was a skill she honed in her past or one that came naturally. Other than learning about these elves, though, they hadn't done much of interest. All they had done was move from where she first remembered waking up all the way to the shore, with some hunting and gathering along the way. The elves began setting up their camp for the night, the way they always did. She continued to watch them from the edge of the forest for just a moment before leaping into the tree above to nestle into some branches for the night.

As her eyes began to close, she found herself lost in thought, like most nights. On this night, she wondered about her name, as she often did. Sleep began to take her and soon dreams came. Looking around her in the dream, she knew she was in a town full of elves but didn't know its name. Almost every night she was here, and she knew that soon he would be here, too. She had never seen the man's face, but she did know he was an elf. She felt a desire to be near him, but at the same time felt something sinister from him. She turned a corner into an alley and there he was. Only this time, he wasn't alone.

Beside him stood a woman, also an elf, who came to his shoulder. She had long, dark curly hair spilling down and ending just below the small of her back. Her face was hidden in the shadows, like the man, and they seemed happy together. Both were irritated at the interruption, and the new woman reached out towards her, the shadows uncovering her lower face revealing her sneer. As the green-haired elf stepped back to avoid her she stumbled, falling backwards and out of her sleep.

Her head bumped the branch behind her, and she almost fell from the branches when a hand caught her and kept her from losing her balance. A very tiny hand. "You should be more careful if you are going to sleep in trees," a tiny voice said.

The elf glanced around until her eyes fixed on a tiny man that she could hold in her hand, who was flying around with insect-like wings. "What are you?" she asked.

He shook his head. "'What are you?' is quite a rude way to make introductions. I could ask the same of you, after all. I've never seen anyone with green hair."

"I'm an elf," she said. "I think."

"I know you are. The ears gave it away. Although you aren't any kind of elf we have around here." He glanced to the beach where the white elves were sleeping in their camp. "I'm a fairy."

"Thank you for keeping me from falling."

"You're welcome. My name is Dren." The fairy set his feet down on a nearby branch and stopped the flutter of his wings, bringing them to rest down against his back.

She sighed and looked at him sadly. "I don't know my name. I don't remember much of anything before the past three weeks when I woke up near here. Do you live in this tree?"

Dren shook his head. "I don't live in a tree. You're the reason I'm here right now. My father sent me to find the green haired elf he dreamed about." Seeing her reaction, he continued. "For weeks now, every night, he has the same dream. He won't stop talking about the dream, or about the 'beautiful elf girl' that he sees every night while he sleeps. In the dream, you leave here and travel across the sea. I'm supposed to go with you."

"And where do I go and what do I do?"

"I don't know, but my father thinks it's very important that we take this journey."

She thought a moment and shrugged. "Well, I have no reason to stay here. We can set off in the morning."

As she lay back against the branches again, Dren spoke up. "Wait, what should I call you?"

"Let me think about that and I'll tell you in the morning."

Dren took up a spot on a branch and set in for a rougher night's sleep than usual.

*****

"Lina," the elf said to the fairy as they reached the ground and prepared to depart from their temporary camp in the tree.

"What?"

"My name. You can call me Lina."

Dren smiled, "Great! Your memory is coming back. With any luck, you'll remember what you need to do and won't need me around too long."

Lina shook her head. "I don't remember anything at all yet, I just made it up so you'd have something to call me." Dren frowned. "Don't worry, I'm sure it will come back to me. Now where should we head if we're going to cross the ocean?"

"I'll lead the way. Just follow me and I'll see you safely through." Dren began to fly towards the north, at the height of Lina's head. She walked behind and wondered what it would be like to be so small. For the world to be even larger than it already is.

The fairy was right about the safety of the travel, as the hour journey up the coast to the north had been very uneventful. Lina was bored. From the first moment she remembered, she was busy studying those strange elves and never had any moments that felt like they dragged on for such a long time. "This has been quite a dull trip."

"Better than the alternative," Dren said. "We have our lives and haven't been set upon by any strange creatures or people. Besides, if you want some excitement, you're about to have some. Duck down so you aren't seen." He stopped flying and fluttered in mid-air, pointing over at the shoreline and a camp that was set up on the beach as Lina knelt, covered by the tall grass.

There were brown canvas tents set up on the sand near a cave and men were moving all around. Some had shovels and other tools, and many were shirtless and sweaty. They looked like they had been hard at work.

"Pirates," Dren said as he landed on her shoulder.

"What are pirates? They look like men to me."

"They are men, but being pirates is their criminal occupation. They steal, murder, kidnap, and commit all sorts of other crimes. The fairies know everyone who comes and goes throughout Atim."

"Atim?"

"That's the country we're in. Those pirates aren't from Atim, though, and their ship is going to take us where we need to go."

Lina looked out across the beach and saw the ship Dren mentioned. It was a large boat with many masts, and she had no idea what it was. "Is that a ship?"

"Yes, that's their ship, and it's going to take us where we need to go. The land of Maruun."

"And how are we going to get on it? Are we going to pay them to take us?"

"If only it were that easy." Dren breathed in a moment, steeling his nerves. "We are going to sneak on and hide until we get there."

"Are you crazy?!"

"Shh!" They both looked back to the shore. They were a good distance away, and no one seemed to have heard Lina. "I'm not crazy, but they will discover us if you make too much noise. I have a plan. It's dangerous, but from what I've been led to believe, you're powerful, and I have a bit of magic myself. Together we can see this through."

Lina was unconvinced. "Tell me this plan."

*****

The moons were high in the night sky and most of the pirates slept in their tents on the beach. The rowboats they had brought to shore were undisturbed, as taking one of the them would give away that Lina and Dren were going to be stowing away. Instead, Lina was swimming out to the ship while Dren flew low beside her, just above the water. She didn't know why she remembered how to swim, but it came to her naturally, as did some of her magic. They hadn't departed from the beach where the pirates slept, but from further up the coast to hopefully avoid detection. This plan of Dren's was riskier than Lina would like, and she was very nervous as she swam along, but the few pirates keeping watch on the beach weren't focused on the ocean since their worry was on people on the land finding their camp.

"Finally," Lina whispered as they reached the pirate's ship. Her arms and legs were already tired from the swim. "Now, how do we get on it?"

"Use your magic to get up there. I'll fly up and make sure the coast is clear." Dren took off to the deck of the ship. After a moment, he looked down at Lina waved for her to come up.

Lina closed her eyes and tried to feel for the power to leap up and onto the ship but realized she couldn't. This was different than when she used her magic to leap into the trees. Then, she physically jumped as well, but here she had no footing. If there was a magical way for her to rise from the water and onto the ship, she did not know what it was. "I can't," she said, looking back up at Dren.

Dren flew back down by her side to talk. "What do you mean?"

"I mean I can't figure out how to use magic to get up there." Lina felt embarrassed at her inability.

"It's okay." Dren looked over and spotted the rope from the anchor. "Do you think you can climb?" He pointed to the thick rope.

She didn't want to climb. Her arms and legs already felt like they were burning after the swim to the ship, but it was her only option. "I can do it."

"Good. I'll fly back up and keep watch in case something happens." Dren flew up towards the deck near the anchor while Lina began to swim to the rope to begin her ascent.

Lina's muscles weren't ready to give up yet as she began to climb up the rope. She found that it wasn't too difficult but looked forward to getting a chance to sit and rest. As she neared the hole where the anchor lowered into the ocean, she wondered how she would make it from there to the deck of the ship. Right as she was about to peer into the hole, Dren rushed down beside her and whispered in her ear, "There's someone on the deck."

"I thought they were all in the camp?"

Dren shook his head. "I have an idea." He quickly disappeared, flying into the hole Lina was looking at. In a moment he returned. "It's clear inside. Do you think you can fit through here?" He gestured to the opening.

It did look like there was plenty of room, even with the anchor's rope, and Lina needed to get on this ship to go to Maruun. "I think so." She began to climb in. It wasn't too tight of a squeeze, but she did wish she had a little more room to work with. When her feet were on the floor inside, she looked around the inner deck of the ship. Dren was soon at her side.

Unmade beds revealed they were in the crew's sleeping quarters, and the clothes strewn about showed their slovenly nature. This was not a good place for the two of them to hide out if the crew would be spending some time here when they returned to the ship. As they began to wander around Dren spotted stairs leading below. Again, he left Lina to scout ahead, and she waited patiently for his return. "No one is down below. It looks like a storage space. I think we can safely hide there."

"Do you really think we can stay here unnoticed?" Lina asked as she walked onto the deck below, looking around. "They'll be bringing their tents and tools from their camp on the beach into this area of the ship for sure when they return. How can we stay hidden?"

"I told you I have magic. I can make us invisible when they return. But only as long as you stay still. If you start moving around it will wear off, quick." Lina was not excited about this plan at all.

Made in the USA
Columbia, SC
15 June 2019